I0619572

THE BOX
BABY

LARRY CUNNINGHAM

Copyright © 2021 Larry Cunningham or Cynthia Berry
All cover art copyright © 2021
All Rights Reserved

This is a work of fiction. Names, places, characters and incidents are either the product of the author's imagination or are used fictitiously, and any resemblance to any actual persons, living or dead, businesses, organizations, events or locales is entirely coincidental.

No part of this book may be reproduced or transmitted in any form or by any means, electronic or mechanical, including photocopying, recording, or by any information storage and retrieval system, without permission in writing from the author.

Cover Design – Jaycee DeLorenzo
Publishing Coordinator – Sharon Kizziah-Holmes

Paperback-Press
an imprint of A & S Publishing
A & S Holmes, Inc.

ISBN -13: 978-1-951772-85-7

CHAPTER ONE

IN THE BEGINNING

December 14, nine-thirty in the evening, no more than minutes after birth a box containing a baby girl, umbilical cord still attached arrived at a Springfield, Missouri hospital emergency entrance. A fleeting figure dressed in dark hooded sweats placed the box at the entryway and sprinted quickly away from observation of surveillance cameras.

Two hospital security officers noted the peculiar transaction and rushed outside in time to see a car, license plate covered with tape, speed from sight. The officers inspected the box, noted the contents and immediately called for assistance.

The emergency room rushed the baby to Neo-Natal. The nurse with the best record for 'Inny' belly buttons reduced and tied the umbilical cord. The Box Baby made national news for two days. No parent came forward to claim the baby.

The hospital, several weeks after the baby's health

stabilized and after she gained the necessary weight, transferred the child to the state Division of Family Services to be placed, according to regulation, for adoption.

January 28, fifty-nine days after advent of the box baby, a wealthy and politically well-connected middle-aged couple from Cheyenne, Wyoming used political power and money to selfishly jump the line of applicants and adopted the baby. The child became Emily Prindiville, daughter of R. Frederick Prindiville, 45 and his wife, Ethel, 39. Mrs. Prindiville, unable to conceive after the difficult birth of her son, fancied that the enjoyable activities and company of another child would provide support for her ever-diminishing prospects of happiness. Ethel had become a casualty of early-age Alzheimer's. She and her husband recognized that her future activities would become restricted to home and R. Frederick agreed to let her adopt, believing, self-interestedly, as he seldom lived at home, that a little girl would serve his wife's long-term needs better than a pet or a boy. Emily grew to be a most pleasant and accommodating girl, providing more love and care than the Prindivilles probably ever deserved. The little girl flourished. Mrs. Prindiville did not. Her health failed steadily, relegating her to an electric wheelchair by age 45.

Emily became the care responsibility of the Prindiville family maid, an illegal Mexican immigrant who Mrs. Prindiville named Marie. The name carried over for the remainder of Marie's tenure at Eagle's Nest.

Eagle's Nest, a name R. Frederick chose to emphasize

his estate's prominent position on the elevated terrain on the western outskirts of Cheyenne, looking down on the town as he looked down on the entire world.

The Prindivilles had produced a son by natural birth, Robby, three years older than Emily and R. Frederick's obvious favorite. Robby died at fourteen, the victim of scarlet fever. R. Frederick blamed Emily as she had come home from school sick two day before Robby fell ill. Emily recovered without damage. Robby died within two weeks. The Prindivilles erected an ostentatious monument in their garden near Robby's gravesite. R. Frederick sat alone near that shrine for hours, the hours extending into days, and the days into years mourning the boy he had envisaged as successor to his vast business empire, mostly mining and mineral interests.

Emily never once received the love and esteem R. Frederick lavished on Robby. Not ever. Neither of the Prindivilles ever revealed to Emily her adopted status.

The Prindiville family customarily assembled only once a year to celebrate anything, and that happened annually on the Fourteenth day of December. The yearly ceremony was a contrived show of affection on the occasion of Christmas, and not coincidentally Emily's birth date. R. Frederick demanded that they observe both events the same day, December fourteenth, thereby discharging in a practical manner the nuisance of repetitious sentiment.

On this day, the fourteenth, sixteen years after Emily's bizarre birth circumstances, she sat cross-legged on a silk cushion amid fragments of festive wrapping paper scattered about the rough-hewn floor of the Prindiville mansion's enormous den. Emily, now fully grown at sixteen, was tiny, an inch short of being five feet tall. Her delicate features, lustrous brunette hair and enormous dark eyes blended in flawless harmony, not unlike a great artist's portrayal of extraordinary feminine loveliness. Few onlookers who ever set eyes on Emily Prindiville failed to comment on her beauty.

A blaze in the den's massive fireplace flickered luxuriously in the background, serving as centerpiece for an extravagant array of holiday candles shimmering from sills in front of frosted windows. The overall effect saturated the scene in soft, huggable warmth. A fifteen-foot Christmas tree, erected by the gardener and decorated by the housekeeper, embellished the gracious setting, providing the pleasant, if somewhat pungent smell of evergreen.

Emily sat motionless, waiting, hands folded on her lap, eyes sparkling with teenage anticipation. At that moment her father–overweight, balding and attired in a black silk evening robe– stepped into the room bearing the final offering of the celebration, a gift he had chosen exclusively for her birthday. *The crowning moment.* His birthday present always eclipsed the other birthday-Christmas gifts, providing justification to save it for last. He placed the offering on her lap, retrieved his pipe from a nearby humidor, assumed a casual leaning position against the fireplace, and then, smiling imperiously, pointed with the pipe stem and said, "I went to a lot of trouble to get that."

"Oh, thank you, Daddy." Emily hesitated, eyes on her father, caressing the soft, satin-textured paper, awaiting his license to open the magnificent package. He clamped his teeth on the pipe and nodded. She favored him with what any unsuspecting onlooker would describe as a radiant smile. She then smoothed the excitement from her face with her hands and wiggled into a stable position on the pillow. With eyes firmly closed, she pretended to concentrate, fingertips pressed lightly on the package as if to divine the contents. The charade collapsed within moments as traces of an unruly smile crept from the corners of her mouth and spread. Her eyes popped open and she ripped the splendid paper away.

R. Frederick, an arrogant, preoccupied man, too self-important to realize his daughter's demonstration of delight was fabricated, a dutiful ritual she performed every year for the unveiling of his special gift. The obedient, compliant girl had long known her father expected profound gratefulness and she delivered. Emily would do almost anything to please him—until of late. Lately she brooded and worried about the growing frequency of his suggestive comments, always when they were alone. And the touching. He had never bothered to touch her before. She woke one night to find him sitting on her bed. She began to worry about his stealthy presence outside her bedroom door—a door she now locked. And his eyes. She felt his eyes following her.

As the final piece of shimmering gold paper fell away, she gingerly lifted an exposed wooden container. "It's so heavy, Daddy," she exclaimed, puzzled by the size and weight of the handsome box.

Frederick's perpetually stern expression relaxed slightly, displaced for the moment by a self-satisfied smile. He removed the unlighted briar pipe from his mouth and said, "Oh, you'll like it, Honey. It came all the way from England."

"England?" she whispered breathlessly, eyes glistening, lingering over the gift, stroking the smooth, burnished teakwood, prolonging the moment deliberately to validate the feigned extent of her appreciation. She then cautiously opened the brass latch and lifted the hinged lid, pausing at the half-open position to peek.

"Good heavens, Emily! It won't bite! For Heaven's sake open it!" her mother prompted from across the room. "Do you plan to keep me in suspense forever?" The words were not harsh, rather an indication of anxiety, for R. Frederick, as usual, had kept the secret to himself. "Open it," she urged. "I'm dying of curiosity." Ethel Prindiville's gnarled, trembling fingers nudged the control toggle on the arm of her wheelchair as she maneuvering the conveyance closer.

Frederick raised a camera and prepared to record the moment for the family album. Emily paused briefly as the gilded lid locked in the open position. She then slowly lifted a dictionary-sized book from the box, surveying the gift intently, baffled at first. Suddenly she smiled as only a delighted adolescent girl can–a smile to bring joy to the heart of any father, even R. Frederick.

"It's the diary!" she exclaimed, looking up, beaming as the camera flashed. "Just like the one we saw in the movie, Daddy! You remembered! Oh, thank you! This is the best birthday present ever. Oh, thank you." Her show of gratitude was not an act.

Frederick smiled confidently, directed the pipe stem at the diary, and declared, "I knew you would like it. That's a ten-year diary. Just think, you will be twenty-six when you make the last entry."

She rose from the pillow, hugging the wonderful journal to her bosom, and rushed to place the expected kiss on her father's cheek. She then whirled joyously through the profusion of discarded wrapping papers littering the floor.

Ethel remarked, "It's just magnificent, Emily, covered in rose-colored brocade and all trimmed with gold. It is so ornate. Let me–"

R. Frederick interrupted, "That diary is designed to record seven days on each page. You won't have space to write much about trivial things."

Emily opened the diary and discovered two dainty key attached to an exquisite gold chain hidden beneath the cover. Upon discovering the keys, she held them aloft and exclaimed, "Look, Mother, it locks!"

Emily made her first diary entry, and the longest she would ever record, on the fifteenth day of December, the day after she received the splendid volume.

Dear Diary: My life changed today at the local hangout with my three best friends. Lindsay, Vanessa and Paige. This is what happened:

Paige suddenly leaned over the table and whispered, "Oh-My-God!" She covered her mouth with one hand while pointing out the window with the other. "No, don't look. He's watching. It's Colin. Colin freakin' Kelly."

Colin Kelly, coming junior, all-state everything, honor student and easily the most admired and by far the best looking boy in school. So mysterious. There he was, Colin Kelly, sitting alone at a table in the courtyard. He smirked. He knew we were talking about him.

Vanessa said, "Oh, please, just kill me right now. He is soooo cute."

Paige said. "Cute does not describe Colin Kelly. He is way, waaaaay, way beyond cute."

Lindsay scoffed and said, "Yeah. Well, girls, don't worry about Colin. He wouldn't give any of us the time of day. Such a jerk."

I said, "He's probably waiting for what's-her-face. You know, the senior cheerleader he hangs with."

Lindsay groaned. "Miss Marvelous. The bouncy boobs–bouncy hair–bouncy, bouncy."

I spoke without thinking, "He is not a jerk!" Oh, Diary, I have secretly pined over him for the entire year. Colin lives somewhere beyond my house. I see him riding a bike to school every day. He's in my class in school, but oceans away in life. I think about him all the time. He doesn't know I am alive.

Lindsay noticed me blushing and said, "Well, well. Look here. Emily is beet red." She held up a finger for silence. "Oh, I get it. You and Colin Kelly? Really, Emily? Really?"

My three friends broke up laughing and jeering.

"You and Colin?"

"You dreamer."

"Tell us, Emily, are you two going out now?"

"Does his tongue get stuck in you braces? Is that the attraction?"

I felt tears pooling and wanted to leave. Instead I said, "Colin is a nice guy. He is *not* stuck up." I hugged myself, sat back and turned to look out the window, straight into Colin Kelly's eyes. He had watched the entire performance.

Lindsay reached across and pulled my arms apart. "Okay, Emily. Prove it!

Prove Mister Perfect is not a perfect jerk. Prove it!"

I stared at her. "What are you saying?"

"Yeah, Emily, "Vanessa added. "I dare you to go out there and say something to your perfect Colin."

And there it was. I didn't think. I slipped out of that booth, walked directly to the door, out of the cafe and onto the patio, and there stopped. Okay, I was brain-locked. I took some deep breaths, turned toward the street and headed straight for home. Something angry from deep inside stopped me. I turned around and marched straight over to face Colin Kelly.

He saw me coming, stood and pulled a chair out, smiling all the time. "Hi, Emily. Have a seat. Let's talk."

He knew my name!

Colin took my arm and turned me to the chair. "Sit!" he ordered.

I couldn't look at him. Okay, I was terrified. He sat and leaned close, all smiles and confident. "So, tell me, Emily. What was the bet? Come on. I know what's going on."

I murmured, "Nothing like that. Just–"

"Come on. Tell me. They dared you, didn't they?"

I sighed and nodded. "Look, I'm sorry." I glanced up at him and said, "I'm really sorry." My hand automatically covered the braces.

He pulled my hand down. "Look at me," he commanded. "And smile. Smile, Emily." He squeezed my hand. "I'm serious. Your friends are watching. Smile. There, that's better." He patted my hand, propped a long leg over the table and causally leaned back, the picture of confidence. "All right, Emily, let's do this right."

"I.... What?"

"Let's throw the dare back in their faces."

"I don't.... What?" His leg dropped and he leaned close. I could smell his breath.

"Look over at them, Emily. Wave and smile."

I had to force a smile. My friends were glued to the window.

"That's good. Okay, now look at me. Let's put something together. Here's the deal. In a minute or two I'm going to kiss you. No! Don't frown! Keep smiling. Look at me. Okay, I'm going to kiss you like we are really tight. Like we have known each other forever. After that, you go back to your friends and keep the secret."

My world came to a screeching stop. All sound faded. My heart literally ran away. "Keep what secret?"

"How will they know we really don't know each other if you don't tell them? I won't tell, Emily. That's all there is to it. After the kiss, you go back in there and keep the secret. Let them think what they will. Are you in?"

The idea was shocking. "You mean?" I pointed at my mouth.

He nodded. "Exactly." His eyes narrowed. He leaned closer. "You do know how to kiss, right?"

He didn't wait for my answer. Thank Heaven.

"Time's up, Emily. You in or out?"

"I...ahhh."

Tick, tick, tick. tick.

"Okay."

Bang! Just like that. The old Emily would never have the courage. I said, "Sure. Why not." I really wasn't all that confident.

He stood and pulled me up. "No strings attached, Emily. Just for fun."

I nodded, uncertain about how to deal with what was coming next. I had never... not really. No boy had ever even tried to....

Oh, God.

He took me in his arms, tilted my head back and said, "It's easy. Open your mouth a little, like this. No! Don't pull away. Now, when I kiss you, just act natural. Then just go back to your friends."

After we broke apart, I walked away patting myself on my chest, laughing. Laughing? Yes! I was thrilled. The moment I stepped inside I patted myself again and said loud enough for everyone to hear, "Oh, heart, heart!" My astonished friends ran to me. We held and danced in a tight circle.

Colin Kelly. He really is a nice guy.

They dated occasionally during their senior year, always at school dances, but only if Colin could get off work. He worked nights as clean-up and stocker at a grocery store. His mother was an invalid living in a mobile home in a ratty trailer park on the edge of town. Spending money on a date was not in Colin's comfort zone. The relationship never really matured beyond being just friends.

R. Frederick somehow learned that Emily had been nominated by the junior class for homecoming queen. He demanded that she retract her name. She argued with him for the first time in her life. Her mother was too sick to be of help. R. Frederick forbade her to go to the ceremony or the dance and that ended it. Another long diary entry.

Emily graduated as Valedictorian the next year and Colin received a full-boat football scholarship to UCLA. He asked her out one summer afternoon before leaving for college, for a ride in the country in his shiny new convertible. Emily learned more about Colin that day than she wanted to know. He drove to a remote abandoned home well away from town. Colin didn't waste time on preliminaries and began kissing her as his hands roamed all over her body. She struggled to get away, begging him to stop. Emily began screaming as his hand snaked under her blouse and to her breast. He laughed and kept tugging at her clothes. Emily could not handle his strength. She was boxed in by his strength and size, completely at his mercy.

Her terror abated somewhat when she saw a raggedy, haggard old man step from the house, rubbing sleep from his eyes. He didn't say anything, just pulled a pistol out of his coat pocket, walked up to Colin's blind side and rapped him forcefully on the side of the head with the pistol. He pulled the door open and instructed Colin to get out of the car. "Stand over there!" He waved the pistol to the side of the road. After Colin stopped, he closed the door and said, "Now, young lady, are you from Cheyenne?" She nodded. "Then you jes' go on back home and leave this asshole out here. You can drive, cantcha?" She nodded. "All right, move over here and take the car. You go on home. I ain't gonna kill him or nuthin'. He can get a ride when he gits to the highway. Now you git. I mean it! Go!"

She called Vanessa for a ride home and left Colin's car at the trailer park. She never saw Colin again. Emily learned later that the bouncy cheerleader left school because she was pregnant.

She also learned that at the beginning of her college sophomore year, and Colin's first year as the starting quarterback at UCLA, that the shiny new car led NCAA investigators to an alumni club's illegal money bribe. That ended Colin's football career before it started.

So much for Colin Kelly.

Emily's mother became confined to bed, requiring twenty-four-hour care. Emily cared for her at night and Marie during the day. Emily began nurses training at the local college, terribly disappointed because she desperately wanted to get away from her father's suffocating demands. R. Frederick bought an older car so she could get to and from school and shop for home needs.

Her mother died two years later. Two miserable years. Emily maintained a pleasant bearing throughout the ordeal and suffered no self-condemning shame from the experience. She had demonstrated strength of character far beyond her age.

And then, a month after her mother died, on the fifth day of January, the final family connection collapsed. It happened when Marie asked R. Frederick for better pay. He refused and she quit. Marie, Emily's lifetime friend and counselor was going back to Mexico. Emily was losing her friend-in-need throughout the travails of being a Prindiville. Emily begged her father to keep Marie. Once again, he refused.

"No! She doesn't have that much to do now that your mother is gone. No! She is just trying to wrangle more money to send back to Mexico. No!"

"You owe her, Daddy. She has been very loyal. I could not have managed without her. We owe her."

"No, dammit! No! And that's final. Mind your own business."

"Are you planning to hire someone else?"

He looked surprised. "Why would I? Can't you handle it? Again, no."

Now I'm the housekeeper.

Emily went to Marie's room that evening. They held each other and cried. She helped as Marie packed. When finished, Marie said, "I need to show you something, girl. Have a seat and take a deep breath. What I have to show you is going to hurt." She reached into her vest pocket and handed Emily a key; a key matching the two keys to her diary.

Emily stared at the key, stunned for a few moments. She ran to her room to see if it worked. It did. The other two keys were still in her sock drawer. She dropped to the floor, staggered by the realization that her father had, or could have known everything she had done or even thought about doing since the day he gave her the diary.

Marie slipped in and told Emily that she had known about the key for almost a year but kept the secret because of the family situation with her mother. "I never intended to keep what I knew from you, Child. I just couldn't do it during your grief. I planned to tell you, and now I have."

"Oh, Marie, this is so distressing. Thank you for being honest. What you have told me makes many things clear. That's why he knew so much about my life. That's why he knew things I didn't tell him. He always knew just the right questions to ask. He always knew what I was doing and planned to do. He knew who I was seeing and who I was thinking about. He even knew what I was thinking. This is so awful, Marie. This is the worst kind of betrayal. I'm sick to my stomach. I need to think."

"I'm sorry, Emily, but there is more. There is much more."

"It surely can't be worse."

"Oh, but it is. I'll be right back." She returned a few moments later with a folder and handed it to Emily.

It didn't take her long to recognize that the paperwork revealed her true relationship to the Prindiville family.

Adopted? "Oh-my-god! Can this be true? How did you…?"

"Your father called me from Washington DC during one of his business trips just after your mother died. He needed something from his wall safe and she was gone. He gave me the combination and asked me to read some information to him for a contract or something. I know it was wrong to take advantage of the opportunity, but I looked through the safe and made copies of those papers in the folder because I knew they never told you about being adopted. I was sworn to secrecy. I'm sorry, Emily. I am so sorry."

"Oh, don't be, Marie. I needed to know. Yes, I desperately need to know this. Thank you so much."

Emily drove Marie to the bus station the next morning after giving her a thousand dollars from her father's account. They never saw each other again.

Two months later, the day after finishing her third year of nurses training, Emily placed her car keys, cell phone, credit cards and most of her clothes and jewelry on R. Frederick's bed. She left a note telling him that she was keeping her medical insurance for a few months. Emily left the diary and a short letter revealing everything she had learned from the safe and asked him not to look for her.

She called a taxi, went to the bus station and took an overnight bus to Springfield, Missouri. She had only enough money for food and a place to stay for a few weeks. She had school records, adoption papers, birth certificate, health insurance papers and enough clothes in a large suitcase to last a week without laundering. She felt free. She no longer felt boxed in. She felt like a liberated woman, all alone in the world and soon to be independent. Free! Free and on the way to find her birth mother; on the way to discover why her mother gave her away; on the way to start life over.

Emily arrived in Springfield late the next day and took a motel room for two days. She felt real fright for the first time since leaving home and stewed over her impulsive decisions. *Worry about that tomorrow, Scarlett.*

She awoke in the middle of the night with a raging temperature, vomiting and diarrhea. She collapsed in the bathroom, too sick to move from the fouled bathroom floor until noon the next day. Only then did she have the energy to crawl toward the bed, but not enough strength to get up. She pulled the covers off and over her and lay on the floor, often unconscious and too weak to move. The maid came at Ten O'clock on the final day to prepare the room for the next occupant. She found Emily still on the floor and called management. They immediately called for an ambulance. Emily spent the next two days at the hospital, hydrating and regaining strength from food poisoning. Upon release, the hospital provided transportation to the motel so she could reclaim her luggage. The suitcase had been broken into and her meager stash of money stolen.

The motel manager said, "I don't know nuthin' about that, but I do know you ain't stayin' here, missy. Now, you done cost me a bunch to clean up after you and I got to replace that rug. Took me half day to clean the place and it stills smells. I can't rent this room!"

He drove her to a city overnight shelter. The shelter took homeless people only if the temperature was predicted to go below freezing. Emily was officially homeless, broke, alone, frightened and too weak to care if she lived or died.

CHAPTER TWO

THE OLD MAN

He noticed her while on his way to town on a frigidly cold morning: A girl or very small woman with a scarf over her hair, struggling with a too-large rolling suitcase. She apparently had just departed the local overnight shelter for the homeless. She was trailing well behind an also just-released group of homeless vagabonds half a block ahead. He knew the shelter opened at sundown on nights predicted below freezing. He also knew that the mostly homeless lodgers were turned out by eight in the mornings. The old man had long made it a practice to pick up people in obvious need, particularly any woman with too much to carry or in bad weather. He didn't go looking for them, but once noticed he usually pulled over and offered help. He was whited- headed, wrinkled and clearly elderly; most street people accepted his help. The COVID epidemic had rendered him careful of the virus and he drove on by, hating himself for the being prudent.

The next morning dawned well below freezing and found him guilt-ridden, sitting at the kitchen table with a bowl of cold cereal and coffee, his thoughts still fixed on the girl. His attentions had returned to her over and again since driving by the day before. He checked the clock, finished eating, poured the coffee out and drove to town to see if she might be somewhere near the shelter. The drive didn't take long. He located her on the first pass, a couple of blocks east of the shelter; this time just beyond a run-down business district. He cruised by, exasperated by a troublesome deference to caution that countered his longing to stop. A block later, frustrated by indecision, he angrily yanked the truck around, drove back and parked across the street from her. He sat watching for a minute, making up his mind, wrestling with the urge to help. She had not moved. She could have been a statue, head down, motionless, either resting or sick he figured.

Maybe she's waiting for someone? So, just ask her, dumbass. How hard is this?

He sighed deeply, put his COVID mask on, got out and hurried across the busy street to advance within a few steps. She either ignored him or didn't hear or see his approach. He cleared his throat. Still no movement.

"Excuse me, Miss."

No reaction.

He stepped closer and cleared his throat loudly to attract her attention. She whirled to face him, eyes wide with fright, a trace of fresh tears smeared over her soiled surgical mask

Oh, man. She is so young. Not a kid, though.

He stepped back a little, thinking more distance would seem less threatening. "Could you use some help, Miss?"

She stared at him briefly, an older man, tall and

slender, a baseball cap in hand, his silvery hair back-lit in the morning sun. She addressed him angrily, frightened, thinking he probably wanted to take advantage of her circumstances. "No! You need to get away from me. No one is going to stop to help me with you here. Just go away!"

He respected her wariness and stepped farther back. "That's why I'm here. I stopped to help you. Are you waiting for someone?"

She instinctively began creating a wall of defense. "That is none of your business."

"Excuse me, Miss, but helping *is* my business. I am here to help you. Look, I'm not dangerous and I am not trying to pick you up. All I want is to help. That's all. Let me help."

The wall between them grew along with her anger. "I don't want your help! I just want you to go away. Leave me alone!" She turned to the side.

He could see fresh tears forming beneath her eyes and began to tear up himself, having become more emotional with age. He sighed, twisted the cap in his hands and turned away slightly, preparing to leave.

One last shot. "Please don't make me leave you here like this."

She screamed, "Look! I am not going anywhere with you! So forget it!"

He began losing what little confidence he had to begin with. "I don't want you to go any place with me. How about some food? Are you hungry? Look, I don't want to leave here without helping."

She yelled, "No! Get away from me!"

He put the cap on, bowed slightly and said, "Sorry to bother you." He sighed, turned away and walked back across the street, defeated. He sat in the truck and watched as she took a seat on the suitcase, sagging more by the moment, and then, eyes closed, she leaned over, put her hand on the concrete and rolled off to lie down on the sidewalk.

He trotted back to investigate. She was not unconscious. He knelt close. "Are you sick?" He thought she said something, too softly for him to understand. "Are you sick?"

"No. I'm so tired. I'll be okay. Please leave me alone."

He stood, looking around. What few homeless people he could still see half a block away were watching him. He sighed and said, "Okay, but you need to get off this sidewalk. Here, let me help you across the street. Come on. You can rest there in the sun. I'm going to get some food for you." She didn't fight as he pulled her up. Once standing but wobbly, she seemed to gather strength. He took the suitcase handle, put an arm around her waist and walked her slowly across the street to the parking lot containing his truck. Once there, gasping for air, she slumped to the ground against a vacant building.

He heard her speak, faintly. He could barely hear the words.

"I just can't go on. I'm so tired."

The wall between them weakened.

"What would you like to eat?"

"I don't care. Anything." She wouldn't look at him.

"All right then. Good." He nodded. "Okay. I'll be right back."

She wasn't in the parking lot when he returned. He looked around and spotted her almost half a block on toward town, collapsed again, sitting on the suitcase, head down, too exhausted to continue. He placed the bag of food on the truck seat, went to her, pulled her up and grabbed the suitcase handle. "Come on. Follow me back across the street. I have something to eat." He pointed toward his truck. She followed, shuffling, losing ground, too weak to pick up her feet. He went back and took her arm.

She gobbled the food while repeatedly glancing at the sack next to him. After a final deep swallow, she pointed and said, "Are you going to eat those fries?"

The wall faded.

She ate the fries without looking up. He offered his coke. She didn't hesitate, though she must have known he had taken a sip or two from the straw. Finished, she leaned back, breathing heavily. "Thank you. I was so hungry."

"When did you eat last?"

"I don't know." She looked over at him, her brow a furrowed question. "Isn't that odd? I really don't remember. I have been so sick."

He stood. "Well, no offense, but you still look pretty sick to me. I'll be right back." He went to the truck, retrieved a travel blanket beneath the passenger seat and draped it over her shoulders. He sat down several feet from her to appear less threatening, leaning against the building. After a moment, he said, "Look, I just need to say a couple of things to you. Will you please just let me have a few words?"

Her eyes remained closed while she spoke. "Maybe you mean well, but I'm not going anywhere with you in that truck." She glanced over at him. Her eyes held.

He nodded. "I don't intend to ask you to go anywhere with me." He smiled, and then to disarm her even more said, "And I really don't want you in my truck, not with this COVID thing going around."

He would have taken her anywhere.

"Now, what I would like to do is get you off this street, though. Nothing good is going to happen to you out here today. The weather is supposed to turn icy. I mean it. An ice storm. Seriously, we are predicted to have ice–lots of it. I can help if you will let me. I won't ask you to do anything against your will."

The wall of uncertainty weakened. She hadn't growled at him. She stared at him for a few moments before saying, "What *is* your deal? Are you with a church or some civic organization?"

"No. I want to help only because I should. It makes me feel good to help someone in trouble. That's my story. And now, for your information, I am going on eighty-seven years old. I pose no threat to you and I have no ulterior motive other than to help, and that's the end of my story. Please, let me help you." He began to tear up.

The wall faded.

"Like what, for instance?"

He nodded, recognizing an opening. "Good. First, what's your name?"

"Emily."

"Hi, Emily. My name is Ben. You look awfully tired, Emily, and you look sick. So let's start there. Would you like a hotel room for a few days to help you recover? Maybe with room service so you can have decent food? You could charge everything to the room. I don't intend to be there with you."

"What? No! I don't have enough money for something like that!"

He held up a restraining hand. "Didn't figure you did. I do, though, and there are no strings attached. Now, how about it?"

The wall regained strength. She was shaking her head.

"I don't want you to go anywhere with me, Emily." He stood, took a twenty from his wallet, stepped near and handed it to her. "Use that. Call a taxi. You can ask him to take you to a decent hotel or motel. I will follow along to register for you and then I intend to leave you with the room keys and drop completely out of your life, unless you need some more help. I want you to be out of harm's way." He waited.

No response.

"Come on, Emily. You really need to get off the streets. Living like this is way beyond dangerous." He held up both hands, palms up, and then stood and said, "Okay. That's all I got. I won't bother you any longer. I wish I could have helped." He turned toward the truck and started to walk. The gambit worked. Her voice stopped him.

"That's a lot of money for someone you don't know. What's in it for you?"

What remained of the wall began to crumble.

He turned back, forcing himself not to smile. "What's in for me? Not one damned thing, Emily. Just something I should do without being asked. I think you need help. No, I'm absolutely certain about that. Let me help you."

A county patrol car rolled to a stop behind him. He sighed, thinking the deputy would probably run him off.

She turned on the flashing parking lights but not the rotating overhead light and stepped out, tall and black and very much in control. "Is there some problem here?" She approached, deliberately waiting until she knew his eyes were on her before punching the vest camera as she neared.

"No, officer. I think this young woman is sick and I think she needs help. Maybe you could lend a hand here?"

"Let me see some identification, Sir." She scanned his driver's license, gave it back and then stepped to Emily to ask for her identification. After handing it back, she said, "Are you homeless?"

Emily seemed confused. "What? No, I.... I'm just tired and sick."

"Did you stay at the homeless shelter down the street last night?"

"Um...yes."

"Well, then you *are* homeless, honey." She turned to Ben. "Okay, Mister Compton. What are you doing here? What's going on?"

"I noticed her on the street and thought she was in trouble. So I stopped. All I want is to help her, Officer. There is some very bad weather coming and she needs to be off the street."

The corporal nodded and said, "You are certainly right about that." She turned to Emily. "Okay, Missy. What's your story?"

Emily rubbed her eyes and pulled the mask back up, delaying for time to think. "I came by bus four days ago–from Cheyenne, Wyoming. I plan to finish school here. I got sick the first night and had to be taken to the hospital. I spent two nights there. When I got back to the motel, my suitcase had been broken into and my money is gone. Most of it anyway. I am still weak and don't know what to do. I'm too tired to think. I just need to rest."

"What kind of sick were you? Or should I say, are you?"

"Throwing up, diarrhea, unconscious. The motel called

the ambulance and I spent two days in ICU. Probably food poisoning. After the hospital released me, they gave me a ride back to the motel. I have very little money left. The motel manager brought me to the shelter and I stayed there the last two nights."

"So, in other words, you are in one mell of a hess." She turned to Ben. "Now, Mister Compton, just how are you planning to help this young woman? Let me hear your ideas. Maybe between the three of us we can put something together. So, tell me." She glared, regarding Ben as questionable, on alert for the safety of the tiny woman.

"I would like to see her in a decent motel or hotel until she feels better. I will pay the bill. If you would take her there, Officer, I will follow along and make the financial arrangements. And then I intend to go home and drop out of her life. I am not trying to pick her up or take advantage of her. It's her choice and I am not trying to get her into my truck. It would sure help if you could transport her if she agrees. I don't want anything from her. That's my story."

The corporal turned to Emily. "And you have a problem with that?"

"I don't know him. I don't want to go anywhere with him."

The corporal turned to Ben. "So?"

"As I said, I don't want her to go with me. I already offered to pay for a taxi to take her to a hotel of her choosing. I have no sinister motive."

The corporal knelt in front of Emily and whispered, "What's the matter with you, kid? I think you are facing a life and death situation here tonight, honey. You are going to die out here, and you are probably going die this very night if you don't get off this street. It's your choice, but I recommend you take this man's offer. Seems to me that you have complete control of the situation. I think the old guy is probably okay. Come on, kid. I'll take you to wherever. Let's get you off the street."

Emily nodded assent.

The corporal stood and looked at Ben. "Well, looks like we have an agreement." She turned to Emily. "Now, you, young woman, hop in the back of my car. I'll put your things in. And you, Sir, tell me again just how you plan to manage this."

"If you will, Officer, take her to the Doubleday Inn. I think it's a nice enough place. I will register for her and pay the bill. I think a few days there with room service so she can recover and eat some decent food will help her recover. I will register for her and then meet you two at the back door on the west side and give you the paperwork and keys to the room. And then, Officer, I plan to go home."

He turned to Emily. "I will never come to your room or call you, Emily."

Ben and Emily had no way of knowing how much their decisions had just changed both of their lives, forever.

He registered, met the two women and gave the corporal the registration paperwork and door key-cards. She studied everything, nodded approval and handed it all to Emily. "Okay. Looks good to me, kid. Good luck to both of you. Now I have to get back to work." She saluted, got in the patrol car and departed.

Ben pulled Emily's suitcase to the elevator. "Do you have a phone, Emily?"

"No. I left it in Wyoming. I plan to get one."

"I think you need a phone."

"I know, but I'll have to do without for a while. Thanks for everything. I may never understand why you are doing this, but I am truly grateful. Thank you."

He waved, walked away and drove straight to a Walmart to buy a pre-paid phone with enough minutes to last a while. He had the desk clerk take the phone and a slip of paper with his phone number to Emily's room.

The phone woke Emily from a deep sleep late that evening. "Hello?"

"Hi, Emily. This is Corporal Henry. Do you have a moment?"

"Oh, hello. First, let me thank you for helping me."

"Glad to help. That's my job. Now, I have something for you, so listen up. The guy who helped you is named Ben Compton. I had the office run a discovery on him. You ready for this?"

"I guess so."

"He looks solid to us, Emily. We don't believe he has any motive other than to help you. Actually, I think he is probably saving your life. We all think you should be cautious of course. We believe he is probably just a plain old decent guy. You should Google him. Ben Compton. A very remarkable guy actually. He filled in a couple of years recently as a county commissioner—appointed by the governor. Oh, and he has a website. bencompton.com. I think you will find that more than a little bit interesting. The hotel has computers you can use. Pull him up. His entire history is there. Seems like a solid citizen to me. You have my numbers if you ever need me. Bye now."

Emily called Ben on the fourth morning of her stay. "Hello, Mister Compton. This is Emily. Are you familiar with the colleges and hospitals in Springfield?"

He smiled and pumped his fist. Once again, as was all too evident in recent years, he felt the onset of tears. "Yes. I am very familiar with those institutions. I graduated from Missouri State and have spent lots of time with family and friends in all of the Springfield hospitals."

"I would like talk with you about Springfield in general. Perhaps we could meet?"

"I would like that. When you feel up to it, just give me a call. I suppose we could have something to eat there at the hotel restaurant, if you want to. Something like that?"

"Yes. May I call you tomorrow?"

"Good enough. Call whenever you want to, Emily. And please call me Ben." She thanked him and hung up. He pounded the desk and yelled, "Well, all right!" After a huge sigh, he started laughing, tears welling in his eyes.

She called the morning of day five at the hotel. "Good morning, Ben. It's Emily."

"And a good morning to you, Emily. By the way, what is your last name?"

"Prindiville. Emily Prindiville. No middle name. Ben, I need some pointers about Springfield. I plan to stay here and finish school. Will you be available? I would like to talk you. Maybe today sometime?"

"Any time that suits you. Are you feeling better?"

"Yes, much. First, I think we should both get a COVID test. I called around. We can get in about four this afternoon."

"Done. I'll pick you up at three thirty in the atrium."

Ben was staggered by her appearance. He had not realized just how tiny she was, or, without the mask, how incredibly attractive. Her beauty astonished him. Otherworldly dark eyes– fascinating gypsy eyes. Her hair was dark black and soft as velvet. He caught himself staring and recovered, somewhat embarrassed. "I must say, you certainly clean up well, Emily."

She laughed, put her mask on and they went for the tests. Two hours later, they returned to the hotel and went to the bar cafe. Emily picked an isolated six-place table and sat across from him at the opposite end.

"Social distance, Ben. A temporary arrangement until we get results of the COVID test and until you get vaccinated. I worked at a hospital in Cheyenne, so I have already been vaccinated. You can't infect me but I might infect you. We should both mask up and keep our distance until you are vaccinated, though. Is that okay with you?"

"Perfect. I'm impressed, Emily. I am an old man, you know, and I need to be cautious. Thank you for taking the lead."

"I have finished third year nursing school, Ben, so I have no excuse to be careless."

"Are you working on a nursing degree?"

"I am. I hope to finish it here at Missouri State."

The waiter arrived with menus and they lapsed into silence. Emily declined his offer of a drink. He ordered a beer. A band began playing and ruined any chance for conversation. When finished, he asked for the check and turned to her. "The atrium lobby is spacious, Emily. It's well ventilated and quiet if you are still up for that conversation."

"Yes, I need to ask some questions. I still have some missing pieces, right?" Once seated, she opened by asking about his family.

"One boy. A medical doctor in St. Louis. Heart specialist. He has one son, just beginning a medical internship himself–also in St Louis. That's it. No other family. Before you ask, I left my wife thirty-some years ago."

Her eyebrows raised. "Oh? Divorce?" She started to wave him off, thinking her question pried too much.

He spoke up. "No, separated. Kind of a bad knock on me there. I'm the one who broke the marriage."

She took his comment as an opening. "If you don't mind my asking, why? And, if you do mind me asking, forget I asked."

"I ran off with another woman."

She covered her eyes and peeked through. He was laughing at her. She said, "Really? Should I be sorry I asked?"

"No. It was a mistake. My mistake. I had fallen out of being *in* love with my wife after I retired. We moved to farms we bought while I was in the Corps. My dad had not put up any hay. It was August and I desperately needed her help, just to drive the hay truck for me, that's all. She blew out and went to work in town when I needed her most. That was probably the beginning of the end of the marriage for me. Long story short, I quit seeing the other woman after a short fling, but that ruined my marriage. All on me. I sold all the herds, the machinery, sold or rented the farms and planned to leave. Didn't know where I was going, just leaving. The last thing my spare woman requested from me was to let her know when I was leaving. I called her.

She said, 'When, exactly are you leaving?'

"As soon as I put this phone down. I'm packed and ready."

'Where are you going?'

"Don't know and don't care."

'Can you wait five minutes? I'll call you right back.'

"I guess. Why?"

She hung up. She called back and said, 'I'm going with you.'

"Well, you could have knocked me over with a feather. We lasted about a month. I told her one night that we couldn't go on, that we were building our lives on the ashes of our families. Her boy refused to go to school. Her husband was having heart problems. My son was all strung out trying to take care of his mother's emotional problems. Everything was messed up. Anyway, she called home and her husband agreed to take her back. We packed and I took her home the next morning and took my wife out of a care facility. Our marriage was a shambles. We tried to make a go of it for a few years. I just couldn't do it. And then I met Elena."

"Wow! There is more? Should I be sorry I asked, Ben?"

"Don't be. I had a great life with Elena–the other

woman." He hit his forehead several times with a fist. "I cannot tell you how much I hate that expression–'The other woman.' Anyway, she was my entire life for twenty-five years. She died five years ago. Cancer. I haven't been excited about much since. Living alone is wearing on me, and, of course, it's pretty late in life to even think about starting over with...." He shrugged. "Anyway, now you know."

"You don't look or act all that old to me."

He laughed. "I told you how old I am, and that is way the hell and gone over the hill. Okay, enough about me. What about you? What brings you to Springfield?"

She grimaced. "Ah! Well, I had to know that was coming, didn't I? I'm really not ready to go too deeply into everything, Ben, so maybe a sketch will do for now?"

He nodded and she tipped her hand back and forth. He picked up on the signal. "What would you like?"

"Something smooth and red."

He motioned to the attendant and asked for a mild red wine.

When it came, she raised the wine to him. "Thank you. I'm probably going to need this. I don't drink much, so if I get silly, please stop me. This is a horror story, Ben, so let's just start at the starting place. My life began right here in Springfield, at a hospital, twenty-two years ago. That's the reason I am here. I came to find my mother, and my father if that's possible. I plan to finish my last year of school while I'm at it."

She hit the high points of being left in a box at the entrance, put up for adoption, a few words about her home life and college, and then stopped, pressed fingers to her temples and patted her cheeks briskly. She looked up and told him about the reason she left Cheyenne and how she became destitute. "That's about all there is to it, Ben."

"I'm so sorry, Emily. Things should have been better for you. That business about the diary betrayal leaves me chilled and furious. Damn, that had to hurt."

"Yes. True nonetheless. There is much more in the details of course. My immediate plans are to take a job with a hospital here as a nurse assistant. I am a certified nurse assistant–a CNA. I want to finish schooling and get my RN degree. I have finished three years and should be able to finish in a year. I need to find some paying work while finishing the degree at Missouri State. I have already checked and my previous credits are all good. I scored high enough grades through high school and college. My ACT/SATS scores and college grades qualify me in Missouri for in-state tuition."

"Will you share the scores with me?"

She studied him for several moments. "No. I was valedictorian in high school. That should tell you enough."

"What size school?"

"The largest in Wyoming."

"Okay, I'm impressed. How did your high school years go?"

"High school? Well, for the most part all right. I had some great girlfriends. My father clamped down hard enough, probably thanks to that damned diary, to make dating almost impossible." She shrugged. "And, by the way, I intend to pay you back for all you are doing for me, Ben. Every-single-dollar. And I am keeping track."

He waved her off. "Only if you need to, and certainly not now. I have a good retirement, Emily, and medical paid for life. So, you see, I'm well enough off. You don't need to worry about me being caught short because I'm helping you."

He waited for her to go on. When she didn't, he said, "We covered a lot of ground for one sitting. Perhaps we can do this again sometime?"

"Of course. You are my only contact in Springfield." She chuckled. "Actually, as it turns out, you are about my only contact on this planet. Thank you so much for everything."

He stood. "You look tired, Emily. Off to bed with you. Call whenever you like."

"How about tomorrow after lunch? I need to tour around town and take care of a few things and learn the ropes, but only if you are willing and available."

"You bet." He left her at the elevator. "I think we just might become pretty good friends, Emily. I hope so. See you tomorrow. Call me."

She called just after noon and they spent the day cruising Springfield. When he drove by the hospital, Emily asked him to park near the emergency room entrance. After several moments of staring at the entryway portico, she sighed and motioned for him to go on.

Ben said, "Guess you wouldn't remember that."

They spent the remainder of the afternoon at the Missouri State administration building where she applied for entrance, asked about and applied for possible grants, and applied for student loans. She also appropriated a slate of spring semester classes scheduled to begin in less than three weeks.

Ben got his first genuine impression of her personality as they departed the Admin building that afternoon. Emily skipped and twirled like a little girl. So happy. Playful.

The next day he took her to select a permanent cell phone, and then to open a bank account. Ben deposited several hundred dollars. Emily fussed. He said, "Had to be done. Part of your identification. Now what?"

"Thank you again and again, thank you, Ben. Now, if you have time, I would like to see where you live. And, by the way, I tested negative. You need to call and get your results. Let's do everything we can to stay away from any contact with the virus."

The drive to his home took ten minutes. He lived near the northernmost outskirts of Springfield. Ben pressed a button on the rear-view mirror and a sturdy steel pipe double gate swung open and closed automatically after he drove through. He pulled to a stop in sight of the house after passing a grove of trees.

She exclaimed, "Oh, Ben! What a beautiful setting."

His home was surrounded by a circle of ancient oak trees and an expansive, well-manicured lawn. The fenced yard was surrounded by and interrelated to what appeared to be wide open hayfields. Emily learned later that he rented the sixty acres of fields to a local farmer who took the hay and kept the property trimmed. Their arrangement did not permit cattle.

"You are so isolated."

"Not as far as you might think." He pointed. "Look there. My southern boundary is a river just beyond that tree line. Clear, clean water. The Sac River." He spelled it. "Named after an Indian tribe. The Springfield city limits are on the other side of that river. No bothersome neighbors for me, just a few deer and wild turkeys. I live within five miles of town. I cannot see my closest neighbor's homes. Perfect. Well, it is for me."

The house consisted of two stories and a basement. She could see generous gables on all four sides of the roof. Emily also noticed the magnificent, somewhat elevated covered wrap-around porch on three sides.

She noted that he had not locked the doors as they entered and asked why.

"Locking would just get the windows or a door busted in if someone wanted to get in when I'm gone."

She learned that he only locked at night.

Ben led the tour through the living room into a large kitchen-dining area with an attached utility/bath and back porch–not covered. He led through his study and library and on to the master bedroom. They retreated to the living room again where he pointed to the double staircase with stairs leading up and down. "There is a full basement with a bedroom and gym down there. Lots of storage space. The upstairs has two bedrooms, each with its own bath." He turned to her. "That's it. If you want to make the up and down tour, you go on ahead. I am going to make some tea while you're at it."

She explored and then found him in the kitchen. "I love it, Ben. It's tasteful in a practical sort of way."

He pulled a chair out for her and said, "Practical, you

say? Yeah, I know–bachelor decor. Have a seat, Emily. I'll pour some tea."

"Answer this one question for me, Ben. Why is it so dark? Do you keep the blinds closed for some reason, or just because you were out?"

"Guess I never thought about it. I suppose I like it dark. I never open the blinds."

"I'm not going to let you off that easy. Why not open the blinds?" She noticed that he hesitated, then sighed and looked puzzled, all of a sudden so serious. She decided to change subject by asking about the decorating. "Were all the curtains and paint schemes your idea, Ben?"

He laughed, handed her a glass and sat down. "Lord no. I think it probably has been like this since it was built. The furniture, though, is mostly my son's wife's doing. Fairly recent." He shrugged. "It's pretty bulky. Good enough for me, though."

"How long have you been here?"

"Going on twenty-seven years."

She grimaced. "Ooooo, that long? And by yourself?"

He sighed. "No. I lived here with Elena until she died. Been alone since."

She could tell he was uncomfortable and went back to her original question. "Tell me, Ben, did you keep it this dark when she lived here?"

After a deep sigh, he turned to her and said, "No. She liked it airy and bright." He knew what Emily was doing and nodded. "Honestly? The truth is I have not opened the blinds since the day she died. I like living in a cave. It's cool and quiet. No outside interference. Just me and whatever I'm thinking about. I spend most of my time indoors, writing. The computer is easier on my eyes when it's not bright. Darkness is a comfort to me."

"I will want to know more about Elena and your writing, but right now I wonder if losing her closed your blinds?"

"Maybe, but you are getting pretty close to a place I never go."

"Forgive me. Maybe some other time?"

"Sure. I know I'm a bit of a hermit, but right now I want to talk about you, Emily. I have been thinking about what I am going to say to you since the moment we met." He looked away and cleared his throat, uncomfortable with what came next. "First, I want you to know that I am comfortable with and prepared to continue funding your stay at the hotel, or any other place you choose. And I plan to do just that until you are on your feet with a job and place to stay. But...." He hesitated again, took a deep breath and said, "But I think I know enough about you now to feel comfortable about offering you the option of staying here. I have plenty of space. I hope you know enough about me by now to know that I am no threat and that I have only your interests on my mind. So, to make it formal, it would please me very much if you stayed here until your feet are on the ground." He held up his forefinger for silence. "You don't need to answer that right now. Just something I have been thinking about. I make pretty good company, Emily. I will not mow the yard when you are sleeping, or slam doors or drawers. I won't run the radio or stereo when you need rest. I won't even take a shower. However, I am only a so-so cook. I could go on...." He looked at her hopefully, eyes wide, forehead furrowed.

She put fingertips to her temples. "Oh, Ben. That is way too much to ask of you. You don't need to think of me as your responsibility."

"I know that, but it would suit me just fine if you were. Actually, if you decide to stay, that would make me very happy."

"This is so...so fast. I need some time to think."

"Of course. Even if you don't stay Emily, I would still like to help until you are solid ground, safe and independent. I've grown accustomed to your face." He grimaced. "Don't say it. I know that was cheesy. I don't want to let you just disappear and then worry about you. Anyway, take your time and think it over" He gazed at the ceiling for a moment, groaned, and then back to her. "Okay, I'm not being completely honest. I do have a motive. Simply put, I don't want to go through the rest of my life wondering what happened to you, Emily. I want to know that you made it through your bad times. I want to keep track of what happens to you. I am a wee bit emotionally invested in you. There, I said it. Now, let's get out of here."

"This is all too unexpected for me, Ben. I need to get back to the hotel. Okay?"

"You bet. Let's go. You drive."

"What? No! I can't drive that thing. I don't know—"

"Well, if you do end up staying with me, you're gonna need to know how drive the damned truck, at least until you get your own wheels."

"What about you, Ben? Wouldn't you need a car?"

He got up and pulled her chair out. "Come with me. I want to show you something." They left the house though the garage where he proudly whisked the cover from a very shiny motorcycle. "Here. This is what I will do for wheels. I ride it a lot when the weather is decent, or when someone else needs the truck. Now, let's go."

He walked directly to the passenger side of the truck and got in.

Emily required very little instruction once she struggled her way up and into Ben's four-wheel drive truck. She had to move the seat all the way forward and up, but admitted once underway that it made her feel powerful to look down on almost everyone on the road.

"If you decide to stay, Emily, I will definitely have steps put on. That will help both of us. It's getting to be a bit of stretch for me, too."

CHAPTER THREE

HARMONY

A day later found Emily agonizing over the amount of money Ben had already spent on her, and the efforts he had taken to make her life easier.

He has treated me with more care and concern than my father ever did. Why am I being so guarded? The cops trust him. He has given me time to make my own decision. He isn't pressing me. The fact is, I do trust him. I think he is a decent man. So, it's time to get on or get off. What can I do? The truth hurts, but I can't make it on my own. I'm broke and I don't want to go back to Cheyenne. So?

She called before he finished coffee the next morning.

"Ben, I thought all night about what you said yesterday. Can you pick me up about nine-thirty this morning?"

"Certainly. What's up?"

"Me. I'm up. I am up and packed. If you are still willing, I would like to stay with you, Ben, at least for a while if the offer still good."

There. She held her breath.

He laughed. "Hell yes! Damn straight! Okay, I'll be right there. This is really good news, Emily! I'll see you at nine-thirty." He wiped the beginning of tears away, smiling so broadly that his face hurt.

"Don't be late, Ben. I need to be checked out by ten to save you some money."

Ben saw her the moment he entered the hotel, sitting alone near the registration counter. She bounced up, smiling merrily, closing the distance, swaying from one side to the other, nearly dancing. Seeing her so cheerful and fresh-faced made him stop and smile, thinking, *What a complete difference between now and the first time I saw her.* He wondered if she always seemed so happy and if the behavior was typical. They both put masks in place. She hugged him briefly, holding her breath, face turned away. She stepped back. "This is so exciting, Ben. I am going to mark today as my starting over moment. Can we go? I mean to your home." She laughed and arranged her hands prayerfully. "Please? I can't wait."

Upon arrival, he dropped her suitcase in the middle of his living room and said, "You go on up, Emily. Choose your room. When you're ready, give me a yell and I'll bring your things up. Take your time. Pretend your decision is going to be for the long run."

She stopped at the foot of the stairs. "Which room would you choose in my place, Ben?"

"Depends on whether you are a morning or evening person."

"Why?"

"If you are a night person, the west bedroom will stay darker in the mornings. If you are morning person, the east bedroom will be light early and dark late."

"Ah. Thank you. I am not a morning person." She turned and ran up the stairs.

Ben shrugged and thought. Okay, not a morning person. Guess that means I still drink coffee alone.

Emily took half an hour deciding and found him waiting at the kitchen table, coffee in hand. She chose the West bedroom as Ben hoped she would, separating her farther from his early morning kitchen noises.

"Good choice, Emily. Now, take a couple of days to get settled and think about what personal things you need to be comfortable. I'll be out and about taking a walk. When I get back, I'll make something for lunch. See you later."

"I am in no hurry, Ben, but I will need a few things for the bathroom. I didn't bring much."

"You should probably also think about some jock gear if you are into exercise. I have a mile long trail around the property and a pretty good gym in the basement. If you are taking a hospital job during COVID, it might not hurt to be in good physical shape. Fact is, I don't believe it is ever a bad idea to be in good physical condition." He cocked an eye at her and said, "Only if you are interested."

"Jock gear for girls? Okay, I guess. I am interested, though, and I will need some of your so called jock gear.

Let's call mine Girl Gear. But first, I want to see that trail. These shoes are good enough for that, aren't they? Can we go now?"

Ben kept the trail around the periphery of his property mowed short with a riding lawnmower. When they arrived at the river, Emily stopped and remarked, "This is so peaceful. What I want to know is, where is your bench? Where is your deck? Where do you come to sit?"

"It is pretty, but I generally don't stop. Point A to point B kinda guy. There is no permanent place to sit or put your feet up because the river floods a little beyond those trees." He pointed back toward the house. "Up there. You can see by that line of leaves and limbs in the hayfield just how far the water has been this year."

"Well, this setting is way too good to neglect. I'm going to find a folding chair or something, Ben. I can hang it in the trees in case of a flood. Would that be okay?"

"Of course."

As time went on, they both came, usually separately, to use Emily's chair.

She took his truck that afternoon to shop for clothes and bathroom articles. After the evening meal, he washed and she dried the dishes, all quite relaxed and natural, like old friends.

"Do you have plans this evening, Ben?"

"Nope. What's on your mind?"

"You. I don't really know that much about you, other than I am comfortable around you and I feel safe. But.... But I want to know about your life. Tell me about your life, Ben, from page one if you want to. Oh, and I noticed that you have opened the blinds. Thank you."

"No. Thank you, Emily. It's long past time. Now, about me? You better be sure. You are old enough to know by now just how much guys hate talking about themselves, but I will try to be brief. There is a big easy chair for you in the office. Come on." Once seated he said, "From the beginning? Are you sure? I go a long way back."

She nodded and pulled her feet up.

"Okay. My life began in Nineteen-Thirty-Four near Kit Carson, Colorado. I was born smack in the middle of a Great Depression dust storm. I grew up with three sisters and a brother. My brother died twelve years ago. My sisters all live within twenty miles of me. We don't see much of each other."

"Wait, Ben. Why not? I would think siblings would–"

"Nope. I talk to my older sister at least once a day. She can no longer drive as she is nearly blind. The two of us run around together occasionally, usually shopping or to a doctor visit. We haven't seen each other that much since COVID. The other two...? I don't know, Emily, maybe I'm a little too outspoken about politics. I am not political. Only the candidate counts to me. Not their damned party. My two younger sisters are/were Trump voters. They also do not acknowledge global warming or climate change. And, to me at least, they seem to be easily persuaded by conspiracy theories. I shouldn't take issue with them. I try to avoid arguing about conflicting issues, which leads to isolation. We just haven't been very good friends the past four years. Frankly, I expect we are better off keeping our distance for the time being."

"And your brother?"

"He died nearly twenty years ago. Lung cancer. Another little family get-together problem there, too. He married a Jehovah's Witness and bought into the cult himself, which is okay except his chosen religion left the rest of us out. I'll just leave it there."

"So, in effect, you are nearly isolated from family."

"Oh, yeah. Hard to admit, but true."

"Now, take me back to Kit Carson."

"Okay. Think the middle of the Great Depression and the Dust Bowl. Dad had no way of being successful as a farmer and had to get off the farm. My family had no electricity or running water when we were kids. Dad seldom found decent work and when he did it was mostly nomadic farm work. We moved around like migrants until World War Two came along, moving constantly while Dad went from one temporary job to another. He eventually found a good job in the state of Washington with the Defense Department where he worked for security at the Hanford Atom Bomb complex. In Nineteen-Forty-Six, after the war, we moved from Washington to Missouri and took over my grandfather's ninety-acre rocky farm. That's just twenty miles north of here by the way. We were dirt poor." Ben held up his hands. "And we were also back to square one, living with no running water or electricity and no bathroom. We lived in a two-story log house and raised most of our own food. We five children walked to a one room school where I was the only seventh grader. I attended high school at a little town a few miles just north of here, in a class of eleven kids. I learned how to play ball in high school and not much else. I graduated and entered college where I flunked the math and English entrance exams. It was a teacher's college then; now it's your school, Emily–Missouri State University. I had to take remedial English and Math with the football players. Am I going too fast or too slow for you? Is this too much?"

"I may want to know more, but I find this most entertaining, Ben, if not quite believable. Please go on. I keep forgetting that our lives are three generations apart."

"All true, Emily. My first two years of college were a waste. I played ball and made average grades. I only made average grades by taking easy courses. I didn't step up–just wasting time. And then!" He held his arms up like a touchdown had just been scored. "And then my world completely transformed one spring day in nineteen-fifty-four as I walked alone through the Student Union. I passed near a naval aviator standing by a cardboard cut-out of a naval aviator. A recruiter. Why I stopped, I will never know. I had never been in an airplane or even thought of flying. The recruiter said, 'Do you think you're good enough?'"

Ben paused, watching her for a sign. Emily rolled her hand for more.

"I just stood there like a dummy for a few moments before finally answering, 'I don't know. Why?'"

"It will take you about twenty minutes to find out."

"I just stood there, thinking I guess, and finally said, 'What would I have to do to find out?'"

"Just step back here with me and take a short test.' He directed me to a classroom where I took an IQ test. He graded it, looked up and said, 'Oh, you'll do just fine. When do you want to go?'"

"Dead silence from me, Emily. I thought for a moment, and then for some reason-don't ask because I have no idea-I told him that I couldn't go until I helped my dad through haying season. He nodded, flipped open a tablet, looked up and said, 'How about August the First?'"

"I said okay and signed up. That was the first of the two most important forks in the road of my life. That preposterous, reckless decision has made all the difference in my life, and all for the better."

"Oh, Ben, that is so unbelievable. Go on! More! More!"

"Well, as you can probably imagine, that day changed me. Flight training provided the crucible that molded me into who I could become, not just who I was. I checked into the real world for the first time in my life and totally applied myself. I got my wings but took a commission in the Marine Corps. Same airplanes; same leadership; just different uniforms. Very exciting times. I met my sister's college roommate at age twenty-two while home on leave. After very few dates, when I was twenty-three, we got married and wasted no time starting our family. A boy. I would rather go on with the brief. We can talk about him some other time if you like.

"Anyway, I separated from The Corps at the end of the four year tour I had signed up for; went back and finished college in two years and went back into the Corps. I flew jet fighters, made rank and ended my career eighteen year later as a lieutenant colonel having been the commanding officer of an all-weather fighter attack squadron. I retired in 1977 and started raising beef cattle on several small farms we bought while in the Corps. And then…." He stopped, sighed deeply, and said, "And then I changed everything by running off with another woman."

"Oh, be serious."

"No joke. I broke the vows. I'm not proud of it and it wasn't my idea initially, but that's another long story. We only lasted about a month before deciding we couldn't do it. Our families were falling apart. It all falls into the category of things I definitely should not have done. I sold the herds, the machinery and rented the farms. I left the area and had a hard time trying to settle down after that. I never made it back to living seriously with my wife–just too much damage to overcome. Anyway, I have done a bit of everything since. Taught high school science and physical education, and coached, mostly high school girls. I drove over the road trucks for three months–too long–ran a dude ranch for several years and just wandered around alone for several more years. I once wrote opinion pieces for the Springfield newspaper, until I started writing novels. I have written five novels and a book of poetry. I belong to the Springfield Writers' Guild." He paused, looked up at Emily and said, "I mention the Guild because that's where I first met Elena. Elena and I stayed together nearly twenty-five years. That is a long story for another discussion."

"No, Ben! You cannot stop there! No! Please! I want to know, or is it just too private?"

"No. I will tell you, Emily, but that's a story that needs to stay separate."

"Oh, Ben. Now I'm going to worry about you. I just know something bad–"

"Another time, Emily. Please. Anyway, to wrap up all the disorder, I also belong to the local chapter of the Missouri Poetry Society. I meet friends occasionally for coffee." He clapped and said, "In a nutshell, Emily, there you have it."

"Oh, that is all so amazing. Almost leaves me

breathless. You have led a colorful life. I will definitely want to know more, but I suppose that's enough to digest at one sitting. Thank you. Now, I want to know more about your writing and those novels you spoke of. And, by the way, I googled you and read your website, just so you know. I definitely want to read your novels."

He turned and pointed to the wall to wall, floor to ceiling bookcase behind him. "Right there. Five novels and a book of poetry. I'm still a learning writer."

"Do you mind if I read them?"

"Absolutely not. At your leisure."

"Now, how about that guitar in the corner?"

"Oh, I used to play quite a bit. Usually while on overseas tours. A few of us would get together...kinda like a garage band. Better than drinking all weekend at the officer's club. Do you play an instrument, Emily?"

"Yes. I have played the violin since I was five. Participated in the high school orchestra. Made my way to state competition as a soloist."

"How did that go?"

"I won first place my junior and senior years. I didn't have to be that good because there are not that many high school orchestras in Wyoming."

"Why the violin?"

"My father didn't want me out with the marching band. 'Out there parading around in front of everyone.' His words. So, the violin and instruction at home.

"Any specific kind of violin?"

"Just a regular concert violin. I left it on my father's bed along with other things he paid for, including, unfortunately, my cell phone. I will want to hear you play, Ben, but right now I need to make arrangements to get my books at the university bookstore. And then I need to go to the hospital where my birth certificate came from and see about part time work. I also need to register for their RN classes. They have a nurse training school that fits with the University courses where I will get the RN degree. Can you take me?"

"Be better if you take the truck, Emily. You don't need me trailing along. I'll write out the directions for you."

"I can use the phone."

"Oh, yeah. I forget."

Emily succeeded in meshing a schedule of school and hospital nursing duties during the next two days. She called Ben from the hospital to remind him that she had already taken the COVID vaccination before leaving Wyoming and asked if he had underlying conditions.

"Yes. Why do you ask?"

"I think I can get you signed up for the shot if you do. Are you willing?"

"Great! Yes, I have Pulmonary Fibrosis. I am also nearly eighty-seven. Don't you think that should count as an underlying condition?" He laughed.

"Oh, I'm sorry. I didn't realize about your lungs. How bad is it, Ben? And I don't mean being eighty-seven."

"Bad enough. The doctor who discovered it said I had three to five years to live. That was eleven years ago. The pulmonologists believe I probably contracted it while serving as Air Officer during the siege of Khe Sanh in Vietnam. Another story for you some other time. They think the Agent Orange defoliant we used probably caused it. I have lost about fifty percent of my lung capacity. No cure, but I expect you already knew that, too."

"You don't seem to be limited."

"I am, though, at least from what I used to be. I have adapted."

"I'm sorry, Ben. I would fix it if I could."

"It is also progressive, as I am sure you also know, but thanks. Guess I'm not going to get out of this vale of tears alive. I once believed I might be the world's first immortal. Bullet proof."

"Not funny, Ben. The reason I asked about underlying conditions is because I can probably get the COVID vaccination for you since I am living with you. Just a minute. I want to make sure." He could hear her speaking to someone. "Yes, Ben. Your age and the Agent Orange underlying condition are plenty enough to qualify you. Today at two thirty, if that works for you?"

"Absolutely."

"I'll see you in about fifteen. After she picked him up, she said, "I want to know about combat, Ben. You can tell me on the way."

He seemed reluctant. She prodded him again while crossing town.

"All right. This shouldn't take long, if I can stay away from sea stories. Okay, combat. I served both in the air and on the ground in Vietnam. I was the Air Officer at Khe Sanh during the siege. Dirty, hot, sweaty, bad water and food. Sick all the time. We all went to work anyway. Oh, the living conditions were terrible, but C-rats and the water to drink were worse, what with the malaria meds in it and the requirement to kill the raging bacteria that existed everywhere. I lost thirty-five pounds in five months. Never was so glad to leave something in my life. That's just one form of ground combat. All forms of ground combat are miserable and mine sure wasn't the worst." He paused.

"Go on, Ben. More."

Okay. Air combat. Whole different animal. Exciting. Dangerous. Demanding. But! But after you get into that cockpit, start the engine and close the canopy, you can turn the air conditioner on and everything changes. I was in my natural setting. In control. Getting shot at while flying is worlds apart from being shot at on the ground. You can't hear or see most of the fire coming at you, but the controllers are yelling, 'You're taking fire! You're taking fire.' I actually loved air combat. I wrote a poem about it. Okay, that's enough about combat. I know a ton of side stories, but not now."

She found a new violin on her bed on Friday night. Ben had visited the local music shops during the week to make sure he got a decent instrument and all the accessories. He listened from the kitchen while she tuned the violin and waxed the bow. He teared up when she began playing. She played skillfully, like a state champion soloist.

Emily's following months became a never-ending blur of classes intermingled with nursing assistant (CNA) duties. She spent every free hour and every weekend picking up extra work at the hospital. Ben drove her to and from occasionally, but she had his truck most of the time. She managed to repay most of the money she owed within six months, and then began demanding to pay rent and split food costs.

Emily coaxed Ben into playing the guitar for her and learned that he could barely read music. They visited the music store and found several pieces written for violin and guitar and played together often. He wasn't an expert by any means, but enjoyed music that didn't demand much more than accompanying chords. They played often enough that Ben memorized some pieces to practice while she was gone.

Emily came to understand that if she found Ben sitting on the couch in the living room after supper and before bed time that he wanted to talk and he wanted her there. She would lie on the couch with her head on a pillow next to him and have room left over, often going to sleep listening to him. He would place a hand on Emily's shoulder and pat her before he left. If she didn't move, he placed an Afghan over her.

Emily brooded about her mother during the tumultuous weeks and months following her arrival in Springfield. Her thoughts seldom strayed from why she wasn't beginning the search for her mother. *Am I afraid to start? I should ask some obvious questions. What am I afraid of?* She knew the answer. *There might not be an answer.*

THE BOX BABY

CHAPTER FOUR

ELECTRIC

B en turned eighty-seven in August and asked Emily
if she could take the weekend off. He wanted to
celebrate. He had never, not once in his life, ever
celebrated his own birthday.

"I will ask, Ben. I can probably get a weekend off.
They owe me. COVID is slacking off now and I haven't
had a weekend off in months. Why? What's up?"

"It's my birthday. I want to celebrate. Just hang out
with you."

Emily got the time off and baked a cake. That Friday
evening late, after the cake and a present of sheet music
for beginning players, they were sitting in Ben's office
talking and sipping a glass of wine. Emily was still in
uniform after a half day's work in the nurse's office away
from patients when the front door popped open and
someone yelled, "Hey, Gramps! Where the hell are you!"

Ben smiled broadly, got up and went to the living

room. Emily, mystified by the boisterous interruption, sat for a moment after Ben departed before peeking to see Ben wrapped in the arms of a very tall young man, both laughing and pounding each other on the back. They broke away after the young guy noticed Emily and pointed. He stared for a moment, and then looked at Ben. "Okay, Gramps, you keeping secrets? Who...?" He looked from Ben to Emily and back. "Come on, Gramps. Introduce me." Later, he told them that his first thoughts were that his grandfather was not well and required the services of a nurse.

Emily knew who he was, recognizing his picture from Ben's desk–his only grandchild, visiting from St. Louis. He was taller than Ben, well over six feet, slender with light brown hair. If a man could be pretty, he was pretty. His height was disappointing to Emily. The men she favored always seemed too tall, making her look like a little girl. He obviously spent time being concerned about hair style and apparel. His face and body were refined, almost delicate. She found his jovial personality to be instantly attractive. He was definitely easy to look at.

Ben stepped away, smiling broadly, and then turned to Emily. "There you are, Emily. Mark, this is Emily. She lives here." He watched Mark's puzzled eyes jerk to Emily and back. Ben motioned for Emily to come near. As she approached, somewhat tentatively, he said, "Emily, this is Mark Compton. My grandson."

She offered her hand. As Mark reached–a nanosecond before they touched–a snapping pop instinctively jerked their hands back. They both looked at their hands, and started laughing, believing the jolt to be nothing more than static electricity from rugs. After glancing around, they both realized at the same time that Ben's house had wooden floors that normally did not generate static electricity.

Mark's eyes glanced from Ben to Emily. "Well, that will be unforgettable. Let's try again." He offered his hand. Emily cautiously took it, this time no worse for wear. All three laughed. Mark said, "What a nice surprise you are. Now, how do you fit into this old guy's life? Are you a neighbor?"

Ben started laughing. "Nope. Emily lives here, Mark. She is my roomy."

Mark still held her hand. He turned to Emily and said, "Roomy? Really?"

Emily, recovering from the initial shock, literally and figuratively, said, "Well, maybe boarder would be more accurate. But, yes, we have been together for several months. Just like him not to say anything to you."

Ben patted Mark on the back and said, "Get your things from the car and we'll have a drink. Go!"

After Mark left the house, Emily turned to Ben, patted her chest said, "Oh, my heart, my heart! You sneak! Is he why you set the weekend up?"

Ben couldn't stop smiling. "Yep. Hope you don't mind. Mark makes pretty good company. I expect the two of you will get along just fine. That is, if you don't create an electrical storm and burn the house down."

Emily looked puzzled. "That was weird, wasn't it? All that electricity? Makes me wonder about.... No, I'm not going there. Really strange, though. Anyway, you two will just have to get along without me for a while. I need to put my face on." She ran up the stairs.

When Mark reappeared, the first thing he wanted to know was, "Where is she, Gramps?" And then, "Where did she come from? Who is she? Come on! How long has–"

Ben couldn't stop smiling. "Oh, she's just someone I picked up off the street last winter. Pretty damned slick, though, isn't she?"

"Come on! I'm serious, Gramps. Who? When? Why? What in the hell is going on here?"

Ben went to the kitchen, grabbed his hat and walked right by Mark on the way out, smiling broadly. "You can ask her, Bud. I am going to the station to fill the truck with gas. See you two sometime later." He stopped, turned back to Mark and said, "Emily is about the best thing that ever happened to me, Mark. Just having her here makes my life agreeable and interesting for the first time in years. Just be yourself with her. I'll join you two tomorrow morning. Don't keep me awake all night."

Emily didn't come down for thirty minutes and Mark began to wonder. When she stepped into Ben's office, he stood and stared, paralyzed. He thought she was spectacularly beautiful. At length, after gathering his senses, he whispered, "Oh, My God! I want to keep you."

She laughed. "Well, thank you, Sir. I guess all that primping I just did was worth it. Thank you, but no, you cannot keep me. There is a traditional process, you know. And then maybe we'll see."

He collapsed into Ben's chair. "Oh, this is so, so strange. I have never met anyone who...." He couldn't find words and gazed at her, almost like he had known her but couldn't remember. "Sorry, Emily. Really, I'm not usually this inept. Please forgive me." He stood and asked if she would like a drink.

"Yes, please.' She took her wine glass from Ben's desk, handed it to him and said, "Pour that out. About half. The bottle is on the counter. You should ty it."

After they were settled, Mark spoke first. "When I asked Gramps where you came from, he said, 'I picked her up off the street.' When I pressed, he told me to ask you. So, I'm asking. How did you two end up together? What is your history with my grandfather?"

Emily laughed. "That is so like him. Well, the truth is, he actually did pick me up off the street." She saluted with the glass, took a sip and then recounted her time with Ben. "There it is. Ben has become the father I never had, Mark. I haven't known many, but he is the best guy, by far, who I have ever known. I probably owe my life to him. He is the grandfather I never had, and father and like a brother. Now, Mark, tell me about you. I think Ben has deliberately steered away from telling me about you because he knew this was going to happen. I think he set us up. By the way, where is he?"

Mark shook his head, smiled and murmured, "Oh, Gramps. I expect you're right, Emily. We were, maybe I should say, we *have been* set up, and I, for one, am more than good with that. Oh, he's gone to get gas for the truck. We have been directed not to keep him awake all night. He'll see us in the morning."

Emily sighed. "Oh, I wish he had stayed here with us. He should be here. Ben would love this."

When Ben returned, he found them sitting together on the couch, heads touching cozily as Mark showed her the family photo album. He glanced from one to the other and said, "Is this going to be an all-nighter between you two?"

Mark answered. "Looks like it, Gramps. All your idea,

though, right?"

"Just an accident of nature, Mark. I'll see you two in the morning...or whenever." He smiled knowingly and left them alone.

They left the house with intentions of walking to the gate and back. Mark pulled her to a stop after a long stretch of silence. "This is too hard, Emily. I don't want to wait for your traditional process. That seems too demanding. I am dying here. The tension is about to drive me crazy."

"We have time, Mark."

"No. I desperately want to touch you, to hold you, Emily. It feels like I have known you all my life, and it seems like I knew you were coming, and it feels like I've been waiting for you. Your process can wait, Emily. I cannot."

She stepped close, eyes glistening in the moonlight, put her arms around his neck and pulled him close. She gazed up at him for a moment, and then, after yet another electric surprise, kissed him flush on the mouth, over and over until she had to separate, breathless. "Oh, Mark. What are we doing?"

When Ben awoke and went for coffee, he found Mark asleep on the living room couch. He shook his shoulder. "I expected you to sleep in the off bedroom upstairs."

Mark turned and squinted at Ben. "Oh, Gramps, there is no way I could go to sleep being that close to her."

"Whoa! Are things moving that fast?"

Mark sat up rubbing his eyes. "Oh, yeah. Unbelievable, Gramps. I have never had anyone affect me the way she does."

"Damn, Mark! Are you serious?"

"Absolutely. I would ask her right now if I thought she would come away with me."

"For real?"

"I have never been more certain of anything than how I feel about her."

"That's great, I guess. How about her? Is she aslo…? Do you know?"

"Don't worry. I'm not going to ask for too much too soon."

"Okay, now answer the damned question."

"I think she might. Scares me a little, Gramps. I think she might."Ben turned for the kitchen. "Whew! Well, that sure happened fast."

"You knew it was going to happen, didn't you, Gramps? You knew."

"No, Mark, but I hoped."

Mark put his hands on Ben's shoulders. "Thank you."

The two men stood and said good morning to her as she took a chair. Mark spoke first. "Did you get any sleep?"

"Not a wink. Had too much on my mind."

Ben cleared his throat. "I guess we all do. Want some coffee, Emily?"

"You know I don't drink coffee."

"Might be a good time to learn about coffee."

She placed both elbows on the table, propped her chin

in her hands and considered Mark for a moment before saying, "You look all beat up, Big Guy. Get any sleep?

"Little bit. I recover well from long hours, though, being an intern. You know the drill I'm sure."

She nodded. "Indeed. So, what now, Mark? What happens today? I need some guidance."

"That's easy. I don't intend to be farther than a step away from you for the next twenty four hours. I want to know everything about you before I leave. And you?"

"That works for me." She got up, walked around the table, put her arms around Ben and kissed his neck. "Thank you, Ben. You sneak."

She left the table and headed to the stairs. "I'm going to clean up guys, and then I plan to do it all over."

Ben looked at Mark, smiled and said, "You are in such trouble. You just threw the doors wide open, Bud. She is so different than any other.... Well, you'll see soon enough."

"I know, Gramps. I think she could easily change my entire life. And now, I am also going to clean up. Wouldn't hurt to have some eggs and bacon, Gramps, and then, as the woman said, I intend to do last night all over again." He paused and turned to Ben before leaving the room. "She is the most exciting thing that ever happened to me, Gramps. Thank you." He headed toward the basement to shower and change.

"Do you have protection, Mark."

Mark stopped. He didn't turn to look at Ben, just looked up at the ceiling for a moment, sighed and said, "Stay in your own lane, Gramps."

"I'm just saying."

"That's not going to happen, Gramps. Not this soon and not this time around. Don't worry about her. I got this."

After Emily showered and dressed, she chatted with Ben in the kitchen for a moment before saying, "What could possibly be taking him so long? I'll get him."

She found Mark in the shower, paused for a moment as an impish smile formed, and then yanked the door wide open, reached in and turned the water off.

Mark spun away and started laughing. "Well, well. This is a surprise."

She was standing, hands on hips, trying to look annoyed. "We are waiting breakfast for you." She didn't turn away.

He watched a mischievous smile spread across her face. "What are you thinking, Emily?"

"I'm thinking we only have a day and a half left, Mister. That's what I'm thinking. So move it." She still didn't turn away.

Mark thought, What the hell. He dropped his arms and turned to face her. "Pretty much standard male equipment, wouldn't you say, Nurse Prindiville? Is this what you're waiting for?"

She laughed, tossed her head and walked away. "You'll do. Now hurry up. Breakfast is waiting."

Ben was chuckling when she returned. "What's so funny?"

"How did you get all wet, Emily?" He started

laughing.

"Well, someone had to turn the shower off."

"Oh, Emily. You two make me happy." He stepped back from the skillet and looked at her. "Is he on the way?"

The impish smile returned. "He should make an appearance any time. Maybe with some clothes on."

"Ah! Caught him ill-equipped, did you?"

She smiled, more for her own entertainment. "Oh, little Marky turned out just fine, Ben."

They were both still giggling when Mark made his appearance.

"What's so damned funny?" He glanced from one to the other. The look on their faces revealed everything. Ben knew. "Oh, I get it." He stared at Emily until she looked at him. "Two can play that game, Emily."

"I know. Sorry, Mark. Maybe we should just move along."

"You wish. Retribution will be mine, you jerk."

After breakfast, Ben asked if anyone wanted to go to the river. They did. Upon entering the trees along the river, Emily stopped, stared ahead, and then turned to Ben. "Oh, Ben! A sanctuary! A place to unwind. Thank you so much." She hugged him and ran wildly toward the elevated platform he had constructed for her during the past week.

Mark watched her go. "What's going on, Gramps?"

"Oh, hell. I should have done it a year ago. She mentioned it, so I got off my butt and built a place for her."

The two-foot-high platform was large enough to contain four or five people easily. Ben had covered the deck with all-weather turf surrounded on all sides by built-in sturdy wooden benches.

When the men arrived, Emily was standing on one of the benches, arms spread, "Welcome to my church. This is the church of happy!"

The weekend passed quickly. Ben watched from the distance as Mark and Emily spent the days exploring each other. Inseparable. Growing closer. Before Mark left for St. Louis they were clearly functioning as a couple, exhibiting all of the familiar signs of new love–unrestrained and openly happy.

CHAPTER FIVE

MARK AND BEN

Mark found Ben waiting at the kitchen table on Sunday morning. "You're up early, Gramps. What's on your mind?"

"You call this early? Unlike some people I know, I get plenty of sleep. I would like to have some time with you today, though. Kinda hoped you might show up early."

"I set the alarm to make time for you. I'm sorry, Gramps. I've been involved in my own world. I guess you know what's going on between me and Emily is pretty intense. Anyway, I am sorry about ignoring you. What's on your mind?"

"Never mind me. I think I know what's happening to you and wouldn't have it any other way. I'm not going to pry into your personal life." He threw up his hands. "That's a laugh. The whole world can see. There is a glow around the two of you. I would like to have a few words about you and your work, though. And then maybe we can switch back to your present distraction. So, how is your work going?"

"I'm on schedule to receive the MD degree the first of the year. Eight long years, Gramps. Just four more months and I get the MD."

"All right! Great! And then what?"

Mark sighed. "Well, that's when the final phase begins. I will serve as an intern for about a year under other doctors, and then residency. I will still be learning and being monitored as a resident, but somewhat independent until I am fully qualified to be on my own as a doctor of whatever my specialty is."

"Are you looking forward to all that? I hear it's tough. The price of doing business, I guess."

"Oh, it will be a slog, no doubt. On call all the time, day and night. Always on someone else's schedule. It's a grind, Gramps, but I am committed."

"I remember all that with your dad. I wondered at the time if it was worth it to him. Now I suppose I will wonder about you."

"I can't imagine Dad ever thinking it wasn't worth it. I don't remember him ever taking time off, either. He sure missed my childhood. He still doesn't take time off. His vacations are nothing but a series of lectures. He flies all over the world giving lectures. He's legendary. I hear the speaker's pay is also very lucrative."

"I know. I keep up with him through your mother. She gave up being frustrated years ago and learned to organize her own life. I have always been somewhat surprised that you decided to take up the profession, knowing how demanding it is. Do you ever have second thoughts?"

Mark studied his grandfather, brow wrinkled, thinking, and then said. "No, Gramps, I don't think so. Not really. I plugged right into the routine. It all seemed natural to me. The routine and challenges suit me. Well, at least they did until...." He drifted off, involved with his own thoughts.

Ben waited long enough to become uncomfortable. "So? Until what? What are you thinking, Mark?" He closed his eyes with a grimace. "Oh, I expect I know what's bothering you. Emily. Damn! Should I be sorry?"

Mark shook his head, still lost in thought. His face suddenly reversed into a smile. "No, Gramps. Absolutely not. All you did was arrange twenty-four hours that have been the most interesting and enlightening time of my life. For the first time, I have come face to face with the prospects of a future that I really have never thought much about–a future with a woman. Emily brings an entirely new dimension to my life. I need to take a step back from what I have been doing and take a new look. I need some time to analyze the possibility of an entirely new voyage." He slapped his face smartly with both hands. "Time for Mark to join the real world, I guess. You know, Gramps, I never thought about how someone like Emily could affect me, or for that matter I never speculated about someone like her being part of my life, or, I suppose, that someone like her even existed. No woman has ever affected me like she does. I have been so wrapped up in the medical journey. Sharing my life with someone has not been part of the equation."

"And now?"

"Right. And now? Oh, man." He shook his head, almost sadly. "And now I need to face the possibility that I'm not on this journey alone." He closed his eyes and let his head drop. When he looked up, he was smiling. "And now, Gramps, there is nothing more important than thinking about that red flashing likelihood that she may already be part of a life I have really never seriously considered. Right now, nothing seems as important as she does, and that stops me in my tracks. It's sobering. Mind-boggling, in fact. If this experience with Emily is as real as it seems, and there is no doubt in my mind that it is, then I cannot imagine going through life with her being secondary to my work. I am already thinking– fantasizing maybe–about a life with her." He leaned closer. "But not the way Mom is to Dad, Gramps. I want a closer relationship than that with whoever I end up with. I want her, whoever she may be, to be the defining feature of my life. I cannot envision, at this point, Gramps, that Emily could ever become secondary to my job. I am not my Dad. I am not a humanoid. I want to be totally committed to someone, not to something."

"I suppose you realize, Mark, this conversation began when I asked about your job. Have you had enough experience with women to recognize that what you feel for Emily is different than other relationships?"

"I have. I have known some marvelous women, Gramps. Bright, beautiful women; desirable, available women, and I can say without a doubt that none of them have ever affected me the way Emily does. She makes all of the fundamental elements that have been my life seem trivial, including my chosen profession."

Ben whistled. "Well, I suppose it's a good thing she came along at this juncture in your career then." He leaned closer. "So, what in the hell *are* you thinking, Mark?"

"Thinking? Nothing and everything. I'm just treading water. My thoughts are too scattered to form an intelligent opinion, let alone a plan. It seems like I am caught in an avalanche of decisions that I am clearly not ready to make. To tell the truth, I'm stunned, Gramps. I'm dead in the water. It is obvious to me that it has never occurred to me that a woman could affect me this way, or that I have even thought about how a woman like her could affect my plans. I have always known that I didn't want to be as dedicated to a job as Dad is, but I have been sincere about medical school. I don't feel half-hearted about being a doctor, Gramps. I'm still all-in about medicine. But, if what I feel for Emily is real and lasting.... Well, then I need to do some serious thinking about the specialty I have chosen, don't you think?"

"I didn't know you have chosen a specialty, Mark."

"I have. Cardiology. I realize it is very demanding and time-consuming. Several more years of training even after I get the MD–up to seven more years. Now I wonder. Now I'm not sure."

"Are you thinking about changing?"

"Too soon to say that for sure, Gramps, but I sure won't be thinking about anything else for a while." He sat back and exhaled. "Okay, that's enough about me. Now, I want to hear what you think about Emily. Be honest."

Ben smiled and leaned back. "Mark, the truth is Emily is like a daughter. She makes me that happy. I am comfortable with her. Being with Emily keeps me in high spirits. I would do anything for her. There, you wanted honesty."

"Thanks, Gramps. After the short time I have spent around her, it's easy to identify with what you just said. I have some deep thinking to do."

"I don't envy you, Mark, and I encourage you to take your time. This may be the biggest decision you ever make. Don't rush it."

After making coffee, Ben returned to the kitchen table and Mark opened an entirely new conversation.

"I realize this may not be the appropriate time, Gramps, but there is something else I want to talk to you about. This has been on my mind for weeks." He shifted uncomfortably, rubbed his face, and then heaved a deep sigh. "Elena. You have never talked to me about Elena, Gramps." He studied the pained look on Ben's face. "I know it's my fault that I even need to say that, because I have never asked about her. She always seemed to be out of bounds. Dad and Mom kept your relationship with her under the rug. They never talked about her, at least not in front of me, but I have always recognized the always present undertones of disapproval. You were…still are, I guess, somewhat notorious around home. But, when I think back, I have been a little too content to leave it there. I'm sorry. I admit being egocentric and way too involved with my own life to ask you about her. I want to know about Elena, Gramps. I want to hear about her from you."

"Nothing in the world will please me more, Mark. I would like to sit with you at a better time, though, when you are relaxed and when you have more time for me than you do at the moment. I don't expect you to take time from Emily in my favor. Not right now. Will that work?"

"Sure. Whenever you're ready. The sooner the better. I think, what with my involvement with Emily, now might be a good time, though. I would like to understand more about the emotions and decisions that made you leave Grandma."

"Right, and I will be happy to tell you, but, speaking of Emily, I hear her, so let's break this off. Thanks for the visit, Mark. Let me know what you decide to do about your internship. I feel better for having this conversation and I think you are more receptive now to personal talks. I'm glad you asked me about Emily first, though. She has changed my life, Mark. I was despondent before she entered; just passing time; waiting to run out of time. She made my life a great deal better." He paused, looking over the top of his glasses. "And, by the way, she is the reason you are here. I wanted you to meet her. I suppose, being smart enough to be a doctor, you probably figured that out."

Mark spent the entire day with Emily. They then stayed up most of the night again, and when he departed Sunday afternoon for St. Louis it came coupled with a cascade of mingled tears, his included. He had never seen Ben tear up. Emily's tears were running steadily when he finally separated and got into the car. She hid her eyes with her hands and sat in the grass beside the car after he closed the door and started the engine. Mark couldn't drive away. He turned the engine off and sat with her in a rocking embrace until she shooed him on his way. He drove straight through, his thoughts centered on Emily and what to do about his medical career.

Mark unexpectedly took the next two days off and returned to Springfield on Monday to apply with Cox hospitals for an internship in Family Practice. He met

Emily for lunch in the hospital cafeteria.

"What? Why didn't you tell me what you were thinking? Oh, Mark, this is all too drastic. Are you sure?"

"Never more certain of anything. I don't want to spend the rest of my life like my father; working day and night year after year, gone all the time. I want a better life than that. I want to spend my life with and for someone, not for some*thing*. I need more time with you, Emily. Lots of time. Maybe a lifetime of time. I am not asking you for a commitment now, and I am not asking you to make any kind of a decision. If my application is approved, and after I get my MD, I am going to be closer than your skin unless you run me off."

"I am thrilled, Mark. You just made me very happy. But Family Practice? Are you sure?"

"Yes. I might eventually open my own offices." He leaned close. "And I suppose I will need a nurse."

"Mark? This is too fast."

"Well, none of it is going to happen tomorrow, is it? We have four months before I am here permanently. We will have plenty of time to be certain about a lot of things."

"Are you that sure about us, Mark?"

"No doubt in my mind about us, Emily"

"The fact remains that we have only known each other for two days. Don't you think we should spend some time together before making life decisions? Of course we should. Nah, let's just jump right in. As Ben would say, 'What the hell.'"

He could tell she was teasing. "Someone has to be the adult in the room, Emily."

"What? You? You, the guy who just blew out of a cardiology internship after one weekend with a woman you had never met or knew anything about? One weekend, Mark, and you didn't even try to get laid? That guy? That guy is going to be the adult in the room? Really?"

On the next Monday Mark was back in Springfield to apply for the internship. Emily introduced him to her shift mates. As she walked him through the hospital on the way to his car, he stopped, placed his hands on her shoulders and said, "I am desperately in love with you, Emily."

She covered her face with both hands and wept, standing in the hallway in the noon lunch crowd. Mark held her until she pushed away and sat down leaning against the wall, intermittently crying and laughing. A whispering crowd assembled. A security officer stopped by and asked Mark what was going on.

"Nothing to worry about, Officer. I think she's just happy."

The officer shrugged. "Really? This is happy? Okay, but you should probably get her up now and clear the way. Yeah, let's get her up."

When Mark left her a few moments later, she was smiling through the tears. He drove to tell Ben.

"Not surprised to see you, Mark. Been wondering how long it would take you to get back here."

"I'm not back permanently, Gramps, not until after I

get the MD, and not until the hospital here accepts me for internship. But my applications are in."

"I suppose we can expect you about the first of the year then, right?"

"Yes, hopefully. I should have things tied it up in St. Louis by then. Emily can fill you in on my plans. Right now I have to get back to St. Louis and finish that MD."

He called Emily on the way. "Just so you know what I'm thinking. I'm going to have protection the next time I get you alone."

"Yay! If something doesn't happen very soon, Mark, I am going to need some psychiatric help. But you won't need protection. I took care of that early this morning. The chemistry should be in full effect the next time I see you."

CHAPTER SIX

IRIS

After high school, Iris Brooks attended a Christian college at one of Springfield, Missouri's three religious schools. She majored in music with intentions of becoming a high school teacher. Her diminutive size, less than five feet, furnished limited options upon graduation. Two small and very remote country schools made substandard financial offers. She returned to school, finished an advanced degree in music the following year, and then applied for teaching positions again, demanding pay commensurate with her education. No takers. Her father suggested, rather gruffly, that she needed to get a job and support herself. "I can't afford to keep you in college. You are old enough to take care of yourself. There are more jobs out there than being a teacher."

Life for Iris Brooks became drudgery. She worked for a temp agency for two years and picked up extra money playing the organ and piano for a small church. A major church discovered her talent and offered a position as assistant music and choir director. She was happy, though still struggling fiscally, living in a one room apartment with a shared hallway bath. Her music reputation grew, primarily for her voice. She had a pure, effortless soprano voice that served religious music well. A local gospel singing group invited her to join. She connected with other groups and solo personalities. She soon began singing on radio shows, sometimes solo, sometimes with groups.

Mathew Driscoll spotted her on her twenty-eighth birthday. They dated a few times during the following years. He loved to talk about his plans for a church. Iris found him dynamic and interesting, and she believed that Mathew truly loved the Lord. He announced early in their relationship that he wanted to remain chaste until after marriage. She was both relieved and impressed. Iris married Mathew on the first day of her thirty-first year.

She had the marriage annulled one month later.

The Reverend Doctor Mathew Driscoll was impotent and had known it for many years. Mathew had deliberately kept his enfeeblement secret from Iris, thinking perhaps that living with a woman for a period of time would heal his disability.

It did not.

Iris left him and went back to a life of fast food drudgery while teaching piano to little kids in their homes. Mathew still asked her on occasional dates, and she more often than not accepted just for the company. Though hardly constant companions, they were generally accepted as a continuous couple. No one knew about the annulment. They were both embarrassed to admit it.

Mathew had opened his church and radio show the

year before marrying Iris. He spared her the listless life
of waitressing, teaching piano and singing for small
churches. He hired her permanently and she soon became
an indispensable part of his show. Her sweet voice and
ability to play keyboard in all of its modes were a
valuable and entertaining addition. His growing
membership, both on the radio and in person, adored her.
She became his main side attraction, other than his
relentless beseeching sales pitches for Christian vitamins
in bottles with supplement descriptions that did not
correspond to the actual contents. He also sold products,
usually pharmaceutical, some laced with oxycodone, a
drug he obtained from shady sources in Mexico. The
products Mathew peddled, he sold for many times his
costs. He also pushed a liquid concoction for seniors that,
when tested by the federal government, registered
eighteen percent alcohol.

Lawsuits followed.

His lawyers contained the legal battles while
Mathew's celebrity and bank accounts continued to
swell. His star rose regionally, and then a national radio
corporation offered a contract. He found a nationwide
audience, and then the program went international.
Mathew became wealthy beyond his fondest dreams. Iris
also benefited after her five-year contract expired.
Lawyers fought over her contract. Her attorney won. She
bought her own modest home and within a few years had
salted away enough money to last comfortably for a
lifetime.

Mathew also exploited Iris's natural talents as an
accountant and tax advisor. She could locate anything:
drug factory sources, what the feds were investigating
and what lawyers Mathew could hire to hold the

investigations at bay. She knew that Mathew, at that juncture of his ministry, figured that if he could just last for two more years he could live out his life on the beaches of Mexico. Iris planned her life accordingly, to be independent by the time Mathew crashed. She had learned to despise Mathew. She knew him as no other person did. He was a lawbreaker and a religious pretender. He did not love or serve the Lord. Mathew Driscoll served only himself.

Iris needed more than money. She desperately needed someone. Not just any someone. She wanted a bed partner. Iris craved the physical company of a man.

After all of their times together, from the first time Mathew saw her until the present, Iris had nothing to show for the relationship other than her modest home and the comfort of assured retirement benefits.

Not enough.

She knew her working relationship with Mathew was a house of cards supported by crafty lawyers and felt certain he was going to run out of time before realizing his dream of wealth.

Mathew played upon the knowledge that most people who knew them believed he and Iris were married. The ruse worked because Iris didn't object. She had learned how to play Mathew's game. Their deception worked simply because Mathew never said or did anything to relieve his believers of the idea that they were not married.

Iris played along. The money was good.

Iris knew everything about Mathew's organization.

Everything. She knew about the differing copies of expense and income accounts; the amount of money spent on lawyers to keep the feds from the truth; the criminal past of his two associates–both with penitentiary time. The two associates were also Mathew's lifetime friends and both were dependent upon his generosity.

Iris needed more.

She found more living right next door. A nice looking middle-aged divorced ex major league baseball player had moved in. They coupled. She loved him completely, living together until she got pregnant at forty-three.

He moved to California.

Iris suffered weeks of intense emotional conflicts about keeping the baby. She waited too long to have an abortion and decided to keep the pregnancy secret from Mathew until it became too obvious. That worked until the sixth month. She was too tiny to hide a truth that, as it turned out, Mathew also desperately wanted to keep secret.

Iris did not want the baby–or any baby. A baby would destroy the life she imagined and planned for. She decided to place it up for adoption. Mathew disagreed, but only because keeping such an arrangement secret seemed unlikely. They decided, jointly and decisively, to take the baby to a hospital the moment it was born.

Mathew improvised Iris's part in his show by playing recorded spots from past performances. He hired another young woman to fill in for his local Sunday televised theater shows until Iris could return.

Iris was working church financial accounts with Mathew late one evening at his new estate when birth pangs began. Her water broke and the birth began instantly. Mathew panicked. His assistant, Chuck, called a friend, a rest home worker who showed up within minutes to act as midwife. Mathew gave Iris pain killing drugs from his private medicine cabinet. The drugs not only seemed to anesthetize her pain, but her ability to think clearly. She seemed barely conscious throughout the ordeal and later said she could not remember the actual birth.

Iris lied. She remembered every moment perfectly.

After many hours of pretending near coma, Iris appeared to regain her wits. Mathew was there.

"I'm so tired, Mathew. Where…? I want…. Where is my baby? Is the baby all right, Mathew?"

"Sshhh. Just relax. The baby is fine. Go back to sleep now. You need rest. Just relax. Everything has been taken care of."

"No! Where is my baby, Mathew! I want to see my baby!"

"What? Don't give me that, Iris. You know very well what we did with the baby. We did exactly what we agreed to do. Oh, come on! You can't blame this on me. It was your idea. You are not going to blame this on me."

Iris resumed her place on the show two weeks later. Her tears were all the more believable. World viewers and the hometown crowds loved her. People across the world believed in her, and they were right; her tears were sincere. She grieved over her lost baby and hated herself for letting the baby go. Iris welcomed the opportunity to bare her emotions.

And then the roof of the ministry fell in. The feds came—lots of them. Men and women wearing windbreakers with identification letters on the back representing several factions of the federal government. The FBI led the list. Mathew spent most of his remaining millions paying fines while attempting to stay out of jail. He survived. His ministry did not. Mathew would wait five long years before trying again.

Iris didn't need the money after Mathew's fall. She had siphoned a very substantial amount of ministry cash away while keeping the books; enough to last for a lifetime of luxury. She went back to work as a waitress just to have something to do. She also played piano and sang for a small church for no pay. Iris was forty-three.

CHAPTER SEVEN

MOTHER DEAR

E mily's thoughts seldom strayed from Mark during the following weeks. Their work prevented another visit. They supplemented by spending an inordinate amount of time on the phone talking and texting.

On her daily visit to the hospital cafeteria, Emily seldom passed the records office without realizing that the path to her birth mother might be just inside. She paused more than once, only to move on; reluctant to begin the search; afraid the investigation could end; or worse, that it could initiate a look into her past that might be unpleasant.

Emily brooded. Weeks passed and then months while she agonized about initiating the search for her mother.

Ben encouraged her to get on with it. "How hard is it? Just do it, Emy. Do it! I'll go with you if you want me to. I'll do the newspaper research for you."

She took two days off from work and spent the time at the Library Center researching news items from the date of her birth until she could find no additional articles. Her birth had created a print storm. Finally, without forethought, while walking by the records office one afternoon after work, she abruptly stopped and said aloud, "Just do it!" She took a deep breath and entered.

A beyond-middle-aged woman sitting at the closest desk to the door said, "Over here, Hon. May I help you?"

After introducing herself, Emily said, "I was not born here, but my birth records should be here. I wonder if I could see them."

"Wait. That is much too fast for me. Please explain."

Emily related the story about her birth certificate and the lack of identifiable parents, and of being left at the emergency entrance.

The woman suddenly placed both hands on her cheeks and exclaimed, "Oh, for heaven's sake! You're the box baby! I wondered if I would ever find, and I made the entry. Now you just wait right there." Several women in the office had stopped working to watch and listen, murmuring to themselves while Emily waited.

"Here it is!" her collaborator announced, out of breath, waving a folder. She plopped into her chair and opened the folder. "Yes, here it is. December the Fourteenth, Nineteen-Ninety-Nine. Nine-Thirty PM." She held up a restraining finger. "Now wait. Let me think." She looked up. "If my math is correct, you will be twenty- three this coming December, right?" She flipped pages, read for a few moments, looked up again and said, "You were taken from Emergency to the Neo Natal ward, held there for two months, and then transferred to the state facility for adoption. That is about all I can tell you." She snapped the folder closed.

Emily moaned. "Oh, I really hoped to find out who my

mother is."

"Sorry. We never did get that information. The hospital reported the incident to the newspaper and other news outlets, asking for information leading to the mother. After a period of time, the hospital had to send the baby–you, as it turns out–to the state adoption center. I doubt if the adoption service will give parental information to you, but if I were you I would ask. I sure would if I were in your shoes. Let me get their numbers for you."

Emily was dispirited but not surprised. The next day as she snaked through traffic in the hallway, once again leaving the hospital after work, the records clerk stopped her.

"Miss Prindiville! Over here! I have been waiting for you. Hoped you might be along about the same time. This has to be quick, Honey. Quick, step in here with me." She looked up and down the hallway." I can't be seen speaking to you." She checked the hall both ways again and pulled Emily into a refreshment machine area. "Now, you listen carefully because I won't be talking to you again. I have always been pretty sure that I know who your mother is. I knew that long before I saw you yesterday. But now, after seeing you, I am almost certain of it. You could be identical twins." She stepped close and whispered, "I will get fired if the hospital ever learns that I told you even that much. I'm not going to give you her name or address. Please remember that in case anyone ever asks how you found out. Okay, this is what I think I know." She checked the hallway again, cleared her throat and said, "I think your mother called a few times the week after leaving you here that night. She was crying and begging to know if a newborn baby had been left. It broke my heart to hear her, and I told her that someone did leave a baby but the baby had been sent to the state adoption center. I copied her phone number and called from a pay phone at Walmart so she wouldn't know who I was. Now, if you want to know who I believe your mother is, just turn your radio on at Nine O'clock in the morning on any weekday. I can't remember the exact station numbers, but it's in the 550 AM range. You can't miss it. She is also on television at Ten O'clock in the morning on Sunday. She's on Channel Eleven. That's all I know. I always thought she was your mother, but now I'm sure of it. Goodbye and good luck. Please don't try to talk to me again. I told you everything I know."

Emily told Ben about the encounter the moment she got home. Ben did not look happy. He frowned, sat back and said, "Well I'll be damned. I'll just be damned. I will bet you anything, Emily, that I know who your mother is."

Emily quickly sat in the chair next to him. "Be serious, Ben. Are you kidding me?"

"No. I wish I was kidding. I remember seeing parts of that show a couple of times. I never could watch it much past the announcements, though. Oh, Emily, if she is your mother, you are not going to believe how much you favor her. I'm surprised I haven't already put two and two together." He shook his head and smiled. "I'll be damned. Well, okay, let me tell you what I know about her. She and her husband were very popular television evangelists at one time, and I mean worldwide popular. I don't know the details, but they–I'm not sure she was involved–so let's just say he got into some trouble with the feds for advertising all manner of medical items that apparently had not been approved or were proven to be phony. They lost credibility and their television and radio shows went belly up for lack of sponsors and the loss of believers. They have been attempting to make a comeback over the last year or two–mostly on radio. I read recently that their radio show is going nationwide again, and soon. It seems like I heard they are also trying to make it on nationwide television again. They have recently opened a regional television show. I'm sure he is trying to work his way back. He allegedly made a ton of money while on national television previously. He lives in what I am told is an impressive estate on the eastern outskirts of Springfield. Really not too far from here."

"Do you think she could actually be my mother, Ben?"

"Well, if similarity in looks has anything to do with it, yes. Wait just a minute." He reached for his cell phone and pulled Iris up on Google. "Here. Take a look for yourself, Emily. I want to watch your face."

Emily looked up from her phone a few moments later. "Good grief! Okay, now it's my turn to be damned. This is scary. That could be me in what, in thirty years?" She handed the phone to Ben.

"Yeah, it is scary, and that is the Iris Driscoll I remember seeing years ago. Remarkable resemblance to you, don't you think? So, what now, Emily? Are you going to pursue this? Her husband's name is Matthew Driscoll, by the way."

"Her husband? Isn't that odd, Ben? I never think about who my father is. I only think about my mother. Oh, Ben, I do want to know about them. Maybe I should start by going to their church on Sunday just to see her in person. Do you think I can get in? Is there an audience?"

"I believe so. You should probably do some serious research, Emily. Actually, I think you should study about this long and hard before you decide to make yourself known, if that's on your mind. Seems to me there was, and may still be, some legal unpleasantness involved in their history. I'm not sure exactly what, but I have some sketchy recall about a national network television exposure show. I remember that a celebrity reporter interviewed a disgruntled Driscoll ex-employee who ratted Driscoll out. If my memory is correct, the results of the federal investigation information were part of that show. I didn't watch it, but it made local news for a few days. Pretty much ruined the Reverend Doctor Driscoll. He went off the air."

"Ben, I have no way of knowing without asking her if she is my mother and I can also ask her if Driscoll is my father. That's another reason to meet her. Seems logical that Mathew Driscoll is my father, don't you think? Seems to me he is a reasonable prospect. They married."

"If you go ahead with meeting Iris, I expect information about your father will come naturally. First things first, Emily. One thing at a time."

Emily spent her evening off-times at the city's main library reviewing news items about the Driscolls. She had to work through the Nine O'clock weekday radio shows, but watched the Driscoll's television show with Ben on the coming Sunday. Afterward, she said, "I have to see for myself, Ben. I'm going next Sunday."

She entered an ancient downtown movie theater the following Sunday. The theater had been transformed into a church dominated by lights, cameras and an enormous sound system. Emily arrived early and sat in the second row, watching as the theater filled mostly with older people featuring silver hair and glasses. Iris entered the stage first and played soothing religious music on a huge keyboard. She played well. When the theater lights flashed, she stopped playing and sat perfectly still.

An announcer's voice boomed over the sound system. "The Reverend Doctor Matthew Driscoll!" Emily had learned from library research that he was not a doctor of anything other than his imagination. She also learned that he was not a minister affiliated with or recognized by any established religious organization.

Driscoll stepped from behind a convenient curtain and took the pulpit. The Reverend Doctor welcomed the crowd, arms spread majestically and launched immediately into a sales pitch hyping a bottle of liquid protein and vitamin. Emily didn't pay attention after downgrading him to an annoying delay while waiting for Iris to play and sing. The Reverend impressed her as nothing more than a cheap carnival barker. He did have a glorious head of wavy silver hair. Her eyes remained locked on Iris. With the sales pitch finished, Matthew turned to Iris and asked for a song before the sermon. She played extremely well and sang beautifully, permitting what appeared to be a sincere display of emotion to run free. She seemed in a trance, eyes closed, looking toward heaven, singing and playing, tears streaming without restraint. Emily was captivated. The crowd was captivated. Iris was no amateur.

The sermon ran on and on. Iris sat still in the beginning, listening intently, and then, almost imperceptibly, raised her arms. Members of the crowd began following suit. When Iris began swaying her arms from side to side, members in the front rows caught on, unconsciously imitating. Emily suspected that most of the front row seats were occupied by regular attendees who were familiar with the routine. The ceremony ended after yet another sales pitch, the passing of collection plates, and yet another imploring appeal for support from the radio audience. The Driscoll's then took positions at ground level on either side of the stage to greet the flock. Emily waited until the line thinned before making her way forward.

She took the hand Iris offered, watching her face for a hint of recognition. Iris seemed more engaged by the next person in line.

Emily didn't release Iris's hand. "Mrs. Driscoll...Iris. I have waited a long time for this moment. I would like a few moments in private with you if that's possible."

Iris turned to engage. "I'm sorry. What did you say your name is?"

"Emily. Please, could you find a free moment for me? Please?"

Iris's expression indicated nothing more than annoyance. "I don't usually...." She frowned, "What is this about?"

"I need a moment, that's all. A private moment. I can wait until the line is—"

"No! If you have something for me young lady, just tell me. What is it?"

Emily recognized that time was not in her favor. She

decided to put her cards, all of them, on the fabled table. "Here is a newspaper article I think you might be interested in."

Emily had copied a short article in the December 15th, 1999 Newspaper article headlined, THE BOX BABY, reporting an unknown person had abandoned a newborn at the hospital emergency room entrance the night before. At print time, the baby had not been claimed. The hospital would keep the baby for an unspecified period and transfer her to the state adoption bureau if not claimed by a legally recognized parent.

After concluding that Iris, clearly irritated by the intrusion, was not going to read the article, Emily said, "I would like to ask you about the evening of December the Fourteenth, Nineteen-Ninety-Nine. That's the day I was born."

Iris looked puzzled for a moment.

She stared at Emily.

Her mouth dropped wide open.

Her face coloring turned ashen.

She collapsed.

Two stagehand-equipment operators noticed the commotion and rushed to her aid. The Reverend Doctor took the podium and ordered everyone to leave the church immediately. "We have an emergency, folks. Please hurry."

Emily decided to leave and come back the next Sunday.

Later, while Iris recovered in her backstage prep room, Driscoll interrogated his two helpers.

"Who was she? Have you ever seen her before?"

They both shrugged.

"Answer me!"

The short guy said, "No, but she sure looked a lot like Iris, Boss. I mean, a lot like Iris."

Driscoll walked away muttering to himself. *"Always wondered if something like this would happen. Son of a...."* He returned to the men. "Okay, now I'm serious. Do either one of you have any idea who that woman was Iris was talking to is?"

The two men, serving as his studio crew and security, had been with the Reverend from the beginning, or at least until he fell out with the feds. The shorter man, Al, dark complexioned and muscular, when forced from the Reverend's bounty, had made his way by hook and crook into the Iowa state penitentiary system, serving five years for armed robbery. The Reverend retained Chuck, his childhood friend and lifetime companion, by offering free room and board along with barely enough money to live on.

Chuck took the lead. "I have to tell you, Matthew, Al is right. There was a spooky resemblance. Actually, that girl could be...well, you know what I mean. She could be that kid Iris...."

Oh, Mathew knew, but he did not want to believe. "There is just no way. No. You two are imagining. There is just no way."

The two men glanced at each other and shrugged. Mathew seldom changed his mind and often flew into rages for slight disagreements. Better just to move on.

Mathew called for them later that evening. They were easily available, living in luxurious apartments over his six-car garage. "Okay, I want to know who she is, and I need to know as soon as possible. Check with the parking lot camera guy first. I know he runs those things at night, but I don't know about in daylight. See if he had those cameras on this morning. Now! Move it! This could be a game-changer if she is…. Go! Now!"

The cameras had not been operating.

Mathew started thinking about how to control the situation. *A warning of some kind? I need to get control of this in a hurry, one way or another. If she is Iris's kid, she could ruin me.*

"Oh, Ben, you should have seen her. I so wish I had taken you. I am *her*, Ben! This is so strange. I just don't know what to think. This is so exciting!"

"Slow down, Emily. Sit down and tell me everything."

"She is my *mother*, Ben. I know that. I felt it and I could tell she did. Well, maybe not at first, but when she did, she passed out. Out cold. Oh, she knew, Ben! She knew. What do I do now? What can I do? I don't want to walk away now, not when I am this close. I don't want to let her go. Not now. Help me."

"All right. Just slow down. Let's take a snack and a bottle and head to your church. This may take some time, Emily." They went to the river and talked.

After hours with Ben, Emily decided to go back the next Sunday. She recognized his uncertainty and could tell he did not endorse another visit even though he kept his thoughts to himself. Emily went again on the next Sunday. She sat closer to the rear and watched Iris walk onto the stage, stop and stand still while surveying the audience. Her gaze stopped for a moment when she reached Emily–just for an instant, and then she turned and went quickly backstage before returning to take her place. She never looked toward Emily again, not even a glance.

Okay, I'm on their radar.

At the end of the service, Emily went forward again, sat down and waited as the line of well-wishers paraded by. Iris looked up as the line of people shortened to two, looking directly at Emily for a moment, and then abruptly climbed the stairs and left the stage. Emily took a seat in the front pew and waited for ten minutes before departing in Ben's truck.

She noticed that the only car left in the parking lot had pulled out behind her and believed it was following. After changing streets a few times it became obvious that the car was shadowing. She drove to the hospital, parked near the front entrance, went in and observed through the lobby windows. The car circled through the lot twice, stopping behind Ben's truck for a moment, probably to take a photo of his license number, and then back onto the street and out of sight. She waited ten minutes before feeling safe, and then drove home.

She found Ben in his office and relayed the information.

"Well, crap. That's just a little too much intrigue for me, Emily. Are you thinking about going back out there?"

"No. I got the message, Ben. That's enough. I wish, though, in a way, that things could have turned out differently. Guess I'll never know."

Late the next afternoon, Emily called from the hospital. "Ben! I think someone just tried to bomb your truck."

"Where are you, Emily? Are you okay?"

"I'm still at the hospital and I am okay. The police have been here, Ben. They took your truck. They just now loaded it and left."

"Okay, let's start at square one, nice and slow, Emily. What in the hell is going on? Where did you park the truck?"

"I parked on the second level of the West garage. Someone apparently saw two men under your truck and reported to security. The men ran off when security showed up. One of the security guys looked under the truck and saw hanging wires. They called the city police who came right away. Now get this, Ben. They came with a bomb squad. Anyway, we are officially without wheels."

"You take an Uber home, Emily, and I will take the bike to police headquarters. Have the Uber pick you up at the East entrance, just in case. No one can sneak up on you there."

He managed to get his truck back after much questioning and investigating. The bomb squad thought someone may have been in the act of wiring the starter to attach an explosive. "Looks like they were going to install the explosive on the passenger side, though. That makes us believe that maybe they didn't intend to kill anyone. Depends on how much of a bang they were going to attach. Never know, though. Lucky someone saw them.

Do you have any idea who would do something like that? Do you have enemies?"

"I don't know of anyone who would target me. A friend of mine has been driving the truck lately. I can't imagine why anyone would want to hurt her, but you should probably take that up with her." They asked more questions and gave his truck back, advising him to have Emily contact the detective department in the morning. "Never know, Sir, it might be nothing but a mistake, or a prank, or maybe a warning, but you need to be careful. Something like this is nothing to fool around with."

Ben took Emily to work and picked her up after that. The detectives found no evidence to follow other than Emily's visits to the church. Both detectives looked at each other knowingly the first time Emily mentioned the Driscolls. They asked for Emily first, and then the Reverend and Iris to come to headquarters for questioning. Emily reluctantly revealed the possibility of her relationship to Iris, but she did not tell where she got the information, other than Ben thought she looked like Iris and that he also remembered the box baby incident. They advised her not to return to the church. They also told her they would have the Driscolls in for another visit.

The Driscolls were not cooperative.

Emily slept infrequently for several nights thinking about the Driscolls. She apologized to Ben and teared up. "I should have left well enough alone. I'm sorry about your truck, Ben."

"They didn't hurt my damned truck, but they sure as

hell hurt my feelings. Pissed me off. Maybe their police visits will stop all the crap."

He dropped Emily at the hospital the next day and traded his motorcycle in on a low-slung used Japanese car. *"There, let 'em try to get under that."*

She fussed. He told her it was well past time to get rid of the bike anyway. His doctor had warned him for years, "If you drop that thing, you will probably break a hip, Ben. If that happens, I'll give you a year to live at most. You are too damned old to be toying with a broken hip. It's time to let it go. Past time in my estimation, by about thirty years."

"Anyway, Emily. It was time for a change and it is done. Your name is on the car title. Now let's move on."

"No, Ben. I want to pay for the car. I need to."

"Fair enough. Pay whenever you like. I am not hurting for money, Emily, you know that. Anyway, that bike was worth a bunch more than your car. I would advise you to park somewhere different each day, though, maybe outside in front where the cameras are more prevalent. And check behind your tires. If they are screwing with you, they might leave something sharp there to cause more trouble."

"She's driving a little Honda now, boss, and I know where she lives. She was easy to follow."

"Okay. She has the cops asking questions now and that could lead to the feds again. We need to shut her up. I need some time to think. I have to get control of this, and I mean right now!"

Iris pretended illness for the next two weeks, spending her days at the main library reading every snippet of news from the 14th of December 23 years ago. She searched the records onward for two months, but found just the one article. That was enough. She knew the young woman was her baby.

The box baby was her baby.

Mathew and his two helpers flew to California to arrange marketing for a pilot television show for a major network. Iris quietly and deliberately spent the following days plotting how and when she would ruin Mathew Driscoll. She planned to get him out of her life forever. He was the condemning connection to the truth she agonized over and desperately wanted to keep secret. If news reached the public that the box baby was alive and well and living in Springfield, and connected to Iris, her life would be ruined. People might believe Mathew's story about the baby. He would say it was her idea to give the baby away. She planned to ruin him first, and then no one would believe anything he said. There would be no connection to her. Iris knew everything about his organization and could provide the federal government with an exact roadmap to his illegal transactions and falsehoods. She began copying files and letters, phone numbers and names, deposits and withdrawals, contracts and bank accounts. She smiled when finished, confident that any federal investigation based on her information would only take about ten minutes. She placed the records in her bank box.

Iris had another task to complete. She had also learned from Mathew's notes that one of his men had followed Ben's white truck from the hospital after the failed bombing. Iris now knew where Ben lived and left a note in his mailbox with her phone number and went home to wait. She had signed the note IRIS.

CHAPTER EIGHT

ON LOVE

Mark arrived unexpectedly from St. Louis on Friday afternoon.

"I'm not staying with you tonight, Gramps. I have taken a suite down on the lake at Big Cedar Lodge for the weekend. Emily is going with me." He pumped a fist, smiling broadly.

Ben looked up. "Well, you two lasted longer than I would have. I'm happy for you, Mark. That should be good for both of you."

"I have all afternoon with nothing to do before she gets off work. So, if you're game, I would like hear about life from your perspective, Gramps. I want to know what you think about.... Well, everything. Is this a good time?"

Ben studied Mark for several seconds before nodding. "Yeah, I guess it is, Mark. As good a time as any. Where do I start?"

"First, since this weekend is going to be about Emily, give me your thoughts about love, Gramps. I know you write love stories. Emily has told me about your books. I want to know what your take on love is."

Ben looked surprised. "Love? That would be a very long and complicated conversation, Mark. My take is relatively simple, though. I have loved many things and many people, but to me loving and being *in* love are entirely different books. Being *in* love is all-consuming. Loving someone is easy, but being *in* love is losing control of your life. In my case, voluntarily and happily. I have done it twice."

Mark nodded, but didn't appear to be won over.

Ben noticed. "Okay, let me start with my wife. I was *in* love with her for many years. We had some wonderful years." Ben held his hands out, palms up, surrendering. "Until I wasn't. When the ending came, it came well defined and I knew it. She became someone I no longer understood. She became someone I too often didn't enjoy. She turned into her mother. Her mother and I always got along, but we didn't like each other. There were other reasons why I drifted away and I expect your grandmother's take on why I blew out would be different than mine. I would really rather not go there, Mark. No reason to disrespect her; nothing to be gained by that. We both changed. I suppose that sums it up, but I changed the most and I wanted something different from life. I wanted to be *in* love again. She loved life in the Corps and she was very good at it. In fact, probably better at it than I was. But I made a promise to my father about retiring from the Corps at twenty years. I promised to come home and take over the farms. I kept that promise. I expect that effectively ended the *in* love part of our marriage, at least it probably did for her. She had always made it clear that she didn't want to give up the life we had and truthfully, I knew very well that she had never exhibited any interest in farming. Other reasons popped up and other consequences materialized until I found myself alone on the farms. She went to town to find work when I desperately needed her.

"A few years passed that way, until I opened the door to a neighbor woman. Nothing like that ever happened to me before. I had never allowed *that* door to open. Not once in all the overseas tours to Japan, Korea, the Philippines, Vietnam, Spain Norway. I never opened that door to any of the attractive women I associated with stateside. Opening that door was the beginning of the end of my marriage. I could not see plodding through the rest of my life without feeling the kind of love I once knew."

"What happened to Grandma after you left?"

Ben's expression revealed nothing more than genuine astonishment. "You don't know?"

"No, Gramps. What has she done? I know she lives in California. I know my folks don't see about her. Did she ever want to remarry? What?"

"We never divorced, Mark. She filed. I signed. She couldn't go through with it. I suppose the retirement benefits and security had a lot to do with that, and maybe she held hopes that we might.... It was easier for me to let things go that way instead of opening the emotional issues again that put her in the hospital after I left the first time. We are still friends. She calls. My retirement still goes to a joint account and she writes a check to me for half each month. My sometimes relationship with your father, in my opinion, is mostly because of how he believes I mistreated his mother. Your father never asked for the reasons why we split up and I never told him." Ben shrugged. "Not sure my reasons would influence his disapproval in my favor anyway. He has always been very open about his verdict. I am guilty in his eyes."

"Wait! And so you are still married?"

"Yup. It wouldn't hurt to talk to your parents occasionally, Mark. My relationship with your grandmother is common knowledge. Has been forever. "

"What about Elena? How did she fit into that? Didn't that bother her?"

"Oh, yeah. She finally recognized that I was not going to divorce and decided to take what I could give. Once she made that decision, we were solid. No debate or quarrel. She never once brought it up again. Being separated for as long as I have been is not the kiss of death to new relationships."

"Amazing. Damn! I really don't know anything about you. Has your life worked out the way you wanted?"

"Hell no. Life could have been easier. I could have been a better man. I wouldn't change what happened, though, just how I managed it. I could have been a better guy for both women."

"Whew! Well, as if I don't have enough to think about already, tell me about Elena."

Ben rubbed his eyes viciously, got up and went to the kitchen. "I'm going to have a drink, Mark. You need anything?"

"No thanks. I better save it for tonight."

Ben laughed.

"What's funny about that?"

"I have to tell you, Mark, Emily is a cheap date. She can't hold her liquor. One glass of wine and she's about as good as she's gonna get. Actually, about half a glass puts her to sleep. Best way in the world to ruin an interesting evening with Emily is to pour too much wine.

She's tiny and she doesn't drink much or often. Be careful with her."

After Ben returned, and after he had taken a couple of swallows, he took some deep breaths, swiveled his chair and gazed out the window for what seemed like an eternity to Mark. When he returned, Ben was smiling. "All right, let's do this. Elena, from square one. She came to me completely unexpected. I first met her at the local Writers' Guild where she was serving as president. Could not take my eyes from her. One of those things you hear about. Never happened to me before. When I look back at that moment, I recognize that was one of the two major forks in my road of life. We said Hi in passing as she left the Guild that day. She was leaving with another woman and didn't stop. But I did. I stopped and turned to watch her. I don't know why I stopped. I suppose there was something about her that attracted me. She kept walking but looked back and smiled. That was it, Mark. We both admitted, as time went by, that exact moment was the beginning. The attraction never went away. It got stronger.

"Anyway, I ran into Elena at the next Guild meeting and caught myself watching her to such an extent that I don't remember anything about the meeting. Our eyes always connected. Just glances really, not quite intentional. I couldn't keep my eyes from her. Some of the people there who knew both of us recognized what was going on before we did. I heard about it later. They said the atmosphere was electric because of what was happening between me and Elena. It affected our friends. They sensed it.

"That started years of innocent encounters at Guild functions. At least I like to think they were not calculated because we were both married. And then…." He sighed, deep and broken. "And then several years later–let's see, I had known her for six years by then. We traveled to a writer's conference together, the only writers from the Springfield Writers' Guild as it turned out. We sat together; we ate together; we waited for the next lecture together; all quite proper. And then…." Ben paused and clapped his hands sharply just once. "And then I deliberately changed everything." He paused, shook his head reproachfully and said, "To be perfectly honest, I have never done anything more intentionally in my life. Nothing that ever happened between Elena and I after that was anything but calculated on my part.

"I handed her a poem, Mark. A poem I wrote the night before just for her. I knew enough about her family life by then to know that she was unhappy, and I certainly was not happy. Anyway, that poem began what grew to be an-out-of-control landslide toward each other. A year or so passed while we grew closer. Still just friends. We were no longer exactly innocent as we were seeing each other alone occasionally. We were not blameless. We were obviously creating a closer relationship. And then all of fooling around, the secrecy and mystery came to a screeching stop. She called one night from a motel to tell me she had just left her marriage."

Ben sat back and slapped the desk and said, "Bang!"

"Her husband kicked her out because she flinched when he tried to hold her. Oh, he knew why she cringed. I expect he knew all along. Well, you can imagine my reaction. I sure as hell wasn't expecting that. I don't know that either of us had planned on breaking up our marriages as that was certainly nothing we ever talked about. But there it was–get on or get off time. I packed up and left home a couple of days later and spent the next twenty-five years with her. I remained *in* love with her until she died. Some of the best years of my life. She died from cancer and I have been alone since."

"Sorry, Gramps. I should have known all of that. I can't imagine not knowing. I'm embarrassed."

"Ah, no matter. Your father and mother never tried to accommodate my choice, so you were just left out. They probably thought you would be better off without me in your life. You still might be better off. Their disapproval ruined what modest opportunity you and I had for a connection, though, which, frankly, was also probably my fault."

"There are usually two sides to every story, Gramps. Grandma would never talk about it."

"True. I won't say I agree with your dad's resentment of me. He made it difficult for me to nurture a close relationship with him, or for me to be on familiar terms with your mother. Not really his fault. I was absent most of his life; gone at least two thirds of his life on overseas tours. Even while stationed stateside I had constant weapons training deployments and away from home at least half the time I was stationed in the states. Your dad was in college before I retired from the Corps. He protested the war while I was in it, and that hurt. I always took it as his way of protesting me. And then he turned to religion. It seemed to me like he turned toward any and every thing opposed to the military. And then I ran off with Elena and that damned sure sealed the deal. That's why you and I ended up where we are right now, Mark. That effectively prevented any chance of me having a relationship with you. Your dad and I just never made it past Elena. We ended up poles apart, morally and politically. Not his fault. Those are just the truths I live with."

"Do you think there is any chance you will ever be family with my parents again?"

"No. Not from my point of view. Not after the way they chose to treat Elena. There has never been a time I could sit with him and tell the things I just told you, Mark."

Ben got up and went to the bedroom. Upon return, he slapped his book of poetry on the desk in front of Mark. "Read that when you have time. You can gain some insight into my thoughts about practically everything. Many of those poems are windows to my world, a world your father would not recognize."

"Thank You, Gramps. I look forward to this."

"I wrote the beginning poem about that window to my world. I can do it from memory."

"Go ahead. Please."

"Okay. The title is, *WINDOW WORLD*.

I see you there, looking for answers,
watching the world from your window.
The clouds and sun, birds and rain,
gloom and pain, it's all the same
from every window everywhere.
What I wish, watching you there,
is for you to turn from that window
and begin reading the book of poems
in your hand. The book I wrote for you.
A look at the world from my window.

"That's it, Mark."

"Oh, I like that, Gramps. I'm looking forward to this."

He held the book aloft.

"I was an old man and tired, Mark, living alone with memories until Emily came along. She has made life good for me again. I might even write a happy poem someday."

"Has Emily read this?"

"No. Not yet. I wanted to wait for a happier time. I have other books you know, Mark. Four Novels. She has read all of the novels. I also have a website. Are you aware of that?"

Mark sat back and grimaced. "I do know that, but only because Mom told me recently. I'm sorry to say that I have not read your books. Too busy with my own life. I'm sorry, Gramps"

"Never mind that. I have learned not to expect much from family. I doubt if your mother or father have read my works. They sure keep it to themselves if they have. I will admit that it is painful. My friends, and a lot of people I don't know, readers, reward me, but not my family." He sighed. "Sorry to lay a bummer on you, Mark, but I think most writers have about the same experience with family. I may be different from most only because I am so damned old. No one ever expected me to write novels or poetry. Publishers are sure not interested in writers my age."

Mark thumbed through the poetry book, closed it and said, "Now, back to the original subject. I wanted to know your take on love."

"Ah, yes, love. I have been *in* love more than once, Mark. To me there is nothing to compare *in* love with. I would say the greatest gift of my life has been the times I have been *in* love. I love many things, Mark. I loved flying, great ships, good friends, cattle ranching and teaching school. I love being alone in the wilderness, just not for too long. I love any body of water and mountains. I hate that I cannot go to the mountains now, what with this damned pulmonary fibrosis. I love motorcycles and kids and hard work and sweat and I love this house and writing. What I have loved most of all, though, is being *in* love. Being *in* love has provided the highpoints of my life. Those are the memories I live for.

"Falling *out* of love effectively ended my marriage, Mark. I hungered for being *in* love again, as I was for many years with your grandmother. I needed that feeling. I still do. I needed that closeness and I found it. I found it because I was looking for it. I found it because I once had it and knew what to look for. For me, that kind of love can only happen with a woman. My wife touched me that way for years, and then Elena affected me the same way. The difference between being *in* love and love is simple: Once you have it, craving the feeling never goes away. Being *in* love, particularly in the beginning, hurts. Days and nights apart are torment. I hope you experience the same suffering so you will know what I am telling you is true. Being *in* love is different.

"I expect a person can go through life living with ordinary, comfortable love just fine, and I also expect most people do. Being *in* love is crazy. You will do foolish things to be with her. You will sacrifice for and crave the feeling. You will cherish her because she is the bridge to that feeling."

Ben sat back and laughed. "My God! Did you understand anything I just said? Here I am, well into my eighties and I probably sound like a lovesick teenager to you."

"Not to me, Gramps. I hope what you just talked about

happens to me. I want that."

"I am afflicted, Mark. I am afflicted by good enough health, by looking and acting much younger than my age, and by desires that should have expired years ago. I am afflicted by the life I led; the fighter squadron life; the great airplanes and ships. I am afflicted by a life with magnificent friends and exciting jobs. Yes, afflicted even by war. I loved parts of serving in that damned war. Some combat situations test the strength of human moral fiber. If you serve in real combat, the dirty, tiresome, out-of-control-near-death combat, the I-don't-care-if I do die combat, you will come away either tormented and shaken or content and confident with yourself. Combat didn't bother me. I am also plagued by never being forced by nature to submit to the customary life patterns of old people, which is probably a damned curse. Old people my age usually act like...well, old people. Most of my friends are much younger than I.

"My imagination, coupled with great experiences, have cost me, Mark. I find it difficult to be content with normal. The mundane smothers me. I find the monotony of everyday life to be a reality I must live with, but find it to be suffocating.

The two men spent their remaining time together talking about Ben's books. Mark checked his watch repeatedly, finally deciding he needed to leave.

"I may not stop by on the way back, Gramps. I need to be in St. Louis early Monday."

They stood and shook hands.

"You don't need to stop by, Mark. This is way out of

route for you. Emily can fill me in on your weekend." He punched Mark on the shoulder. "Maybe she will and maybe she won't, right?"

Mark gazed at Ben for a moment, smiling. "We aren't going to become subjects for your fiction are we, Gramps?"

'Not possible. Fiction needs to be believable. You two are pressing the limits. "

Mark called to tell Emily that he was trapped on the interstate overpass. "A semi is all the way across the road. Jack-knifed. I can't back up because the damned traffic is jammed behind me. The cops are not here yet. It's going to be a while, Emily."

"Oh! Why would something like this…. Okay, I guess there is nothing to be done but wait it out. I'm still inside the hospital. I'll wait here until you let me know you are on the way."

An hour later, Mark called Ben. "I can't get Emily on her phone, Gramps. Have you heard anything from her?"

Ben's alarm bells rang.

"No. Not a word, why? Any idea what's going on?"

"I don't know. Nothing good from what I can gather. Her car was unlocked when I got here, Gramps. Her phone and purse were on the front seat. Her keys were on the floor. This is not like her. I left a note and went in to check with her team. They said she left work on time.

That would have been an hour ago. I have looked in the cafeteria. I am at her car now and I'm going to stay right here. This is very troubling."

"Yeah, it is. I suppose you should stick around there. I suppose I should probably stay here. Let's hope she shows up soon. There must be a good reason. Has to be. Emily is not scatterbrained."
"Right. If she doesn't show up within the hour, I'm going to call the police. If that happens, they will probably want her car for possible clues. Since it is unlocked, I'm going to park next to it when the spot opens up. I don't know what else to do."

CHAPTER NINE

BEYOND

Emily waited at the nurse's station for ten minutes after Mark's call, too nervous to stand still or sit. Her thoughts were centered on the coming weekend. She decided to get her cosmetic kit from the car and headed for the parking garage, noting on the way that clouds had covered what little sunlight remained.

No moon tonight.

Nightfall was already replacing the balmy late summer evening. As she reached her car, a voice from behind yelled, "Hey, Miss! Did you drop this?" She turned to see a man trotting toward her, closing fast, waving something that looked like a surgical facemask. Before she could answer, the sliding door to the van backed in next to her car screeched open. She turned to face a masked man already in the act of reaching for her to muffle what little sound she was able to make. The other man arrived at the same time and the two wrestled her quickly into the van.

The larger of the two, the man from the van, held her

tightly, his hand clamped roughly over her mouth while the other accomplice ran to the driver's side. The man holding her from behind growled, "You need to stop fighting me, lady. Don't make me hurt you. You need to calm down. Nothing you can do is going to change anything. Stop fighting me! I mean it! If you fight I will hurt you. Stop fighting!" He jerked her head back.

The guy gripping her ordered the other to put Emily's cell phone and purse in her car. "Throw her keys on the floor! Leave it unlocked! Come on! Move it!"

The driver drove to the top of the parking garage where few cars remained. The man holding Emily ordered his partner to come around and help. They forced Emily's arms behind her back and fastened two sets of plastic zip ties around her wrists.

"Not too tight. He doesn't want her hurt."

They then covered her mouth and eyes with duct tape and reclined her seat all the way down. Nothing happened. They just sat quietly, smoking. No one spoke. Emily couldn't understand what they were doing or why they were not moving. They sat for what seemed like forever.

What are they waiting for? Must be waiting for someone. What is happening? Are they going to hurt me? Do they have the wrong person?

She trembled and cried silently, tears pooling over her eyes beneath the tape. Her nose began swelling from crying and she had trouble getting enough air.

The driver finally spoke. "It's dark enough, don't you think?"

"Yeah. Let's get this over with. Time to hit the road. Don't make any mistakes. We sure as hell don't want to attract any attention with her all tied up. Just a nice

Sunday drive."

Ten minutes later, Emily assumed they were out of the city as the van picked up speed and they made no further stops for traffic lights. The man in the seat next to her leaned close and said, "Look, we don't intend to hurt you. Not unless you make us. What we are doing is just a warning. We are doing this for your own good. Just a warning. You need to think about what the hell you've been doing, lady, and then you need to back the hell off. If you keep snooping around, we will be forced to do something more permanent, and that means hurting you. Now, that's all I'm going to say. You damned well know what I'm talking about."

A warning? Should I believe him? This must be a mistake. Why would they be warning me? About what?

Emily's fright diminished with time as her thoughts focused on what he said. She didn't need to think long before considering the only possible answers to her predicament were either that they made a mistake and snatched the wrong person, or that her recent encounter with the church had stirred something sinister.

Must be something about the church. Is this about Iris? Her reaction to me was certainly odd. Why would she pass out? What have I done? Ben was right to be skeptical.

Time did not fly. The journey lasted for what seemed like hours. Emily listened closely to their conversations but they spoke very little, usually only about directions. "Is this the turn?" Later the man next to her yelled, "You just drove by the damned road, Al! Turn around."

Al? Remember that.

Ten minutes later her captor said, "Okay, slow down some. We need to select one of these fire roads." They drove on and on. "Here! This one! Nice and slow now. It's probably going to be rough as hell."

"Jesus! This is too much for the van. You sure about this?"

"Yeah. This is the right place. I tagged one of the trees at the entrance. Not much farther."

Emily began trembling again as what they were going to do with her was apparently imminent.

"Stop here! Let's leave the road and walk from here. Turn the van around first."

The van lurched and changed gears, and then stopped. "Now what?"

"Now we hike, like the man said. Bring that bag of snacks and let's get this over with."

The door beside Emily skidded open and the men wrestled her out. They started walking, each holding her by an arm. She stumbled repeatedly. The men holding her managed to stop most of her tumbles. They walked up and down long hills for what seemed like hours, and then climbed a steep hill. She could tell they were no longer on a trail or road as a thick bed of leaves crunched beneath their feet. On and on they went. Emily tired until she could no longer pick her feet up. They dragged her for a few minutes before one said, "Screw this. This is far enough, don't you think?"

"No. I know where we are. We just need to let her rest. I'm going to take the tape off now."

"I don't know, man. He said not to."

"Well, he ain't here, is he? Do you want to carry her? Because that's where we are. She's worn-out. She's done about all she's gonna do."

"Yeah, but he said leave the tape on."

"She can walk better with it off. Look, I'm about out

of juice, too. So let's just get this over with."

The tape came off along with most of her eyebrows and some skin. Emily could feel blood flowing on her cheeks. She could not see anything in the darkness; not the men; not the woods; nothing but darkness. One of her captors flipped an extremely bright light on and she briefly saw the other guy flinching and holding his hand in front of his face.

"Jesus, Chuck. Not on me! Point that damned thing somewhere else!"

Emily said, "I need to pee."

They both laughed. "Go ahead." More laughter.

"Seriously. I need to–"

"What the hell. Okay, but we ain't gonna untie you. One of us will have to pull your pants down. You good with that?"

She realized that her predicament was hopeless. One way or another, she was at their mercy. "Yes."

"Okay, just relax. We are not going to do anything to you. Here we go." With that, he pulled her dress up and moved her panties down to her knees. "Go on. Squat down."

She was too tired to balance and the guy holding her had to provide support. When she struggled back to her feet, he pulled her panties up and they started walking again. Both men had strong flashlights. Emily was able to see well enough to keep from stumbling so much. Her feet and legs were weak and raw. She could feel blood squishing in her shoes. They kept pulling her.

They finally stopped.

"What do you think? Far enough?"

"Yeah. This should do it."

"We gonna untie her?"

"No. He said either she lives or she dies. Up to her. Let's get out of here."

"Her shoes. He said to take her shoes."

"Aw, man. That's aint gonna make no difference. She's not going anywhere."

"No, dammit! Take her damned shoes!"

After that, she watched and listened as their lights and walking noises diminished. A few minutes later she could hear nothing but night noises—an almost deafening silence. Emily started after them, attempting to keep their light in sight. Her sore feet and a brutal fall ended the pursuit. Her nose bled until she worried about losing too much blood. She could tell that her feet were bleeding. Emily gave up and lay on the forest floor for a long time, weeping silently, nearly sleeping, just not quite. When daylight began peeking through the trees, she sat up and began struggling with the zip ties, only to finally realize that the only way out would be to force her hands beneath her body and legs. The effort took her remaining strength. She managed to contort and wiggle enough to slowly force her hands beneath her butt. Cramps stopped her several times. She had to pause and try to relax until the unbearable cramps relented. Finally, with a gasp of relief, her arms and hands were free and in front of her. She laughed. She laughed until the laughter became weeping.

Later, after suffering through bouts of hopelessness and despair, she began to think about the best way to get out. She climbed the nearest hill and sat listening for sounds of human industry.

Nothing.

Emily decided to keep the sun in front and started walking, hoping to stay in a straight line. She chose east, wrong or right. She didn't have enough strength remaining to waste it walking in circles. She attempted to stay on course using the sun until it was too high to determine direction. She stopped to rest, snoozing off and on, waiting for the sun to go down so she could establish direction again, and then she planned to begin walking, this time away from the sun.

Emily struggled on until darkness before collapsing, out of breath and too weak to walk any farther. Her feet had lost feeling and strength. She couldn't feel anything but numb. Sleep came fleetingly and unreliably. She could hear night sounds from every direction. Disturbing sounds. She was certain that she could hear animals walking, breathing and snorting. She imagined animals on all sides. She learned later that she may have encountered feral hogs, animals dangerous to humans, particularly helpless bleeding humans.

Emily wondered what Ben and Mark were thinking and worried about how her absence would torture Ben. She didn't know Mark well enough to know how her disappearance would affect him, but she certainly knew how Ben would take it. He would be heartbroken. She cried thinking about Ben and worried about Mark.

Ben and Mark went back to the hospital the next morning, Saturday, and searched the grounds and parking garages for clues. Mark noticed tears on Ben's face more than once. Ben seemed locked in his own world. The two men spoke very little after the initial discussions, attempting to consider, each in his own way, possible reasons for her absence.

The police were of little help. They had already exhausted the only potential lead–Emily's meeting with Iris at Driscoll's church. Both evangelists expressed surprise and distress, but provided no information.

After the meeting, one of the detectives told the other, "I don't know about him, but that woman sure was twitchy. I say she knows something but won't say it around him. Something like that. I think there is something going on there and we should probably have the heavies bring them in separately."

Ben attended the church on Sunday, going forward after the service to hand Driscoll an envelope. "There is a little something in there for you." He left without looking back.

Driscoll didn't open the envelope until later, thinking it probably just another contribution. He found no money. The note read: *I will kill you if she doesn't show up soon. That I swear.*

Ben did not share his church visit or the contents of the note with Mark.

Dawn of the second morning found Emily sick, dehydrated, starving and too weak to go on. She lay in the leaves until the sun was almost overhead before struggling to her feet. She wasn't sure at first, but an almost imperceptible noise attracted her attention. A familiar noise; a long-way-off noise. It sounded like a truck engine. She wasn't sure and cupped her ears to listen. The noise seemed to be moving from her right to left. She listened until the noise faded off to her left and then began walking with renewed energy and, for the first time in days, finally with a reason to hope.

Emily arrived at a narrow blacktop road just before sunset and sat down to wait. So happy. So happy that she could not stop crying; thrilled to realize that the nightmare was near an end. It ended thirty minutes later as a pickup truck containing a middle-aged couple stopped. The woman ran to her.

"Oh, honey, you look hurt! How did you get to be so hurt? What happened to you?"

"Oh, for God's sake Sarah! Get her in the damned truck! We need to get her some help!"

They decided to go to the nearest town, Bradleyville, a tiny town with nothing more than a convenience store and post office. The woman called ahead on her cell phone and the store owner in turn called the county sheriff's office.

Upon arrival, the store owner's wife led Emily to the restroom to clean her wounds. Emily balked.

"Please, not yet. I need to call someone. Please. I need a phone." She called Ben.

Ben put his phone on speaker. "Mark is here, Emily. Are you all right?"

"Hi, Mark. I think I'm going to be okay, Ben. Two men grabbed me in the parking garage. Oh, let me wait to tell you everything that happened. It is unbelievable. I am okay now. I am in a little town. Just a minute." She held the phone out so Ben could hear and asked the owner's wife, "Where am I?"

"You are in Bradleyville."

"Did you hear that, Ben? I don't know where Bradleyville is. Do you?"

"Yes. What are you doing down there, Emily? What happened?"

"I was taken hostage and dumped in the woods. They tied me up and left me. I have been lost in the woods for...I forget...two days? Three? I really can't remember. We can talk later. The sheriff is on the way here. An ambulance is also on the way. They are going to take me to the hospital in Branson. Can you meet me there?"

"Absolutely. What do you need? Can we bring anything?"

"Yes, please. I need some clean clothes and shoes. They threw my shoes away, Ben. Bring my running shoes. Wait. No. Maybe your slippers and loose socks because my feet are swollen and bloody. The shoes need to be loose. And I need some loose clothes to wear. Jock gear. Sweats. My legs are scratched and bruised. I have been without shoes the whole time, Ben. My feet are cut up and terribly sore. I cannot stand. I'll see both of you soon. I need to go now. The sheriff just got here."

The sheriff didn't stay long. "This is going to fall under Greene County jurisdiction since that's where you were abducted. I'll call and give them what I know. They will be in contact. Let me have a phone number."

She gave him Ben's numbers.

The ambulance arrived soon after the sheriff departed.

Ben and Mark arrived at the hospital within the hour. They came in Mark's car. Ben cried openly, pressing his forehead to hers before pulling away to make room for

Mark. He left her with Mark until the hospital released her four hours later, after removing the hydration needle from her arm.

"No reason to keep you. You are still seriously dehydrated, so you need to drink water. Drink a lot of fluids. We have taken care of the wounds so there should be no infection. You will definitely need a wheelchair to keep the weight off your feet. It will take at least a week to get you back on your feet. I'm sure you know the deal, being a nurse. Good luck."

"One of you needs to ride back here with me. I need some human warmth."

Mark and Ben looked at each other, each waiting for the other to volunteer. Mark motioned toward the back with his thumb. "You, Gramps. Get back there."

Emily lay with her head on Ben's lap. Before sleeping, she murmured, "I love you, Ben."

"I know. I know, baby. Now sleep."

She slept all the way home.

The next morning, Mark bought medicine, healing salve and rented a wheel chair. Ben visited the college to gather Emily's school assignments for a week.

Emily agreed to sit for newspaper and television interviews. When Ben questioned her motives, she said, "Yes. I absolutely want to do it. I don't care how dreadful I look. I want the world to know what happened."

"Do you have any idea who could be behind what happened?"

"Yes I do, and so do you. I need to think about what I am going to say to the police."

"Do you want to talk about it first, Emy? This could be important. You need to be sure."

"No. Thanks, Ben. I need to do this."

The interviews took place on Ben's porch.

"Miss Prindiville, do you have any idea who is responsible for what happened to you. Do you know why you were abducted?"

"Yes, I definitely do, to both questions. However, I am not free to reveal my suspicions. The City Police and State Patrol are presently conducting an investigation and I have been informed that the FBI will soon be involved. I am not going to speculate."

National news outlets ran the coverage for two days.

"We have been foiled yet again, Mark. I can't go anywhere for at least a week or ten days. The police and State Patrol are demanding that I remain nearby for the time being. Oh, and by the way, the FBI is coming for an interview this afternoon."

"I could possibly take the rest of the week off and stay here to help you get around."

Mark didn't seem all that firm to Emily. "That would be wonderful, Mark, but you should go on with your plans. I'm going to be useless. If you stayed we would have to ship Ben off for a few days."

"Emily, I'm not surprised that you and Gramps are close, but he sure teared up a lot last night. And I noticed it at breakfast this morning. Is he usually that emotional around you?"

"He is, but not necessarily about me. He tears up when I get him to talk about Elena. The truth is, even watching the traditional feel-good moment on the evening news brings him to tears. I don't think he is suffering, though. I think he is content, in a way, that he is still that close to her and that his emotions are not hidden. It's all about Elena and getting old, Mark. He thinks getting old has something to do with exposed emotions. His tears are not about me. He told me that losing Elena changed him. But you are correct thinking he is very emotional. Are you good with that? I mean, are you worried about him medically?"

"Not really. He cried several times last night, Emily. He lost control in the hospital room with you, and I saw tears a few times on the way home when oncoming car lights lit up his face."

"Oh, I don't think Ben loses control. I think crying probably makes him happy, in a way, not to be so locked in by macho crap. He's okay, Mark. Really he is."

"You two have a great relationship. Both of you seem at ease and comfortable with each other."

"Oh, it's much better than that, Mark. I love him more than I have ever loved anyone. Ben is the father I never had. He is my rock. He saved me, Mark, and I mean literally. But that's not why I care so much about him. He would do anything for me, no questions asked. I know that is true and I feel the same about him. He has opened an entirely new and wonderful world of what it should be like to be human just by being himself. He was my way to you, Mark. Even you are thanks to Ben. He is my family. He is, or was, everything to me. And now, Ta DA! I have the promise of you. The last three days were terrifying and will always be with me, but I could not be happier than I am at this moment. Oh, maybe I could stand a little less sore and being so dinged up."

Mark laughed, "So, am I in competition with my Grandpa?"

"Nope. You are in another league, big guy. I plan to molest you. I plan to live on you. I expect to become part of you. I would smother you right now with kisses if I could feel my mouth. No, Mark, I have plans for you that do not include your grandfather."

"You are really beat-up, Emily. It doesn't seem to matter, though, because you are still pretty, even though you are beat up. The bruising is already coming to the surface. You are going to be a mess for several weeks, maybe a month or two. I'll get some meds to help the healing process."

"Try falling in the dark about a hundred times with your hands tied behind your back, Mark. I don't think my face missed anything. I always seemed to fall face first."

"Why were you so motivated to have the news interviews?"

"I want them, whoever they are, to feel the heat. I want them to be aware that anything that happens to me from here on will come back on them."

Mark said, "Whoever did this will be better off if Ben never finds out who they are. I don't see him as being timid about much of anything, let alone someone messing with you. "

"Oh, I would bet anything Ben has no doubt about who did it. He knows exactly who is behind what happened to me, and why. I am as sure as I can be of that. Oh, he knows. Ben knows. I worry about him, Mark. He might do…. No, I don't want to think about that."

CHAPTER TEN

COLIN, AGAIN

Mark was at the kitchen table Tuesday morning with Ben when Emily arrived, still struggling to master the wheelchair. Ben demanded that she sleep in his room to put a stop to laboring up and down the stairs. Ben had changed the bedding and moved to the basement as soon as she returned from the terror of her National Forest adventure.

"Just until you can manage the stairs, Emily. It's a done deal so quit griping about it. You are welcome."

Mark cleared his throat after breakfast. "I have to get back to St. Louis today. I need to finish some courses and concentrate on work with my instructor. I'm still on schedule to get the MD the first part of January. And I have decided to finish my residence there, as originally planned."

Ben stopped eating and looked confused.

Emily was speechless.

What?

Ben said, "Whoa! What happened to finishing up your

residency here? I thought you had already made arrangements."

"Of course you're right. I did." He cleared his throat, glancing from Ben to Emily, clearly uneasy. "I decided last week to stay with the original plan. I really haven't had time to tell you, what with everything…well, you know." He glanced from Emily to Ben and back.

Emily, while stunned and momentarily sick to her stomach, was not all that confused. "Well, Mark, what about our plans for the weekend at Big Cedar? Hmm? When were you planning to tell me about *your* decision? Or were you planning to go and perhaps tell me there? How romantic."

"I'm sorry, Emily. I was on the way to tell you on Friday evening. I was going to tell you and then go back to St. Louis after that."

"Wow! Just like that. I was so planning on…." She struggled to stand. "Oh, to hell with it! Just so you know, none of this is all right with me. You were not thinking about me, *Mark*. What happened? Did you get cold feet, *Mark*. And now I want to know if you had already cancelled the room at Big Cedar? Yes, I want to know about that! You had you already cancelled, right?" She glared at him, waiting for an answer.

He couldn't look at her, but nodded. "Yeah, I cancelled. Look, I know I should have–"

"You rat! Are you kidding me? "What happened, Mark! I thought we…."

No one said anything for the longest time. Emily stared at Mark, attempting in vain to suppress the flow of tears. Ben, looking down, wished he could be any other place on the planet. Mark got up, stood watching Emily for a moment, and then whispered, "I'm sorry."

He left the house.

Emily went to bed.

Ben sat on the front porch.

They seldom ever spoke about Mark after that morning. Mark did not call, or send a letter, or text, or return to face her.

Emily went back to work and school on Wednesday, well before Ben thought she should. He lifted her into the truck, loaded the wheelchair, dropped her off at the hospital's main entrance and then wheeled her through the hospital to the nursing school classroom. He took a seat in the back to wait. Emily noticed that the instructor, Doctor Wentz, was also sitting in the back of the room. She had seen the guy standing at the speaker's podium before, attending her hospital and University classes. He never seemed to be by himself, always laughing and joking. Obviously a student. Colin something-or-other.

Oh, God. Another Colin.

He waited until Emily found a place to park the wheelchair and said, "Good morning. I am Colin Hilton. Doctor Wentz has asked me to do this session on Immediate Medical Attention as I have some pertinent background to share. First, emergency medical care under extreme circumstances is my specialty. My job for the past couple of years has been moving desperately injured or sick people to hospital care without letting them die."

He looked up from his notes. "The–without letting them die– part is what this session will be all about. I recently separated, honorably according to my enlistment agreement, from the Navy after three combat tours in Afghanistan. Combat tours with the Marines as a Navy corpsman. I plan to become an emergency room RN and eventually a Physician Assistant–a PA. That said, please feel free to stop me any time you want more or better information. Doctor Wentz is here for the better information part."

He looked around the room, smiling. Emily was well aware that he never stopped smiling. None of what had happened to her during the past week leaked in to spoil the moment. He was a happy guy. Very tall. Too tall with maybe a little too much facial hair in the form of a closely trimmed beard. She didn't like beards.

"All right, then! We begin. I served as a combat medic. Marines just call us Corpsmen. In the middle of combat, if a Marine yells 'Corpsman!' we show up. It doesn't matter how dire the setting or how scared we are, we show up. We show up and do what needs to be done to see that wounded men make it to the hospital alive. Many of you will experience similar circumstances, possibly many times, during your career, particularly you Emergency Medical Technicians and emergency room nurses. On many occasions, there will be no time for detailed analysis. You will do what is necessary and you will do it in a hurry. Get the heart stabilized, stop the bleeding, stabilize the patient, whatever needs to be done quickly. It may not be a gaping wound or anything visible, but you must be able to assess the situation immediately and then do what needs to be done to get the patient to the hospital alive.

"Okay. First things first. Get them out of the danger zone–off the street, out of the burning car, out of the water, the list goes on–out of the burning sun. In my case it was usually out of the field of enemy fire. In your case, off the road in the middle of traffic." He held up a finger. "More on that. First responders are killed and maimed way too often because they have not cleared the patient from the danger of their surroundings. Get off the damned road! Get out of the water! Move away from danger. "

Emily, like the other thirty students, remained intensely focused on his presentation. When finished, he said, "I know there will be many questions. I am going to be here for the remainder of the course. Doctor Wentz and I will remain in the room until it's time for the next class. Thank you."

The class smothered him with attention. Doctor Wentz remained seated, smiling at the class reaction. He eventually rose and called an end to the excited discussions.

Colin, once free, walked directly to Ben. "Hi. I'm Colin Hilton. I noticed you here and assume you are you waiting to take Miss Prindiville to the university. Am I correct?"

"Yep, that is my intent. Nice presentation, by the way." He offered his hand. "I am a retired Marine, Colin. Ben Compton. "

"Ah, we have more than Emily in common. If you two are okay with this, I will be happy to transport Emily to and bring her back from the university" He pointed to Emily as she maneuvered the wheelchair to a stop next to him. "That is, if she approves. No sense in more than one vehicle being involved." He faced Emily. "Would you be okay with that?"

Emily looked to Ben. He shrugged. When she turned back to Colin, his hands were on his chest, his eyes pleading.

"How nice of you to offer, Colin. Sure, if that's not too much trouble. Ben can take the rest of the day off."

Colin said, "Great. If you want to travel with me until you are back on your feet, I would like that very much. Will that work?"

She took time to think. "All right, Colin. I'll probably be back on my feet some time next week, though. Thank you." She turned to Ben. "Is this okay with you, Ben?"

"I guess. You two work it out. I'll get you here and take you home." He turned to Colin. "I'll bring her to the West entrance, Colin. Can you pick her up there, or do I need to wheel her in here each morning?

"I'll be there."

"And that's where I can expect to find her later today, right?"

Emily and Ben both watched Colin. He nodded and said. "Yes. Perfect."

After the second hospital class, Colin pushed her to the cafeteria. They became friends easily, openly casual and natural from the beginning. He wheeled her to the West entrance after lunch, retrieved his truck-a vehicle twice the size of Ben's truck. He lifted her onto the seat easily, loaded her wheelchair and drove to the university, talking and laughing all the way. They repeated the routine the remainder of the week and the first two days of the following week.

Emily knew where he was from, about his family and where he lived, all before the end of the first day. No immediate attraction, but she liked him well enough. A nice guy.

"You said you live north of town, Colin. How far north?"

"Not far. Just east of Willard on the Sac river."

The Sac river. Hmmmm. "Where is Willard?"

"About seven miles from Springfield. I live on a small farm."

She called Mark late one night after thinking about him for days. "Have you got a few moments for me, Mark?"

"Certainly. Go ahead, Emily. I know I probably deserve what's coming."

"Oh, I didn't call to fuss at you, but you damned sure deserve it. Several things have occurred to me that only you can answer, Mark. First: Do you realize that you never touched me in any sexual way? Not my breasts; nothing more than my face or shoulders. No tongue when kissing. Nothing all that intimate. Does that strike you as odd, considering how close we seemed to be?"

He started to answer. She interrupted.

"You just wait until I'm through. Why didn't you bother to tell me you were thinking about dropping out of a Springfield residency? You didn't tell me you were going to stick with cardiology, either. You have not read Ben's books, and I find that inconceivable, Mark. I read his books the first thing. All of them. You could learn a lot about your grandfather by reading those books. The fact that you don't know Ben, your own grandfather, nearly as well as I do is also inconceivable. Why did you let Ben come to the back seat with me on the way home from Branson, Mark? I needed you. I wanted *you*, not Ben. And what about sex, Mark? I practically threw myself at you. You managed to avoid sex, and I find that a wee bit weird, Mark. Now, answer me this, and I am serious, what do you do with your free time, Mark? What do you do for fun?"

"I usually try to catch up on sleep. I occasionally catch a movie. Sometimes I eat out at a different nice place. Mostly I spend free time recuperating and getting ready for what comes next."

"That figures. I hate to ask, but everything I know about you makes me want to ask this. Is there is any chance you might be gay?"

"No! What would make you think that?"

"Oh, just about everything I just asked that you haven't answered."

They both remained silent for a long time. Too long. Mark cleared his throat.

Emily said, "Thank you, Mark. Maybe I'll see you around. Have a good life."

She told Ben about the conversation.

"What have you learned, Emily?"

"I have learned that old sayings are sometimes all too true. How about, 'All that glitters is not gold?' I hope, if I ever meet someone who affects me the way Mark did, that I hold on to some of my cards. I was so sure, Ben. A lesson learned the hard way."

The next day at lunch, she asked Colin, "What do you do with your spare time, Colin? What do you do for fun?"

"I try never to have spare time, Emily. In my off-work time I race dirt bikes through the woods. Enduro racing we call it, and that's because it takes endurance. I play ball on a team during every season. Flag football, baseball, basketball. I join leagues. Some teams are for men and women– Co Ed teams. You should join. Great fun. I ski some in the winter, spend a lot of time on the water in the summer, and I chase girls all year round. Yes I do. And, just so you won't think I sneaked up on you, I intend to make myself not only desirable but available to you, Emily. That should be fun, don't you think?" He laughed good-naturedly. He laughed a lot.

"Well, Colin. I am somewhat involved at the present time."

"Really? Somewhat? Somewhat is not going to keep me from trying."

"All right, then I am pretty sure I am not available."

He laughed. "Nope. I'm pretty sure that pretty sure is not going to keep me from knocking on your door, either."

"What will it take to convince you?"

"Well, first things first. A ring? I don't see a ring, Emily. I suppose a ring would slow me down." He laughed again. "Nah! I'm probably going to hang around until you run me off. Anyway, you would have blown me off in a second if you were with another guy."

"Don't you have any pride, Colin? Look at me. I am a walking bruise, bandaged all over my body. And I can-not-walk, in case you missed that. I am more purple than white."

He laughed. "Ah, but you forget, Madam. I have seen you before, and I damned sure noticed you the moment I saw you. Waiting for you to clear up is no problem. I remember exactly what you look like." He stood and said, "We better get moving. Let's go." On the way to the university, he glanced at her several times, and laughed.

Emily thought, Oh- My-God! Two weeks ago I didn't

know a guy and now I have dumped one and this guy is nothing if not available. I'm turning into a trollop. Hey, good for me.

The last day of their travel arrangement did not come without regret. Emily enjoyed his company. "You know all about me, Colin. Now it's my turn. Are you seeing anyone?"

"Yes. I live with someone, Emily." He laughed.

Long pause. "A her?"

"Yes." He laughed.

Emily suffered instant disappointment and thought while looking through the side window that Colin laughed a lot. He laughed at everything. He laughed when Emily couldn't see anything funny. His laughter was or would soon become annoying.

"Yeah. I have known her all my life."

Emily didn't reply for a while, still looking through the side window, thinking. "Sorry I'm being nosey, Colin. I didn't mean to pry."

"Yes you did. Of course you did. Now go on. Finish it."

She turned to him. "Finish what?"

"Oh, who is she? Do you know her? You know–the usual." He laughed.

"You are playing with me now, Colin. Just tell me." She thought he was enjoying the exchange a little too much.

"Her name is Velda. I have known her all my life. She loves me completely." More laughter.

"Come on! Are you engaged? What?"

He laughed, pounding the steering wheel. "No. At least not in the usual way. Her last name is Hilton, by the way." He waited expectantly, glancing from the road to Emily.

"So? Go on."

"Hilton! You didn't get that part? I live with her, Emily. She is my grandmother." He laughed.

"You are joking."

"No." He laughed. He couldn't stop laughing. "When I got back from Afghanistan and after I got out of the Navy, she asked me to stay with her. She's in her eighties now and lives alone on a farm. She still keeps some chickens, a dog and cats, and a small herd of cattle. My folks live nearby. They set her up to ask me. I think they were tired of seeing after her every day."

"You really are joking, aren't you?"

"Nope. She makes a great roomy, Emily. She is happy. She cooks, cleans, and she thinks I walk on water. She is easy to live with and right now I am happy to have a place to stay."

Emily could feel anger swelling. "Nice try. I am not believing any of that for a moment, Colin. Why don't we just change the subject?"

"Look, Emily, I know I joke around, and you probably should be skeptical, but I am serious this time. You have to come meet her. Say when. She would love to meet you."

"Why would she? She doesn't know anything about me."

"Wrong! She knows everything about you that I know. She wants to meet you, Emily."

"What have you been telling her?"

"What little I know, which is just about everything I

know."

Their relationship begins to wane. Colin had little time for her as he spent almost every weekend with his friends, at a bar, racing in the woods, playing ball. When he invited her, she spent most of her time looking for another tag-along woman to talk to.

She thought about the difference between Colin and Mark. Both men were vastly different. While analyzing the two, Emily's thoughts gradually shifted to her own life. She ended up thinking "What is the difference between me and Mark? He works, and then he rests up to go back to work. That is exactly what I do. I work two shifts on weekend and holidays. I don't go out with friends. I really don't have friends, other than Ben and my shift mates. Colin Hilton is just not going to happen. I need to make some drastic life changes."

She told Ben that evening about her thoughts. "I fussed at Mark when he told me what he did on time off. I said, 'That figures.' like I was looking down on him. The problem with that, Ben, is that is exactly what I do. I rest and get ready for the next go-around. I don't have a life, either. What do I do for fun, Ben? I live with you, and you are fun, but I have no outside life."

Emily deliberately changed her life. She celebrated her twenty-third birthday–December 14. She did not celebrate with friends from work, or with Colin. Colin had not been in the picture for weeks by then. She celebrated alone with Ben. Ben and Emily each drank half a glass of wine and let it go.

She graduated during the second week of January and

became Emily Prindiville, Registered Nurse. Much to her dismay, she had learned the hard way that she was not tall or strong enough for emergency room service.

The hospital hired her and she became a practicing nurse on the fourth floor. General all-purpose medicine. She would spend the following months assisting more advanced nurses. Her pay went up appreciably. She borrowed money to pay Ben for the car and her time in the hotel.

Ben attended the graduation ceremony. The graduating class consisted of only seven RNs. The formalities didn't last long. She won student-of-the-year award.

Emily's life became more structured toward her age group. She joined other young nurses and internists for occasional pizza parties and some other likewise loosely organized events. Her cadre of friends increased dramatically. She was happy and everyone she knew remarked about it. Happy, happy.

Someone else noticed.

Allen McDonald.

Emily had also noticed him a few times in the cafeteria–a new doctor. She learned later, from him, that he spotted her soon after moving to Springfield. The smile. Her smile was infectious, he told her. And he loved how she skipped and twirled sometimes when approaching friends. She was an automatic smile. He could tell she affected other people the same way. And petite. So tiny. Allen soon knew all about her work schedule and deliberately made it a practice to be in the cafeteria when she might be there. Her first and lasting impression of Allen McDonald came in the hallway one day as they passed going opposite directions. He smiled, looking directly at her. It was not an incidental smile. He was flirting. She was alone at the time, so no mistaking. She smiled, walked on, and then without slowing turned to look back. He had stopped and was watching her, still smiling. She didn't look back again but waved her ring hand over her shoulder and thought, *Oooo! Game on!*

A week or so later, while at lunch with two new friends, Allen approached with his tray.

"Mind if I join you." He was looking at Emily.

She glanced at her friends, and then to him. "I guess. Sure. Please join us."

He introduced himself and spoke mainly to Emily. Her two friends noticed, glanced at each other, excused themselves and changed tables. Emily didn't object and neither did Allen.

A first-year resident. Doctor Allen McDonald.

The relationship didn't move swiftly as their schedules seldom matched. He stopped her in the hall one cold February day. "I see our time schedules are going to correspond for the coming month. I would like to spend some time with you, Emily. How about it?"

She appraised him, a sly smile forming. "Are you spying on me, Doctor?"

"Only a little. I'm not following you or parking outside your home at night. Nothing like that. Well, not yet."

"Yes. I would like time with you. How about this for starters: four of us, all new nurses, are going to have a pizza party Friday. A quaint little parlor on Commercial Street. I think you will like it. We four women are each supposed to bring someone new. You can be my someone new, Allen. Before you answer that, no, it's not a hen party. It is a mixer. We are only allowed to bring men, and no good old boys are allowed."

His smile sealed the deal before he spoke. "Sounds

good to me. Can I pick you up?"

"Thanks, but no. I live out of town. I'll meet you there. Come casual, but do try to make my choice look good."

They exchanged phone numbers.

That evening at home, Ben noticed her smile. "Something good happened to you today, Emily. I can tell. Your facial expressions are never deceiving. You must be thinking about something far more satisfying than I am, and I am a pretty contented guy right now. Tell me."

She patted her chest. "Oh, my heart! You should see him, Ben. I can't wait for you to meet this guy."

Ben laughed to see her so happy. "A new guy already? Come on, Emily. Out with it."

"It, my dear precious friend, is Doctor Allen McDonald." She smiled, a smile most often seen on the face of jackpot and big game winners.

"Go on. Fill in the blanks"

"He is a new resident. I have seen him around for a week or two. He asked to sit with me at lunch today. He is working on Family Practice Medicine. He's going to be around the hospital for a long time and then plans to remain in the area, eventually opening his own clinic. If looks and manners have anything to do with it, he could be a keeper. Not too tall; not like Colin and Mark. I won't be half of a freak show. Dark hair and eyes. Very, very attractive. Yes, and he is better looking than those other two." She fanned her face. "Whew!"

"What happens now?"

"Pizza party with friends Friday night."

"That's a good way to begin, Emily. I'm happy for you."

CHAPTER ELEVEN

IRIS

Iris read and watched the news accounts of Emily's abduction. She knew the reason for the kidnapping–scare tactics to keep the new threat quiet–and she knew who did it and she knew who was behind it. Iris had decided, even before the law enforcement interrogations about the abduction, that she would not to share her knowledge with the cops. She did not want Mathew out of her reach. Not yet. She need time to take care of her plans first.

The news accounts and interviews captivated her. Iris recorded the television discussions and watched them many times, comparing the girl's face to hers.

That is my baby. My baby.

Ben studied the note Iris left in his mailbox. *Why would*

she want to talk to me? None of this is about me. I need to tell Emily. There can be no secrets between us.

Emily looked up from the note. "Oh, Ben. This is so exciting!"

"Really? Well, it certainly isn't to me. That woman is linked to the people I think are responsible for dumping you in the woods, Emily. My first notion is not to answer. I don't trust her."

"Maybe she doesn't know how to contact me."

"That's not believable and you know it. She contacted me. If she knows who I am and where I live, there is no reason to believe that she wouldn't know that you live here. She has to know where you work, too. How hard is it to follow you? But she left the note addressed to me, Emily. Why would she do that? She could have addressed the note to you. Why me?"

"I don't know. Maybe she really doesn't know where I live. Do you think we should just ignore it?"

"We? I'm just a way to get to you, Emily. This is not about me. She is attempting to use me."

"Okay, Ben. I'll think about it. I won't do anything before telling you. But this is so exciting to me! Come, on! Don't you think it's exciting? She is my mother, Ben."

"I expect it is exciting for you, and in your shoes I would probably be excited, but all I can think about is that she is or has been tied in with people who ran off with you; people who nearly killed you, Emily. Perhaps, if you decide to answer you should probably let me answer the note she wrote to me first. It was addressed to me. That way she would know I am in the mix. She…they would have to worry about me if they are still…well, you know. And, while we are at it, you might also think about the cops. I expect those two detectives would sure be interested in that note. Yep, they would sure be interested to know about this little wrinkle. Anyway, let me know. You're the baby, and you are still in a box."

It took a couple of seconds before Emily smiled and said, "Oh, that was cute, Ben. Puns at a time like this?"

Al rang Iris's doorbell just before dark.

"Al? What a surprise. What can I do for you?"

"I am getting the hell out of Dodge, Iris. I think things are about to get real hot around here and I am not going back to lock-up again. I need to tell you a few things before I split, though. Some things I should have told you years ago."

"Come in. Have a seat. You look so serious. What's on your mind?"

He sat, and then got up, took a couple of steps toward the door, paused, and then went back to the couch. After taking a seat, he said, "I'm too nervous to sit, Iris. Okay, let me get through this." He took a deep breath and blew it out through pursed lips. "All right, first things first. I think the feds, the state and county and the local cops are all about to swoop in on Mathew, Iris. And the reason I am here is to tell you that is that I don't think it's going to be later than sooner. That is one thing. The other thing is about your baby."

Iris covered her mouth, eyes wide with disbelief. "Oh,

I hope this is what I think, Al."

"Depends on your perspective. It's not all that good for me I can tell you." He cleared his throat, got up and stood near the door. "I'm sorry I didn't tell you what I am about to say as soon as I knew it, Iris. Anyway, here goes nothing. I wasn't on the actual scene when it all went down, and it looked to me like you were unconscious when me and Chuck got there–I thought you were unconscious anyway. I don't know exactly what happened afterward, but I do know that your baby was alive, breathing and still wet when Mathew called us in. Mathew had me and Chuck take your baby to the hospital emergency room, Iris. I left her in a box at the entrance and ran." He got up, stepped to the door and opened it a crack. "Just so you know, I'm sorry, Iris."

"Wait! Don't you dare leave me now! Is that all, Al? There has to be more than that!"

He nodded. "Yeah, there is. Me and Chuck think that girl…." He looked down, paused, looked up and said, "You know, the girl who came to the church a couple of weeks ago? You know, the time you passed out? We think she is probably the baby we left at the hospital. We think she is your daughter, Iris. It all fits. And I need to tell you this, too. Chuck pulled out this morning and he is not ever coming back. I don't know where he is headed, but he decided to get out before things go south. I'm not even sure where I'm going, but I ain't sticking around here for the crap I'm pretty sure is headed this way. I hope you don't get dragged into this, Iris, but if I was you, right about now would be a really good time to turn States Evidence before anything goes down. You are probably all right, but if you think you might need an edge with the law, maybe now is the time to get it. I'm just saying. I don't know if the feds could get to you, Iris. I hope you can stay clear." He shrugged. "Anyway, I am sorry for my part about your baby. Goodbye, Iris." He left the house before she could regain control of her senses.

A few moment later, the door opened part way and Al peeked through. "Do you know where she lives, Iris?"

"No. I think I can probably find out, though. I know where the old man I read about in Mathew's notes lives. And I know where she works–all the news reports mentioned that. Why?"

"Did Mathew ever tell you about the death threat he got? Happened right after we dumped her in the forest? Before she got out?"

"I do know about that, Al. I also read that in a note on Mathew's desk ."

"Do you know who the guy is who gave that note to Mathew?"

"I'm almost certain I do. I saw him that day at church, and I know you followed him. I read the license number and the address you gave Mathew on those notes on his desk. I know who he is and where he lives. Why?"

"Because that's where she lives, Iris. She lives with him. That's why." He paused. "We don't know what their relationship is, but you need to be careful. Mathew would turn his own mother in if he thought it would help him." The door snapped closed.

Iris called the local FBI office the very next day after gathering her evidence from the bank lock box. Two FBI agents came to her home within the hour, collected her evidence and transported her to the regional office in Springfield. They ushered her into a conference room containing two additional agents–both women.

Iris soon developed feelings of doubt and panic, wondering if she had opened a door that could put her on the wrong side of the law.

After introductions, the older of the women directed everyone sit. "I am the Springfield office supervising special agent, Miss Brooks. We appreciate your willingness to come forward on a matter that we are presently investigating. Now, tell us as clearly as you can what you have."

Hours later, after opening the packet of Mathew's records; after a delivered bag lunch; after answering what seemed like hundreds of questions that Iris recognized were asked for no other purpose than to corroborate her previous answers; after being advised to keep the lead agent advised of her whereabouts, and after being directed not to leave town without coordinating, Iris returned home convinced that she had done the right thing, even if her intent was revenge. She no longer harbored fears of being detained, or fears about her future. She had signed legal papers attesting to her disclosures and admissions as voluntary States Evidence.

Two days after the FBI visit, Iris received a call from the coordinating agent.

"Miss brooks, this is agent Higgins. I am calling to inform you that the Bureau has apprehended Mathew Driscoll. He is being held without bail as an escape risk. The federal prosecutor has called for a grand jury trial.

Do you have any questions?"

"No, thank you. I desperately needed that information. Will I be called to testify?"

"That information is above my pay grade. You will just have to wait and see."

Iris left home within thirty minutes to place another note in Ben's mailbox. The note not only contained her telephone number, again, but a long message directed to Emily, pleading for a meeting.

"I know who you are, Emily. I think I knew that from the first moment I saw you, but now I am convinced beyond a doubt that you are my baby. I received information yesterday from one of the men who took you in a box to the hospital twenty-three years ago. I have also learned that he was one of the men who kidnapped you recently. I know enough now to be convinced beyond doubt that you are my very own. I desperately want to meet you. We have years to make up. I do not believe I will ever sleep again until we meet. I am begging you with all my heart. Please, Emily. Please."

"Oh, Ben!" Emily held the note in her hand, tears flowing freely. "I just have to call her. I need to call her, Ben. This is so heart-breaking. I want to meet her, and I want you to come with me."

"I think you probably should meet, Emily. I expect it's time. You go ahead and call her. You should meet somewhere, just not at her home, and not somewhere she arranges. Maybe bring her here? That would be all right with me. I could pick her up. I think you should be skeptical until you know more. Up to you, Emy."

"I'm too excited to think straight, Ben. I will probably break down and blubber on the phone. You do it, Ben. Call her for me and set up a meeting. Oh, this is so exciting."

Ben called. "Miss Brooks, this is Ben Compton."

"Oh, I have been so afraid you wouldn't call. Thank you, Ben. Please, just a moment. I'm shaking all over. I need to sit down before you say anything…. There. Okay, go ahead."

"Emily would like to meet you." Iris burst out crying, completely breaking down. Ben waited, frowning, and then put the phone on speaker for a moment so Emily could hear. Emily started crying.

Ben murmured to himself, "Good grief. What a mess." He took the phone off speaker and waited.

After Iris regained control, they agreed to meet at Ben's home the next evening. "I will come for you about five, Miss Brooks, if that suits you. That will give Emily time to come home from work and freshen up."

When Iris opened the door the next afternoon, Ben started laughing. While still laughing, he said, "My, God, it's like meeting Emily in person. You two are identical. This is truly amazing."

Iris offered her hand. "I am so happy to finally meet you, Ben. I hope this is the beginning of a very long friendship. How is Emily?"

"Oh, she's a mess. I don't think she slept a wink. She will be worn out."

Once in his truck and underway, Iris asked to know about Ben's relationship to Emily.

He shook his head and said, "No. I'll let you two discuss that. All I am willing to say right now is this: Emily is the daughter I never had. I'll just leave it there. Now, anything else?"

Before she could answer, Ben's phone rang. He listened before saying, 'We'll be there in about ten minutes.' He clicked off and glanced at Iris. "She's home. This is going to work out perfectly."

"You were right about waiting, Ben. Let's wait for Emily. She needs to hear everything."

Emily was sitting on the front porch when the truck arrived. She met Iris half way to the house. They both froze in place several feet apart and stared. Iris said, "Oh, my. You are so tiny." Ben saw no smiles–no signs of excitement. The two women just stared, holding their hands to their face–everything alike. Emily broke first and ran. They held each other and cried for what seemed like ages to Ben. He tapped them both on the back and said, "Why don't we go inside and get comfortable."

The two women held hands until they reached the chairs Ben suggested at the kitchen table, opposing each other. He took a seat at the end as an interested observer and kept his mouth shut.

Iris opened the conversation. "Who, exactly, is Ben to you, Emily? I want to be aware of your relationship before I tell everything I know."

Emily smiled happily. "Ben? Ben is the father I never had, Iris. He saved my life. He is the best man I have ever known. Is that enough? I could talk about Ben all night, and I might some time, but right now I want to know about you."

"Well, if that isn't enough about Ben, I don't know what would be. There must be a story there."

"Yes, and I will happily tell you. But first, is it okay with you if Ben listens in?"

"Yes. I am happy to have him. Now, before anything else, I want both of you to know what has happened in my life the past few days." She told of her agreement with the FBI and about Mathew's confinement. "He is there at least until after the Grand Jury decision, and then maybe for the rest of his life.

"Oh, and the two men who took you to the National forest, Emily" They are gone. I don't know where to. They both have criminal records and Mathew's present circumstances scared them off. I doubt if we ever encounter them again. And, Al, the better of the two in my estimation, stopped by the night he left and told me all about the night Mathew ordered them to take you to the hospital in a cardboard box. He said you were still wet from birth and still had the umbilical cord attached. That is the first time that I knew for sure that you made it that far alive. Oh, that day I saw you at the church and the newspaper column you gave me were both certainly eye-openers. I thought you could be my baby. I wasn't convinced until Al told me.

"I need to tell you about your birth before we go any farther. I had a baby in the evening of December the Fourteenth, Nineteen-Ninety-Nine. That's your birth date. It happened that night in Mathew's office. I was there helping him with the books when my water broke. You were visibly on the way immediately after that. He called a midwife who arrived as soon as she could–just not soon enough. You were there before she got there. Mathew had given me some pills for pain. I think he mixed pain pills with something like oxycodone or morphine, or maybe something similar, or some other opioid. Mathew had access from Mexico for all kinds of illegal medicines. He made most of his money over the years selling smuggled drugs disguised as legal medicine and vitamins. Anyway, he kept me in a brain fog for a couple of days, but I soon realized you were gone. Mathew didn't want a baby to interfere with our shows. I called all the hospitals trying to find you. They said they could not divulge that information. Those were the worst days of my life. I didn't go back to work for weeks."

Emily reached across the table and held Iris's hands. "I came to Springfield to find out who my mother is. I didn't know you were alive. I found out who you were, quite by accident, at the hospital records office. A clerk there watched your shows and remarked that I could be your sister. She told me about recording the box baby and about the adoption. She didn't know who adopted me, only that the hospital kept me for a period of time waiting for someone to claim me. She remembered your calls asking if the hospital had an unclaimed baby. She knew all about the box baby because the newspaper wrote the story I gave you, and word got around the hospital. She took your number and called back. You answered. That's why she believed you could be my mother, Iris. Is that your real name or a stage name?"

"That is my birth name. I read that article, too, Emily. I called several times before giving up. When you handed me the article at church, I just passed out. That was such a shock."

The discussion went on for hours. Emily told about her life with the Prindivilles, her schooling and nurses training. Ben gave up and went for a long walk. He sat on the porch listening to sounds of their conversation until they decided to sleep. Emily stayed at home and Ben returned Iris to her house. Emily and Ben slept in and then had a long talk, mostly about what the two women didn't talk about the night before. First, who was, or is, Emily's father and other questions to ask Iris.

Ben brought Iris to his home again Saturday morning. The first thing Iris talked about was a network interview offer.

"One of the Big Three networks is proposing an interview on national television. I need to have permission from the FBI I suppose, but it suits me just fine. I want the world to know what he has done, not only to his listeners, but to me. I want to put him out of business forever, if he ever gets out of the penitentiary. They also asked about you, Emily. They want to know if you would consent to be involved. They know about your abduction and the days and nights in the forest."

Ben interrupted. "You two need to slow down. Might be a problem there, little women. If Emily does a reveal show without permission from the law, I would worry. Same goes for you Iris. You will need permission. There really is no proof as to who took her. We know who they were, of course, but there really is no proof yet. I expect Mathew's notes may be revealing, but not until after a trial. I hate to be a spoil-sport, but that is something you both need to think about. I also think there could be consequences from some of Mathew's loyal followers. Something else to think about."

Iris said, "I'll keep that in mind the next time I talk to the FBI. But now! Now I want to say this." She took Emily's hand. "What would you think about a DNA test to seal the covenant that we all already know to be true? Would you, Emily?"

"I have thought about nothing else since seeing you the first time. Yes."

Ben entered the conversation. "You two go on with your visit. I'll research some DNA testing options and let you know."

He interrupted them an hour later. "I think, for your purpose about finding family relationships, that you should order two kits from 23andME. The experts seem to believe they are about as good as it gets. All you have to do is spit in a vial, send it in and wait. Does that sound okay, Iris?"

"Yes, that's fine with me."

"Emily?"

"Yes. Absolutely."

Ben stood and said, "I'm going to order the kits right now. Should be here in a couple of days."

"I want to know who my father, Iris. Wait! What do I call you? Iris does not seem right."

"Iris is good for me, Emily. If you want to call me mother, or Mom, or whatever you decide, that will be okay with me. Now, about your father. Mathew is not your father. Mathew has been impotent his entire life. We were married, but I had the marriage annulled as soon as I found out that he lied. We went on like we were still married to keep the show the way the public saw us.

"As for your real father, he was my next door neighbor, a retired major league baseball player. Not a very good hitter but apparently a great fielder. He lasted ten years as a utility player, whatever that means. A little guy according to average major leaguer sizes. About five feet seven I would guess. He was a nice guy, Emily, very smart and a good companion. We kept close company for about four years. He left for California immediately after I told him I was pregnant. I didn't grieve over him. I was forty-three when you were born. Let's see–forty-three at the time, so now you are twenty-three."

"What was his name, Mom?"

They both laughed. Iris remained Mom from that day on.

"Todd Irving. I have never attempted to locate him electronically. You can if you want to. I don't have anything against him, other than he packed up and left me the moment he felt tied down."

The DNA sample results came in within two weeks. Mother/daughter. No doubt.

As time passed, Iris became an off and on part of

Emily's life. They didn't meet often. Ben remained somewhat aloof. Iris let her hair go grey to separate her by age from Emily. She felt foolish being compared as an older sister. "Older is one thing Forty-three years older is another. I don't want to be your sister."

The Grand Jury wouldn't meet to consider Mathew's case until midsummer. The attending prosecutor did not ask for testimony from Iris. He informed her that the judge or jury conducting the actual trial may have other thoughts. Iris began to worry about becoming involved and vulnerable. She regretted turning States Evidence.

CHAPTER TWELVE

RELOAD

Doctor McDonald arrived a few minutes late. Emily was still busy arranging the room with her friends. She knew the other men: two EMT guys and a nurse from another hospital. The evening promised to be a noisy, genial gathering of friends.

Allen did not disappoint. He was wearing a nice enough sport jacket, a shirt and no tie with Levi's and loafers. He made the introductory rounds by himself, saving Emily for last.

He pulled her in and hugged her from the side. "You look great, Emily." He sniffed her hair and said. "Oh, yeah. I needed this. Looks like a good bunch you have here."

Emily's three friend's eyes followed Allen from the time he entered. She knew they were all watching and whispering about him. Of course they would. A doctor who looked like a movie star.

"We have fun, Allen. This is a very casual affair. We

usually begin at the long table to eat, and then separate to the smaller tables when that seems appropriate, so we can talk without yelling."

A few minutes after pizza and group chatter, Emily stood suddenly and announced, "Allen and I are going for a walk. Be back in a few minutes." She gave Allen her hand and pulled him up. He seemed somewhat surprised but handled the situation smoothly.

Outside on the sidewalk, she said, "I want to spend time alone with you, Allen. Things are going to be too noisy to talk in there. Is this okay?"

"Of course. This suits me. What's on your mind, Emily?" He appeared to be concerned, maybe a bit wary.

"Nothing mysterious. Just general knowledge. I already googled you and I know you went to the University of Virginia. I know you studied primary medicine there, but I don't know anything about your family, or your hometown, or what you do for fun, and I have a long list of intimate little questions that you will probably consider to be private. So, where you are from will be a good place to start."

"All right, but you must follow by answering each question you ask me. Is that fair?"

"Yes. Where did you grow up? Where is home?"

"Woodbridge, Virginia. Just on the southern outskirts of Washington DC. Went all the way through grade and high school there. My father was a civilian contract agent working at the Pentagon. Your turn."

"Not so fast! What about your mother?"

He sighed. "Not much to say there. She divorced Dad when I was six. She left him for a State Department guy and moved to India with him. She's still there as far as I know. If I sometimes seem socially inadequate, you can blame it on my Dad. He never remarried and I have not benefited from a mother's viewpoint. Just so you know."

"No sisters?"

"No. Just me and Dad. I had a great childhood, though. He filled all the blanks. Now it's your turn, but first this one question out of order. "Did you or did you not wave your ring hand deliberately yesterday, Emily?"

"What? Do you think I'm that devious?"

"Hard to answer that politely, but I suppose I do. So?"

"You will never know, Allen." Her eyebrows fluttered playfully.

"All right, but you are still obligated for an answer to the first question."

She sighed and stood. "This really isn't the right time or place for that question, Allen."

"Oh, no you don't!" He pulled her down on the loitering bench in front of a hardware store. "Fair is fair, Emily. Your turn. Come on."

"All right, but let's go back in and excuse ourselves for the night, Allen. What I have to say will take some time and I want to be comfortable."

He stood and pulled her up. "I have all night. Let's do it."

Her friends did not seem surprised, just disappointed. Emily ordered two soft drinks to go and then led Allen to Ben's truck, parked just across the street from the pizza parlor and much closer than his car. "The guy I live with has my car today, Allen. This truck is his, but you will find it quite comfy."

Once settled, Allen, now uneasy and completely confused, said, "The guy you live with? Why don't you start there, Emily?"

She laughed at the sudden change in his demeanor,

from all smiles to clearly ill at ease. "Not that kind of arrangement, Allen. Ben is going on eighty-eight, and he is, for sure, the nicest guy I have ever known. I hope you meet him sometime. Ben Compton. I have lived at his home since coming to Springfield. That is an entirely different story, but associated to what I am going to tell you."

Emily started from the beginning–all the way from being the Box Baby–and brought him up to date. Allen was astonished and stopped her several times to ask questions. She finished the story with her relationship with Ben. "That's it! You are up to date. She looked at her watch. "And we need to go home and sleep. It's Twelve O'clock."

Allen shook his head slowly. "Good grief. That is truly amazing, Emily, and you seem so normal." They both laughed.

"We can go on from there another time, Allen, if you are still interested. I didn't learn much about you this evening. I'm sorry, but I still want to know everything about you."

"Can't happen soon enough, Emily. There is one more thing, though." He moved closer. "I know we are not that familiar with each other yet, but I really want to kiss you. I need to, Emily. I do."

She didn't smile, but faced him and said, "Oh, I suppose, since I am a nurse and you are in need." She smiled and moved closer. "Please do."

She arrived at the kitchen table late the next morning. Ben, as usual, was there reading the newspaper.

He studied her for a few moments before commenting. "You don't look all that unhappy to me, kiddo. A good time last night, I presume?"

"Oh, Ben." She shook her head, smiling and giggling. "This guy I met. He might just end up being a big problem."

"Already? You are a one busy girl, Emily. Hope this one fares better than the others."

"I know. Amazing, isn't it? All those years with no guy friend, and now…. But this guy, Ben. This guy I'm pretty sure is going to end up being a huge problem. But, in his favor, he is definitely providing some great entertainment for me."

"Am I correct in thinking that you are not scheduled for work today?"

"Correct. No schedule. Why? Do you want to do something?"

"Not really. My son called earlier and asked if we, you and me, are going to be around this evening." He watched her face for alarm signs.

She looked puzzled. "Okaaaay?" Trailing the word out. "Is something going on? Do you know why he would ask?"

"Not for sure. Just guessing. I don't think Mark is coming, though, but his mother and father are. I think Marge wants to have a conversation with you about Mark. That's what I'm guessing."

"Well, then I want you to guess out loud, Ben. Is this or is this not going to be about Mark?"

"Not sure, Emily, but, yes, that would be my guess."

"I'm pretty sure I don't want to have a conversation with Mark's parents about Mark, Ben. And I am for absolute sure that I don't want to talk to them about me."

She sat down in a huff, glaring at Ben as if he knew something he wasn't disclosing. "I don't like the way this conversation is going, Ben."

"I understand completely. They are planning to stay here at the house, Emily. If you want to skip it, you need to find a place to stay for a day or two, or I can tell them to find a motel. Your choice. They didn't say anything about how long or for what. Not exactly."

"No, Ben. I'm not running out. Let me move back upstairs to my old room. I can do the stairs with no effort now. Let's change the bedding and take my stuff out. I'll move me up. They can stay in your room tonight, or however long, and then you can move back to your own room after they are gone. I want my old room back. Come on, let's get busy."

After they finished, Emily went to her church in the woods to think. When she returned an hour later, she was no less confused. "What could they possibly want, Ben? Surely you have some idea."

"Okay, here is what I think, but I really have no basis for it other than how you two parted.

I suspect Mark may have said enough to his mother about you and what happened between you and Mark to upset her. Just a guess. She has always coddled him. I suspect she may want to hear your side of the story."

"What? My side? I didn't have a side! Mark just blew out, Ben. You know that. Has she talked to you? Before he arrived the day we were supposed to go to the lake cabin, he had already made permanent moves to return his residency back to St Louis and change back to cardiology. What he did and said to me before that were far more than mere insinuations, Ben. He had already applied to change his residency and come here. And then, without a word to me, he changed everything and left the country! Which one wants to talk about Mark? Is it his mother or father?"

Ben shrugged. "Oh, I know the two of them well enough to say it will definitely be her. She has always overprotected and worried about Mark. Too much pampering for my taste. Stan has not been all that involved in Mark's life over the years. Oh, yeah, you may be sure that Marge will do all the talking."

"I am not happy about this, Ben! Mark has not talked to me about this, either. Neither have his parents. They are using you as a go-between. And now I'm going to face, what? an inquisition? a worried mother? an angry father? What?!"

Ben threw up his hands. "I honestly don't know, Emy."

"Okay, then I'm going to assume that we are all adults and stop worrying about it. Yes! I am going to make friends with Mark's parents. There."

"Good for you, Emy. Maybe we will just have a nice evening. Good for you."

"Emy? I don't mind being called Emy, Ben, but it serves as a great reminder why never to give any of my children names with more than one syllable. Tom, Beth, Sam. Ben. I suppose we need to fix something for the evening meal. So, let's get busy."

She thought, there is no way this evening is going to be pleasant.

After the initial meeting went smoothly, and after a light supper, and after a drink of wine and pleasant conversations, mostly about Emily, Marge asked if she would mind stepping onto the porch.

Okay, here we go.

They sat on the west side in the waning sun and Marge opened the conversation. "Mark and I have always been extremely close, Emily. His father, Stan, has always been…oh, how do I say this? Somewhere else? His work is extremely demanding, as you must know. Anyway, Mark and I are really more like brother and sister. We talk. He tells me everything. We have no secrets."

Crap. She knows everything from Mark's viewpoint. "I presume you are interested in Mark's relationship with me?"

"Yes. I hope you don't mind, but Mark has changed so much since he met you. Well, let's just say he has recently changed so much that I worry. He broods constantly now. He does not come to visit. I am concerned." She covered her face with both hands. "Oh, I don't know how to say what I want to." She cleared her throat, took several deep breaths before facing Emily again." I suppose I need to know what really happened between you two. He is very secretive, but a mother knows. Do you mind, Emily?"

"I do mind, but I also sympathize with your concerns. I can be of little use to you as far as his emotional condition is concerned. He was certainly in control of himself while he was here. But! But I can tell you what happened from my perspective, and it isn't pretty, Marge. You better be sure you want to go on."

"What have you done to my boy?"

Emily nearly fell off the chair.

Oh, this is going to be worse than I thought. "All right, Marge, prepare yourself because this is going to hurt.

Mark is a wonderful person. I had never been in love before, what I consider to be falling in love, until I met Mark. The attraction was instantaneous, Marge, and nothing changed for me until Mark changed it. I honestly believed he was probably the man I would marry. I promise you that he thought the same about me. We clicked. I don't know what Mark has said, if anything, but you should ask Ben. Ben watched us the whole time. We were great together. We were so happy. Ben was there, Marge. He watched us. Ben will tell you what I just said. The attraction between me and Mark was instantaneous and overwhelming. It was real, Marge. I have never been so happy." She paused. "Could you use a drink?"

"Yes, please. A little of that wine we had at supper."

Emily returned with the wine and a glass of water. "Mark made reservations for a weekend on the lake. I have never stayed over with or slept with or been sexually active with a man, Marge. Not ever. But I was thrilled, and I was happy, and I was ready. Has Mark ever mentioned anything about what happened the night we were supposed to go to the lake? About me being kidnapped?"

"He did. How horrible, Emily We watched it on national news. Mark told us about meeting you at the Branson hospital, and how damaged you were."

"Well, did Mark happen to tell you that he had no intention of staying overnight with me that night, even before I was abducted? Did he tell you that he was on the way to tell me the very night that we were going to stay together for the first time that he had cancelled our reservations? or that he had also cancelled his residency in Springfield? or that he had also changed his intent to become a general practitioner and going back to cardiology? Did he tell you any of that, Marge? He sure as hell never bothered to tell me!"

Marge started shaking and spilled her wine. "Is all of that true, Emily? That doesn't sound like Mark."

"I have never lied to anyone, Marge. Ever! But you can ask Ben if you don't believe me. It all happened right in front of him! All of it! Everything I just told you! You surely must know Ben well enough to know he wouldn't fabricate a story like that. Yes, everything I have told you is true. I don't know what Mark told you, but that's exactly the way it went down. He literally blew out, Marge! He blew out and he did it before coming to Springfield that day, and he did it without saying one damned word to me about his decisions. Did you know any of that? Did he tell you that? Is it possible that you knew what was going to happen before I did, Marge?"

"I don't know what to say, Emily."

"You didn't answer the question, Marge."

"He didn't go into that much detail."

"So, did he or didn't he talk to you about those decisions before he came to Springfield?"

"Not to the extent you just conveyed, but yes, we spoke about it a time or two."

Emily sat back, sighed and shook her heads. "I just bet you did. All right. I get it. Now, let me ask you a couple more questions. First: Do you know what Mark does in his time off?" Marge didn't answer. "No? Well I do. He basically does nothing. He has no interests other than his work, Marge. I also asked him, before he left here the last time I saw him, if he might be gay. He said no. Wait before you say anything! I'm not through. He never once touched me intimately, Marge. I think the idea of going to bed with me terrified him. It didn't terrify me, Marge, and I have never been with a man before. I don't think Mark knows who or what he is."

Marge stood, glaring angrily. "That was far more than I asked for, Emily. You need to get help. You are nothing but an angry, spiteful woman who got rejected. I also want to know what you are attempting to do here with Ben. Stan and I think you are taking financial advantage of an old man. We are leaving!" Her nose went up and she whirled away and started for the door.

"No, Marge! No, you-are-not leaving! You don't get to walk out after making those insinuations. No! I do not need Ben's money. I have never taken advantage of Ben. Ask him! I have paid back all the money he ever spent on me. I paid it back against his wishes. Ask him!"

When Emily told Ben about the meeting, he laughed. "Thank you, Emily. Thank you. You just proved that Marge is exactly who I have always thought she was. Well now, let me ask this, did you actually call him gay, Emy? Did you?"

"Not in so many words. I did ask Mark if he thought he *might* be gay. Same thing, I guess."

"No, not the same. I don't think he is gay, actually. I do think he needs some counseling from someone beside his mother, though. Probably wouldn't hurt him to hang out with some guys who have more interest in time-honored relations with women. Well, at least we both have clean beds to sleep in tonight. That's positive."

"How did your evening go with Stan?"

"As usual. He was on the damned phone the entire

time, which, as it turns out, didn't last too long, did it?"

"I'm sorry, Ben. I wish things could have gone better."

"No matter. What the hell."

Emily called Iris to tell her about Allen. She had not been in contact since the relationship with him began. No answer. She left a message on the house phone and tried repeatedly to call on her cell. Iris called the next day.

"I am so sorry, Emily. Things happened so fast. I just decided to go someplace for a vacation. I know I should have told you. We can catch up when I return. Please don't call my cell phone again, Emily. Let's use the house phone. I will leave messages there. Later honey."

When Emily put the phone down. She ran down the stairs and told Ben. "What do you suppose happened? I don't really know her well enough yet to say this is unlike her, but, to me, this is all very odd, don't you think?"

Ben nodded. "Yes. Very odd indeed. When was the last time you spoke to her?"

"About the time I met Allen. What, last Friday? So, I spoke with her Saturday. I told her about Allen. Oh, Ben, I have been so involved, but she didn't seem upset about anything the last time we talked. Something must be wrong."

"Try her again tomorrow. We really don't know her well enough to conclude something has to be wrong. Don't worry too much about her, Emy. She seems pretty self-reliant to me."

"She told me how to find the spare key and wants me to check on her house occasionally."

Ben's frown had deepened throughout the conversation. "Okay. There is this one thing that's bothering me. She isn't supposed to leave the area without approval of the feds. Isn't that right?"

"Yes. Do you suppose she...? Oh, Ben, I hope something hasn't happened to her."

"Why don't you run over there and see about the house. That should keep you from worrying."

"All right, but you have to come with me. Let's go."

They found a real estate FOR SALE sign planted in the front yard.

"Ah, the plot thickens. Did she say anything about that, Emy?"

"Not a word. She just asked me to check the house occasionally. This gets stranger by the minute."

They found the house and property in good order. Before leaving, Ben pointed to the answering machine on Iris's house phone. "It's flashing. I checked. There are three messages."

"Do I dare listen?"

"I think so. She asked you to look after the place, didn't she? Might be something she needs to know, particularly now that there is a real estate sign in the yard."

"Does that give me the liberty to listen to her calls?"

"In your shoes, I would, Emily. Better either record it or take notes if you do listen, though."

"Why? Don't you think I can remember?"

"It's not that, Emy. What I am beginning to worry about is what the feds told her about leaving the area. You have to wonder if she told them anything. I think you have to play it back, Emy, because you could become an unwitting witness–an accessory after the fact.

Yeah, I think you have to play it back. Go ahead."

Emily recorded the messages on a tablet. The first message was her call to tell Iris about Allen. The second message came from an FBI agent just two day ago, asking her to contact them. The third call came from a man named Al.

"Iris, this is Al. You don't answer my damned calls, so I'm leaving this on your house recorder. You and Mathew owe us, Iris. You have stiffed me and Chuck, like forever. You can't use Mathew as an excuse any more. We know he was never really in charge of the money. Me and Chuck want the damned money he promised, Iris. The money *you* were supposed to write checks for, Iris, not Mathew. You are the treasurer. We want to be paid for taking your daughter to the woods. We were really hanging out there, Iris. We took a big chance and Mathew promised five-hundred dollars. And you never paid us for the night he ordered us to take your baby to the hospital either, Iris. He promised a thousand dollars each for that, and you, the person who writes all the checks, never paid. We felt sorry for you and didn't demand the money. That was then, Iris, but this is now. Things are a bunch different now. So here's the deal, and we are not playing around: either you pay up or this information is going to find a way to the feds. Call me, and I mean quick. We'll make arrangements to get the money. You have three days, Iris, Three! We are not fooling around!"

Emily just stared at Ben. She couldn't put all the information together fast enough. "She knew, Ben? Is it possible that she knew all along? Is it possible that she never wanted me? And she is just using Mathew? What am I supposed to think now?"

"I'm sorry, Emy. I really am."

"And I am sure I have heard that voice, Ben. Al's voice. He was one of the men who abducted me. I will never forget his voice. I don't know what to do now."

"Well, Emily, I don't suppose there is any choice about one thing. You are now, without a doubt, an accessory unless you bring this to the feds attention. They will find out if you don't tell, as they always do, right? I would bet anything they have this phone tapped. I think they should find out about the messages from you, even though they probably already know." He waited while Emily wept. "I hate to press, but you really have no choice, Emy. You should probably call them right now. I would."

The FBI didn't wait. The leading agent and a technician arrived within the hour to record the message and question Emily. "Your mother is now wanted, Miss Prindiville. She, apparently, has departed the area without permission. This recording may now be criminal evidence. Also, please let us know if there are more messages, whether recorded here or to you personally. Do not answer a call from her unless we are informed and are able to record the call. Do you understand the seriousness of what I just said? Do not, in any way, involve yourself with Miss Brooks–Iris–without informing us first. Do not answer any call from her until we are with you on the line. Also, we will order the real estate company to pull their sign immediately and stop advertising. Her property is now part of a federal investigation."

Ben and Emily closed the house and went home.

Emily had half a glass of wine mixed with more disappointment and tears.

Ben said, "So, what now, Emy?"

"Now? I will think about that tomorrow, Scarlett. Not much I can do is there?"

"You need some diversion, Emy."

"Thank, you, Ben. You know me too well. I do love you and you are a great diversion, but I'm going to call and see if Allen is available."

"That's who I meant."

She called and asked if he would be busy Sunday afternoon.

"Not if there is a chance I can see you. What's on your mind?"

"A picnic. I know a great place and I have all the fixings. And I desperately need to talk."

Emily gave him the gate numbers. After he arrived she introduced him to Ben before walking to her happy place in the woods. She had already carried a blanket and cooler of food and drink. He held her hand all the way.

"You told me about Ben and this place, but I didn't imagine it being this special. Your Ben seems more like a father figure than your landlord. Seems like a nice guy."

"Oh, Ben is far better than just a nice guy, Allen. Anyway, we spent a lot of time talking about me last the last time, and now it's your turn. But there is this one little thing first. I need some human comfort. I desperately need to be close to somebody warm."

"Perfect! Me too. I have gone about as long as I can

stand being close and not touching you. We need to reach an understanding, about kissing, though, Emily. If you want to kiss around, there should be no more need to ask. Just do it. Is that okay with you?"

"Yes. Yes by all means. Any time. Any place. Any reason. Yes." She pushed him down on the blanked and smothered him with kisses.

Emily told him about Iris. "I just thought she is a secret that I didn't need to keep from you, Allen. I am going to try not to be sad. Actually, I'm not sad, oddly enough. I did what I had to do and now we wait. But, my dear fellow, while we wait, I am not going to be unhappy. I cannot be unhappy around you."

They did get back to some of the questions and answers that she owed him from the night before, but lost interest while slowly erasing a few remaining reservations that Emily Prindiville once had about caressing. She pulled away, breathless. "Oh, Allen. Whew! Let's eat before we lose track of what we came here for. Mercy!" She fanned her face and spread the food and drink. "Now, while we are somewhat settled, I need more answers, please. First, are you a jock?"

"Not really Nothing organized. I jog and lift four or five times a week if I have time. I try to stay trim. Mostly endurance exercises. And you?"

"Ben has me working out. I jog a couple of miles. He has a nice gym in the basement and wants me to do endurance exercises. No bulking up. Yours was a good answer. I didn't want a jock. Are you a Catholic?"

"By birth, yes. By actions? Not so you can tell it. You?"

"No religion. Are you involved with someone, Allen?"

"I would have told you that, Emily. No. I am free.

You?"

"I am also free. "

"Why are you in Springfield, Allen?"

"I wanted to get away from big cities. I wanted to get away from the bustle. I wanted to be someplace more open. Not wide open, but with beauty and lakes and a little slower life. I may want to stay here and open my own clinic. A family practice clinic. You?"

"I came here to finish nurses training and find my mother. I have done both. I am happy being an RN, but I am no longer all that happy about my mother. We can talk about that some other time. Let's just say, for now, that I really don't know enough about her, and, by the same token, a little more than I wanted to know."

"She sounds mysterious."

"You have no idea. Now, back to the business at hand. I want to stay here in Springfield permanently, Allen. I want to live here with Ben as long as I can, or as long he needs and wants me. But more important, I want to know all about you. Oh, one more thing. I may want to train as a PA and specialize in something that will allow a stable home life. Now, your turn."

"Pretty much the same."

"Have you had serious relationships?"

"I suppose I got close a couple of times. Split up by college choices and the demands med school made on my time. Nice girls. Good enough girls. And you?"

"Not really. I have to tell you about Mark, though."

When she finished, Allen, without prompting, said, "He sounds gay to me."

"And you are not?"

He laughed. "No chance. Want me to prove it?"

"Yes, I think I do, just not here and now. Help me

pack and let's spend some time with Ben."

They spent the rest of the evening with Ben before Allen rushed to a hospital to assist with the emergency medical demands of a multiple car wreck.

Ben looked at her with one eye closed. "So, Allen?"

"Oh, you catch on quick, Ben. Yes, Allen. What do you think of him?"

"I suppose I could stand having him around. He told me he's a sax player, by the way. I expect we need to figure out a way to include him in our jam sessions, don't you think?"

She spent time with Allen twice in the evenings during the following week–in his car eating take-out food and more exploratory conversations. While walking in a park and sitting in his car during the last evening, they advanced through the dance of ages, step by gentle unhurried step, until blouses and shirts became unnecessary obstructions to be unbuttoned and moved aside.

"I don't want to make love to you in a car, Emily, but I can and will. I have the emergency room watch this weekend. All day in the shop Saturday and on stand-by that night. I have reserved an on-call bedroom for the night. Meet me there?"

"Stay with you?"

He laughed. "Of course. I want that. Yes, I want to

sleep with you, Emily. I'm pretty sure I will always want to sleep with you."

She didn't need to think. "I want to, Allen, but…well, isn't this awfully fast?"

"No! No! We have completed the respectable preliminaries, don't you think? I have wanted you from the first time I saw you, Emily, and now I am desperate. So, no, this is not too fast. We have spent enough time together to know all we need to know. I'm going to explode if playing around lasts much longer. I want you, Emily. I'll get a key for you. I have the stand-by room from eight until eight. Show up whenever you like. I'll be there when I can get off."

She gazed at him for the longest time before saying, "All right. I'll be there."

Allen didn't get to the room until midnight. He kissed her and took a shower. Emily's heartbeat intensified by the minute. He peeked through the bathroom door and said, "Clothes or no clothes?"

"A towel will do, Allen."

His phone rang.

He stood in the bathroom door with a towel wrapped around his waist. "I'm not going to answer that. No way."

Emily pulled the cover up. She flopped back and sighed. "You have to answer it Allen. You're on emergency call. You have to see who it is."

He let the phone go to message before he crossed the room and picked it up. Emily could tell by watching his face that their evening was over.

"I'll be there in five." He clicked the phone off, looked at Emily and groaned. "God hates me! Sorry, Emily. This didn't end up the way I hoped. The ER is buried and I have to go. Looks like an all-nighter. Lots of casualties. Shootout at a party. I'm sorry."

He dressed and departed within a minute. Emily didn't wait. She straightened the room and went home.

Ben looked up from the Sunday paper as she came down the stairs. She had slipped in after midnight without waking him. Emily stopped behind, put her arms around his chest and kissed his neck.

"I take it you had a nice time?" She had told him she was staying overnight with Allen.

"Nope. Never got to spend time with Allen. He had to spend the night with casualties. Those casualties, she pointed at the newspaper headlines. Our time together was one of the casualties. Oh, well."

"You look tired, Emily. Why don't you take a nap?"

She laughed. "I'm okay, but I need to think. I'm going to my church, Ben. Come down if you like."

The FBI called the next day and asked her to stop by their office when convenient. She stopped on the way home.

"We want to show you a couple of photographs, Miss Prindiville. Maybe you could identify the men."

She didn't recognize the first guy, but she certainly did

recognize Al. She had seen him briefly that night in the woods when they ripped the blindfold tape off. "This guy! I'm pretty sure...no, I know for sure that I saw him. I know it. I will never forget him. He was one of the men who grabbed me. Who is he?"

"That, Miss Prindiville, is a longtime affiliate of Mathew Driscoll. He is, or was, a handyman and apparently a lifetime friend of the Reverend. He also has a long police record. His name is Al Luizo."

"Yes! I heard the other guy call him Al that night, more than once. What happens now?"

"We have tracked Mister Luizo and are ordering one of our affiliates to pick him up. We believe the other man involved with your abduction is either with him at the present, or else Mister Luizo knows where he is."

"Do you know anything yet about my mother? Iris? Miss Brooks?"

"That is not information I am able to share."

"Will you let me know if you find her?"

"Again, too soon to say. If she contacts you...well, you know the drill, right? Call me."

The lead agent called two days later and asked Emily for a time she could appear at city police headquarters.

Upon arrival, they escorted her to a viewing room where she watched through a one-way window as four solemn men were led in single file, halted and ordered to face the window.

She didn't wait. "The first guy is Al. I am sure of it. I saw him that night. That's Al!"

"You are correct. That is Al Luizo, and he worked for

the Driscolls. He has also admitted being promised pay by the Driscolls to abduct you. Do you recognize anyone else?"

She studied the other three men for several moments before replying. "No. But I'm pretty sure the Number Three man is much too small. My impression of the man who physically handled me is of a much larger man than Number Three."

"Again, you are correct." He spoke on a microphone ordering Al and the third man out. He then ordered the two remaining men to give their ages and dates of birth.

"Emily shook her head. "Not sure. The Number Four guy has a deep enough voice and he seems large enough, but I am not certain. Sorry."

"Once again, you are correct. The Number Four man is Chuck Evens. He also worked many years for the Driscolls. He has admitted being part of your abduction and wants to turn states evidence. The other guy works in the garage for us. Thank you, Miss Prindiville. You were obviously a keen observer under the circumstances. Thank you."

Chapter Thirteen

A CHANGE OF FORTUNE

Emily worried about Ben. He had been coughing more lately and had also stopped walking with her. He told her she was too fast and he was unable to catch his breath. She asked him several times to get a physical checkup. He refused.

Emily went ahead and scheduled him and didn't plan to tell him until the day before the physical. She wasn't able to tell the doctor's nurse the last time Ben had a physical. "I don't know and he won't discuss it with me. Let's just go ahead and schedule him. I guess we'll see."

Ben looked up from breakfast one morning and said, "How is it going between you and Allen?"

Emily frowned. "Why would you ask that now, Ben?"

"No good enough reason, I suppose. But there is

something I want you to know. He pulled out his phone and googled R. Frederick Prindiville. "Read that, Emy."

She took her time, looking for something that disturbed Ben. "Okay, Ben. What am I supposed to be looking for? I already know all of this."

"No, Emy, you know *more* than that. What I wanted you to see is what Allen could have known. Let me reiterate: He *could have* known. He could have known all of that even before you met him. Note the date."

She looked. "So?"

"So, that date is well before you met Allen, and while the information he could have read is not up-to-date, he could have known you were the only family R. Frederick Prindiville had remaining, and he could have known how much R. Frederick is worth. If he is a normal person, and if your relationship is going down according to most current social conventions, he probably googled you as soon as he took interest in you. I expect he knew you were possibly going to be R. Frederick's heir before he met you. It says you were R. Fred's only remaining family member. Allen has probably known all along that you were likely going to come into some big bucks. I'm not trying to tell you that he is in the relationship for money, but I am telling you to be aware of what he probably knew. What I am saying is that I find it odd that he hasn't talked to you about what I just showed you. In his shoes, I would have. That's all, Emy. It's your ball game. I'm out."

"Why are you telling me this, Ben?"

He sat back, studied her face for a few moments, and then said, "It's the basis of my life philosophy, Emy. That's why."

"Why haven't we talked about that? Your life

philosophy?"

"Never the right time? Just hasn't come up? I don't really know."

"And now is the right time?"

"I think so. Here it is: My philosophy, if I have one, is not ever having to say-after the fact-that I could have or should have done something that I didn't do. The first morning I saw you, Emy, walking down that bitter cold street away from the heated center for the homeless, I drove on by and despised myself for it. When I turned around and came back, I didn't see you. I came back the next morning and you know the rest of the story. I have always tried to be true to that philosophy. I don't want to feel guilty for not doing something for someone that I should have done. All right, that said, I am a little uneasy about Allen. I don't know why, Emy. I would bet anything that you recognize that I am not completely at ease with him. You don't need to answer that. That's really all I have to say and I'm sorry if it upsets you. If you and Allen go on, Emy, I will be a good friend to him. Now let's get to work."

"What do I do now, Ben? Do I ask him if he googled me? Do I ask if he thought I am going to be filthy rich? How do I do this?"

"There is probably no right way to ask, Emy, but, how the hell hard can it be? Just ask him. Shouldn't come as a big shock to him or anyone, really. I expect googling someone you don't know that well is the usual thing. I probably would have looked you up in his shoes. Wouldn't you? Did you?"

"Point taken, Ben. Yes, I did."

She asked Allen.

He became evasive.

She persisted.

He became angry. "Why is it so important? I don't understand why, all of a sudden, that whether I googled you is important. Of course I did. I wanted to know about you. Now, is that what you wanted to know?"

"Yes, and thank you. Now I don't feel guilty about googling you."

Ben called later that morning and told her that she had an undelivered registered letter at the main post office. "He said you need to pick it up in person, Emily. Must be important."

She managed to get time off and hurried. The letter came from her father. It read:

Suffered serious heart attack two weeks ago. Presently in hospital ICU. The physicians involved tell me there is little chance I will survive. I have maybe a week. If I do not see you before I die, you need to know the combination to my bedroom wall safe. (Two revolutions to the right beginning with zero, stop on 11. Two revolutions left past 11 to 10. One revolution right past ten to 25. Open.) You will find a folder there informing you of my decision about cremation. I do not want burial or funeral services. Do as you wish with the ashes. You will also find a recent accounting of my assets, of

which I have made you the sole heir. You will also find a letter advising you how to keep or liquidate RFP ENTERPRISES, again as you see fit. If you decide to visit, there is a company jet at your disposal. Just Google RFP ENTERPRISES AIR TAXI. Please come, Emily. We should talk.

How did he find me? Well, of course–Prindiville. How many Prindivilles are there? And he knows I found the birth certificate and discovered where I was born. Two plus two. Easy.

Emily called Ben on the way back to the hospital. "Oh, Ben! You have to listen to this." She pulled over and read the letter.

"Whoa! What a shock. What are you thinking, Emily?"

"I want to go as soon as possible, Ben. I'm going to contact the company and request the jet for early tomorrow morning."

"And you now have a private jet?"

"Yes. I suppose it does belong to me now. Good grief! Can you imagine? I want you to come with me, Ben. I need you." He would come. She used the need word. They had agreed that 'need' was all either one ever needed to say. The other would surrender and be happy with it.

She left a message at the emergency room desk asking Allen to call as soon as possible.

His first words after she explained what happened and after she read the letter were, "You have got to be kidding me! Your whole life is a movie fantasy from beginning to end. Are we ever going to get together?"

"I wish. Knowing and being with you has become an

exciting time of my life, Allen. I don't want anything to interfere with what is happening to us right now. Oh, this is such bad timing. I don't know what to expect. I asked Ben to come with me."

"Good thinking. Ben will be a reliable wingman. Well, I suppose that means we are officially on hold. I hate this. I have fallen so hard for you. I wish you luck. I'll be waiting. I don't know how any woman could be more interesting than you are to me. And now this."

"I don't plan to spend much time there, Allen. I don't know what is going to happen. I'll keep you informed."

"I can't imagine your emotional state right now, Emily, but let me add a little more to your dilemma. I hope you are as ready for this as I am. Here it goes, and I am as sure as I can be of what I am going to say. I love you, Emily. I have never been so sure of anything. I know it may be too soon to tell you that, and I realize the timing is bad, but there you have it."

"Oh, Allen. That makes me so happy. I'm going to cry now. I'll be in touch."

Allen put his phone up, a troubled expression on his face. *She didn't say I love you, too, Allen. It did make her happy, though, and she's going to cry. Is that good enough?*

R. Frederick died while Emily was airborne the following day. She went directly from the airport to EAGLE'S ROOST, opened the safe and read through R. Frederick's personal letter first. He apologized for his careless and inadequate attentions toward her and begged forgiveness for all his shortcomings, particularly the diary deceitfulness. She handed Ben each page as she read. At one point she gasped, and said, "Oh my God, Ben! This simply cannot be true! Oh my God." She passed him the company appraisal page.

Ben read and collapsed back into the chair. "Good heavens. Did you have any idea, Emily?"

"No! Not really. Oh, I knew he was wealthy and powerful, but he never talked to me about business. What am I going to do, Ben? This is crazy. I have no idea what to do. This is ridiculous."

"Well, I think we should take our time and read the entire packet first, and then probably see if we can find some decent wine, don't you? You are now the sole heir to a company worth Seven-Hundred and Fifty Million dollars. That is a lifetime of crazy." He started laughing."Damndest thing I ever heard. What the hell?"

"I feel sick, Ben. This whole thing is making me physically ill. I am about to panic. I have no idea what to do."

"Well, when faced with something of this magnitude, right now would be a good time not to do anything, Emily. There are times when doing nothing is the right answer. Let's take a break and come back to this later."

The wine was tolerable and they ended up laughing at the ridiculousness of what little they were aware of. Ben tapped the appraisal sheet with his fingertips and said, "That is one hell of a lot of zeros. Where to start, huh?"

"Unbelievable, Ben. Do think this could be a prank? Is he getting even for the way I blew out?"

The house phone interrupted their conversation. She answered nervously.

"This is Robert Devens, Miss Prindiville. I am the CEO–Corporate Executive Officer– of Prindiville

Enterprises. Please accept my apologies for the call and my sincere condolences for the death of your father. Is there anything I, or we, can do for you?"

Emily turned the phone on speaker. "My assistant is listening in, Mister Devens. I don't need anything at the moment. I am in a state of shock. There is so much to think about. Perhaps we could meet sometime tomorrow."

"Yes. I will set a board meeting at a time of your choice. I would advise as soon as possible. Most board members are already present."

"A board meeting?"

"Yes, Miss Prindiville. Under the circumstances, you being the sole heir, I believe meeting sooner is better, if for no other reason than to become acquainted. Say tomorrow morning at Ten?"

She looked at Ben. He patted his forehead and pointed to her. "Where should I be at Ten, Mister Devens?"

"Our headquarters are no more than fifteen minutes away. I will have a limousine for you at Nine-Thirty. Will that be satisfactory?"

Ben shrugged. She agreed and hung up.

"This is overwhelming, Ben."

"It certainly is to me. What the hell, Emy? " He laughed. "Guess we are going to find out."

They spent the evening reading the packet. Ben finally stood, stretched, and said, "I think it's all probably valid, Emily. You don't have to make any decision about anything right now. Just go and listen. Ask whatever you want to know and then get up, walk out and take all the time you need to think. I believe, depending on what you find out, that it would be a good time to get some legal advice from a major law firm that does this kind of business." He threw up his hands and laughed. "You poor baby."

"I don't want this, Ben. I don't want to change my life in any way. I love my life just the way it is."

"As your life *was*. *Was* is now the operative term, Emily. As I said, What the hell! You can literally do anything you want to."

"I don't want to lose what I have, Ben. Not one single thing."

She called Allen at midnight. "Sorry to wake you, Allen, but I think I finally have enough information to sound intelligent."

"I just got to the room. I'm wide awake. So, tell me. What the devil is going on?"

"Oh, it's no big deal. I just inherited, as sole owner, the entirety of J. Frederick Prindeville Enterprises."

"You told me our first night together a little about your father's business. How big a deal is it? Do you know yet?"

"Oh, it's not a big deal, Allen. It is a colossal deal. It is unbelievable." She told him the value.

"Good grief! And you the sole owner?"

"Yes. I am to meet with my board this morning. *My* board, Allen! I don't have any idea what to do or say. Ben advised me to listen, ask, then get up, walk out and get some good legal advice, just not from my own board. *My* board, Allen. *Mine*! Can you imagine?"

"I can't. Do you have any idea what you are going to do?"

"Yes. As it stands right now, I don't want to change

my life for any reason, Allen. I don't want to be in business, particularly the coal mining business. I have never entertained a single thought about being in business. I think, unless there is a reason that I am not aware of, that I will probably hire a law firm that specializes in sales and liquidation. What do you think?"

"I think Ben is right, Emily. Go and listen. Get up and walk out, and then do whatever the hell you want to. Seven-Hundred and Fifty million dollars? Holy...! I cannot imagine being in that league. Will you still talk to me?"

"Maybe. I don't want too much talking to interfere with loving, though. Good night, Allen."

Allen flopped on the bed and shouted, "She said it! Sort of."

Allen called his father to let him know about Emily. "I met someone, Dad. Someone very special."

"A woman, I hope."

"One-hundred percent all woman. Emily. She is a nurse here at the hospital. I fell in love with her about two weeks before I actually met her. I'm not distorting anything, Dad. I was in love with her even before we met. I fell in love just watching her."

"I suppose that means she's easy to look at?"

"Oh, yes. She is beautiful, but that is not her main attraction. She is happy. Her happiness is captivating. Everyone loves her. She changes everybody's mood just by showing up. And, no, I am not twisting reality. You have to meet her. I have known a few women, in my life, Dad, and I liked some of them well enough, but not like the way I am with Emily."

"Describe her to me."

"She is tiny, and I mean very tiny. Less than five feet. Probably doesn't weigh one-hundred pounds. All parts organized perfectly. Dark black hair. Somewhat oriental eyes, curving up a little on the outside. She is very easy to look at."

"How far along are you two? You haven't been in Springfield that that long, Allen."

"I cannot imagine being more in love."

"How about her?"

"Oh, she went all-in by the end of our second date."

"Meaning?"

"She loves me. She said so. Well, sort of."

"And you?"

"I beat her to it. We put our cards on the table without holding anything back. I cannot imagine ever being happier with anyone. I cannot imagine bothering to look for anyone else. It has been that way with me from the beginning, even before I met her. I knew, without a doubt, that I wanted her in my life."

"Damn, Allen! This sounds serious. Have you talked about your future?"

"Not really. No plans, other than what we think privately. We are still catching up on the past. Her past would make a novel. Seriously, you won't believe her history, or, as it happens, what is going on in her life right now. Unbelievable."

"I need a little more than generalities, Allen."

"Okay. In the beginning, Emily was dumped at the entrance to the emergency room here at a Springfield hospital. Someone placed a cardboard box with her in it at the entrance and ran off. She still had an umbilical cord attached and was wet from birth. No one claimed her. She eventually went up for adoption, but that is an entirely different story that can wait. That is the way her story began and nothing much has changed since. She is Twenty-three. You want to know more now?"

"No. That's enough for now. I want to meet her. I'm excited for you, Allen, even though this seems to be way off your beaten path. I'll let you know when."

"I think you should hear this one more thing, Dad. She is the sole heir to RFP Enterprises. She is worth seven-hundred-and-fifty-million bucks. Google it. Coal mining. See ya."

A stretch Limousine with RFP ENTERPRISES on the doors delivered them to a very modern, almost all-glass, six-story building in downtown Cheyenne, also with RFP ENTERPRISES emblazoned on all sides.

Ben leaned close and whispered, "I think this might be the right place. You think?"

She laughed and while shielding her mouth, whispered, "R. Frederick certainly did love himself. But I already knew that."

A gilded elevator transported them to the top floor where Robert Devens met and led them to a plush conference room. He introduced the eight board members. Three, she learned later, had minimal experience in business, and four of them didn't live in the state of Wyoming. Everyone waited for her to sit before taking their seats.

Devens opened by saying, "I suppose, Miss Prindiville, that we should probably begin by asking what questions you have."

Emily noted that his smile did not appear to be sincere. "Thank you, Mister Devens. I do have a short list. First, I have not received an official death certificate. I need several copies. Was that simply an oversight?" She wasn't smiling. Before Devens could answer, she said, "Please take care of that for me. I would also like to know when, exactly, you knew that I had been designated sole heir and why you, as CEO, did not immediately contact me?" She returned his antiseptic smile and they were off to a poor start.

Devens rummaged for answers before finally saying, "I'm sorry, Miss Prindiville, but I am not at this instant familiar with those numbers. I will have them to you immediately." He left the room and returned within minutes. "The information should be in your hands before we finish here, Miss Prindiville."

"Also, Mister Devens, I would like to have a copy of every document associated with me becoming heir, and all information concerning my father's illness and death."

Devens glanced from one board member to another quickly before saying, "Again, Miss Prindiville, I'm sorry, but I do not have that information immediately available, but I will see that it is delivered straightaway. Is there anything else?"

"Yes. I would like to hear now from the board member in charge of accounting." She looked down at her notes. "Mister Chadwick, I believe, is the CFI." She looked toward Chadwick and asked for the amount outstanding for any loans and other outstanding monies required for normal company operations.

Devens interceded and gave another evasive answer indicating that the information was not immediately available.

Emily turned and looked at Ben, sitting along the wall behind her. He nodded. She addressed the board by introducing Ben as, "Ben Compton is my personal advisor and friend. He is a retired Marine Lieutenant Colonel and knows about as much as I do about business matters concerning an organization of this scale, which is not much. That said, we both would prefer being addressed by our first names. I do not believe we are off to a good start here today, are we?" She turned to Devens. "Have you arranged for a lunch, Robert?"

"Um, no, Miss-ah, sorry-Emily. I did not think we would be—"

"It's not important. Ben and I will find a place nearby." She had listened; she had asked; now she stood. After many confused glances, the board members also stood. She said, "Shall we meet again, say about One-Thirty, Robert? This very afternoon? I would like to begin with answers to the questions I have already asked, and I would then like each board member, without interruption, to provide the status of their particular responsibility. Perhaps, after that, I might know enough to ask the appropriate questions. I would also like documented evidence from each board member of their reports to me this afternoon. I will need that information to make decisions." She turned to Ben. "Shall we?" She left the room. *Listen. Ask. Leave. Think.*

Once in the hall alone, Ben leaned close and whispered, "Say nothing Emily until we are out of here and alone. He held a finger to his lips in the elevator, pointing at the lighted ceiling, shaking his head. Once on the sidewalk, he said, "You were magnificent, Emy! I think you are off to a great start. I would love to be a fly on the wall in that conference room right now."

"Really?" I thought the whole thing was odd. Anyway, I'm glad we had time last night to think about what to say."

"Yes, it was odd, but I bet you will notice one hell of a difference when we convene again. I'm not buying that Deven guy's act, Emily. He is unprepared and just winging it. Probably thought you would be a roll-over. He sure wasn't thinking about you as being his new boss."

Emily's first words at the afternoon session were about a funeral service. "Has anything been arranged, Mister Devens?"

"Ahhh, Um? No, Miss Prindiville, we-I thought you–'

"Good. There will be no service. My father never attended church and frowned on funerals. I will take possession of his ashes. He made arrangements with the mortuary for that. I would also like it if you released an appropriate announcement from me to the entire company this afternoon. The announcement should contain information about my status as owner and some basic chronological information about my father's history with the Enterprise."

At the end of the afternoon session, Emily stood and thanked the board. She announced, to their obvious alarm, that she was undecided about retaining ownership but would advise them as soon as possible.

Devens seemed to panic. "Miss…excuse me, Emily, is there some possibility that you might actually be considering sale or liquidation of the RFP Enterprises? Please tell me that is not true."

"I must be honest with you, Robert. At this moment I do not want my life to change in any way. I am as happy as I have ever been and becoming owner of a company producing coal is possibly the last thing on Earth that would ever appeal to me. So, yes, you may assume that I will probably consider selling."

"I'm not sure what that means."

"Neither am I, Robert. Two days ago I had no knowledge that I was any part of Prindiville Enterprises, and now I am the owner. So you see, Robert, and all of you present, I have a decision to make. I appreciate your concerns and I recognize that what I decide may well upset the course of your lives. I shall try to be practical and prompt. In the meantime, I will announce some form of preliminary decision tomorrow. We should probably meet here again...say at One PM? And, Robert, if you will, I should like to be back in Springfield by nightfall tomorrow as I am on duty the next morning. Please have the air crew informed and prepared."

"Excuse me, Emily, but it seems to me that your decision here may be more critical than–"

"I'm sure it is to you, Robert, but it is not to me. I have a life. I am a nurse and my hospital is overwhelmed by COVID patients. You might consider, if you are interested, putting together an offer to buy me out. I will be happy to give you time to decide and give you the first offer if that is what I decide to do."

Emily and Ben talked well into the night, until he was confident that her decisions would not be hurried and would not be to her disadvantage. He planned to investigate law firms and brokering organizations specializing in selling and closing businesses. She would advise the board of that decision at the coming meeting. She was not going to be hurried. Emily also planned to demand that all company records be locked and preserved the moment the meeting closed.

She called Allen. After the call she advised Ben that she wouldn't be home until the day after returning to Springfield.

"You and Allen, I presume?"

"Oh, you are one sharp Marine, Ben. Yes, Allen."

"Good. I'm happy for you, Emily."

They reviewed and organized notes for the board meeting and both slept well.

The board meeting was a somber affair. The specter of doom lay heavily over a group of privileged people accustomed to doing very little to earn generous compensation just for showing up a few times a year.

After the flight home the next day, Emily took Ben home from the airport, packed a fresh overnight bag and found Allen already in the on-call room at the hospital.

He was not alone.

Emily opened the door and came face-to-face with a very pretty blonde in a slinky party dress. She was crying, pointing to Allen lying on the bed. "I don't know what's wrong with him! I just got here and this is the way I found him. I can't get him to…. I don't know what to do. He's unconscious. Can you help me?"

Emily overcame the shock of the situation and checked Allen's vitals. She called the emergency room and quickly explained the scene. "His vitals are weak and his heart is very irregular. I think the symptoms indicate an overdose. He appears to be in anaphylactic shock. This is an emergency! Bring something for an overdose and hurry!"

After asking the woman what happened, Emily asked for her name and phone number. The girl refused. Emily told her the police might want to hear her story.

"Look, I just got here a minute before you did. I have no idea what is going on. I want to leave. I am leaving." She didn't bother closing the door.

Colin Hilton was first EMT on the scene. He had sprinted all the way through the hospital and didn't wait for Emily to talk. After listening to Allen's heart, and after taking his vital signs, he said, "Drugs. Looks to me like he got some bad drugs. I expect they were probably laced with fentanyl. We need to get his heart and breathing stabilized." He injected Naloxone and began mouth-to-mouth resuscitation. Before the ambulance team appeared, Colin took a breather and told Emily to leave. "I don't need you, Emily. Get out of here! Go down the stairs. The troops will be using the elevator. I'll let you know how this turns out. I mean it. Go! You don't need all the gossip this will create. Go!"

Colin called her an hour later. "I think he's going to be all right. It was, in fact a drug overdose. We can talk about his drug problem sometime. Most of the EMT troops have suspected he is a user."

She told Ben what happened at breakfast.

"You sure have a problem with your men, Emily. I'm sorry. I know you liked him. I hope you get through this without deciding to give up on us. All men are different."

Emily had known all along that Ben was not all that taken by Allen, and Allen had never opened up to Ben. His relationship with Ben resembled that of a wary suitor and vigilant father. Emily had agonized over Ben's reserve, although he never said anything to discourage her.

The RFP board Chief Operating Officer, Frank something-or-other, called three days later and informed her that three board members were attempting to put together the necessary money to make an offer. What would be her bottom line?

Emily had spoken with two major law firms that dealt with corporate sales and formed a good idea of what she could realize by selling the company on the open market.

"Seventy-five percent of the appraised value, Frank. If you cannot offer seventy-five percent, then I intend to hire a firm and place Prindiville Enterprises on the open market."

"There is no way we can meet that figure, Emily."

"I will extend the opening to you exclusively for another week from today, Frank. Please advise as soon as possible."

One week later, amid a meeting with countless opposing lawyers, and after taking into account taxes, Emily became five-hundred million, six-hundred and sixty-two thousand dollars wealthier.

"Now what?" she asked Ben. "I have no idea what to do."

He laughed. "Oh, how I pity you. Too much money is such a problem. Just go back to base thinking in situations like this. Take your time. But for your sake, Emily, keep it secret, and I mean secret from everyone. If this information gets out you will be swamped by people and organizations that you never heard of. Half the population of America will be at your gate asking for money. You will need armed guards. Say nothing."

Emily tapped herself on the forehead with the heel of her hand. "Damn! I told Allen the moment I found out. Just you and Allen."

"I wouldn't worry too much about Allen, but a reminder to him would probably be prudent, if you can find him. Do you know what happened to Allen?"

"Not really. I think he may be back in DC with his father. I know he is no longer working at the hospital. Suspended, I think. I also know the state board is investigating and his license may be denied. Too bad. He seemed like such a nice guy. I really liked him, Ben. I thought we could eventually have something serious. Running into the other woman in his room ended that dream. Well, that and the drug problem. Who knew?"

"Oh, I expect you were probably right about Allen and Mark all along. They are both probably nice guys, but Allen sure has one hell of a problem. Any plans concerning him, Emy?"

"No. I think I know enough about him now to let him go his own way, though. I am very disappointed in me, Ben. I cannot seem to get it right the first time with men. How hard is it, Ben?"

"Not that hard. Just keep moving and looking. Take your time. The right guy will come along. You will learn from what has happened and you will recover and you will be satisfied that you caught it before too late." He rubbed his face viciously before saying, "You might consider not going all-in right away the next time you meet an attractive guy, though. You may be a little too quick to commit. I would sure run off with you in an instant if you were my age. I sure would."

CHAPTER FOURTEEN

ADJUSTMENTS

Two weeks after returning from Wyoming, and after selecting a prestigious law firm from St. Louis, and after discovering what her tax responsibilities would be, and after conferring for hours and days with Ben, Emily had made her final decision about being the owner of a multi-hundred million dollar mining company.

She would not.

She told Ben, "I cannot possibly be more content with my working life than I am right now. I don't want to change anything in my life. I don't want a yacht, or fancy cars, or Mediterranean vacations. I do not want celebrity. I want to stay right here in Springfield doing what I am doing until I am thirty, and then I want to have two babies and quit work. Right here, where we are standing at this moment is where I want to raise my babies, Ben. Right here on this farm with my church. And I want to stay with my kids until they are in middle school and then go back to work, but only with regular hours. No shift work. I want to start as soon as possible training to be a Physician's Assistant. I want to become a PA, Ben."

Ben kept the doctor's appointment without protesting. The report of his health was supposed to come two weeks before Christmas, on Emily's twenty-fourth birthday. It didn't. Emily called. The doctor's secretary told her he wanted to see Ben in his office the day after New Year's holidays. Emily knew at that instant that the report would not be good. She felt certain the doctor was deliberately sparing them the news until after the holidays.

She went with Ben to the appointment. The doctor did not mince words.

"What you have, Mister Compton, is stage four lung cancer now, and that is in addition to the Pulmonary Fibrosis you have been dealing with for years. Stage four means the cancer has metastasized to other internal organs. The bottom line is, as you have known, there is no known cure for interstitial lung diseases–Pulmonary Fibrosis among them. The scars in your lungs cannot be repaired and you will soon require oxygen to breath. Your cancer is incurable and will continue to spread, but we can possibly delay progress. At your age there is little likelihood that, even with chemo, that I can realistically assure more than six months."

Ben didn't seem to be distressed. "And without chemo?"

"Maybe three months. Just possibly. I'm sorry, Mister Compton, but there is no reason to mislead you. Your condition is very advanced. As I said, incurable. You are too old for a lung transplant and the tumors have spread too far to make a transplant reasonable. A transplant attempt would probably kill you."

"Are you telling me that all the warning I get is a damned cough? There should be more to it than that."

"I'm sorry to say that there usually is more warning. However, the coughing that sent you here probably didn't have much to do with the tumors that had already spread. We often find metastatic tumors by accident when we are looking for something else. I won't ask for your decision on chemotherapy now, but you should probably get scheduled to begin chemo as soon as possible. Again, I am sorry. Any questions?"

Ben looked to Emily. She shook her head and began weeping.

Ben refused chemotherapy.

Emily monitored Ben's accelerating physical collapse. After conferring with Ben's son, she made arrangements for in-home hospice three weeks later. He would have a hospice nurse during the days and Emily at night.

Emily cried in his presence and he attempted to console her with his characteristic matter-of-fact fact comments. "The truth is, Emily, I am going on eighty-eight. That is about ten years past my use-by date. Men like me usually flake off about seventy-eight. Don't feel sorry for me or worry about me. Just let me go. I am ready to go. Actually, I am happy to go under the circumstances. Why wait around for weeks of what? Misery? You have been a wonderful to me, Emily. I could not have asked for a better friend. I want to thank you for the great times I have had with you. Until you came along, about all I had left was missing her and memories. That kept me going, but that is a miserable way to grow old. I was an old man and tired until you made my life worthwhile again. Now let me go. I'm not going to fight it. Here I go–all teared up again. Seems to me I do a lot of damned crying."

Ben gave up. He no longer wanted to go to his office. He didn't want to meet with his morning coffee friends. He stopped eating and withered away before her eyes. He quit.

"A couple of things to help out, Emy. When I die, call this number for the county coroner. He will be the one to sign the death certificate and release my body. Then, here, keep this number. Call them after the coroner releases me and they will come and turn me into ashes. They will also deliver the urn to you after it's done. I have a contract with them. " He asked her to make sure his ashes were scattered around the farm. When the pain required morphine, Ben deliberately quit eating and drinking. He went into a coma and died five days later. Emily stayed with him. She held him. She talked to him. She lay on the bed with him at nights, and during the final week, she took leave from work and stayed with him day and night. She did not want him to die alone.

His family finally showed up the day before he died. Marge called Emily away from Ben's bedside and said, "We do not approve of your being on the bed with Ben, Emily. This is family time. You are not family. We can manage from here on."

What is all this family crap? I am his family. They didn't care about him.

"Ben is the only real family I have ever known, Marge. He is like my father. He is the father I always wished for. I want to be with him, Marge. I need to be with him."

Marge insisted. Emily waited for everyone to sleep and slipped in at night anyway.

Ben did not die alone.

Emily's grief kept her from work for days. She had never needed someone as much as she did during those days of grieving. Ben had given her the best times of her life and now she was suffering through the worst time.

Alone again.

And then, a week after Ben died, Marge made it even worse. "Ben is gone now, Emily. The house belongs to us. We have decided not to sell it. You need to move on. We think it would be a good idea if you departed immediately."

"No, Marge! I am paid up for a month in advance. You cannot expect me to move now. And who, exactly is we, Marge? Stan is no longer present. He didn't even wait to see if there would be a ceremony. Who decided not to have the ceremony, Marge? Did Mark have anything to say about that? And by the way, where is Mark? Where has Mark been? Did he go back to St Louis before Ben died? I haven't seen much of Mark around here. I think you are making all the decisions, Marge, and I am paid up for a month. I am not leaving!"

"Oh, but I insist on it. Show me your contract with Ben and I will pay the remainder of what we owe. Mark is still here and I think he wants a word with you sometime later this afternoon. Actually, that's what I came to tell you."

"He can wait. Ben and I did not have a contract, Marge. Ben didn't want or need a contract with me. He trusted me and I trusted him. I paid three-hundred and month and half of the groceries. We didn't need a contract."

"That was then, Emily. Ben no longer has the last word. His will says the house and farm belong to Stan. We want you out within two days. Oh, and we also want to know how much you owe on that car."

"I don't owe anything. I paid Ben for the car. I paid Ben back for every dollar he spent on me. You can look at his bank account and see where he entered the money. And, all of you agreed that I would buy Ben's place. Are you breaking your word?"

"Interesting. There was never a written contract to that effect. As for all of your other claims, all I can find in his checkbook is when he bought the car."

Emily's patience ended. "The car is mine, Marge! It is in my name and I paid for it!"

"Well, that's nice to say, but there is no proof you paid."

"The car is in *my name,* Marge. That is legal proof! It is my car and it is all legal and there is not one damned thing you can do about it. That's the way Ben wanted it!"

"All right. You don't need to be so angry. I won't argue that point. We still want you out in two days. Two days. We think you were taking advantage of an old man. How much money did you take from him?"

"What? Do you have any idea what you are talking about? I don't need Ben's money, Marge. You don't know anything about me because Mark didn't tell you. Do yourself a damned favor and google me. You will find that I am R. Frederick Prindiville's only heir. Google it, Marge! I'm worth millions. And before you run off, What about Mark? You said he wanted to talk to me. Where is he?"

"I'll call him. He should be here within fifteen minutes."

Mark drove in but sat in his car. Emily waited on the porch several minutes before giving up. She went inside and sat at Ben's desk, waiting. Marge finally went to the car and talked Mark into coming inside.

"Well, you finally got the courage to face me. What do you want? Marge said you wanted to talk."

"Are you angry, Emily? I don't understand your attitude."

"That's too damned bad. How much did you know about what Marge is doing to me? She is demanding that I leave! Did you know that, Mark! Marge said you wanted to talk to me. So, talk!"

"I want to know about our relationship. I don't know what happened."

"You don't? Really? You honestly don't? No one can be that damned oblivious, Mark. Okay, I'll tell you what I think. I think your mother happened to our relationship, Mark. I think she thought you had fallen for me and she intervened. Tell me I'm wrong." He wouldn't look at her. "Marge pried you away from me before we had a chance to become too well acquainted. We were so good together that weekend, Mark. You know that's true. I was so taken by you, and then you just disappeared. You escaped by going back to Saint Louis and to your mother. You just faded away, Mark. I don't believe you are prepared to be romantically involved with me or any other woman. You let your mother undermine our relationship because you were too damned weak to run your own life. And I think you misled her about me by letting her innuendoes go without defending me. She is in control of your life, Mark. I no longer have any regard for you. You had your chance and blew it. Please, just go away. I don't ever want to see you again." She turned away and went back to the porch where she found Marge waiting.

"That should please you, Marge. I hope, for Mark's sake that he can grow a pair and get away from you some day." She went to her church and cried.

Emily could not manage packing and work schedules in time to be out in two days and decided not to let Marge control her. She took her time and stayed at Ben's house.

Marge googled Emily that evening. *Oh, my goodness. All that money. Why was she staying with Ben?*

Within the week, upon return to Ben's place after work, she found the gate locked and the entry numbers changed. Her remote was inoperative. Her belongings, computer, clothes, everything she owned, were thrown into cardboard boxes and stacked in the ditch outside of the gate.

How appropriate. My life is back in cardboard boxes where I started. Everything I own is boxed up and thrown in a ditch. The only secure thing in my entire life has been Ben, and I know exactly what he would say: 'What the hell, Emy. How hard is it? It's simple. Just pack it up and start over.' All right, then, Ben. What the hell. Maybe I will take up swearing.

She called Colin and asked him to watch the property for a real estate sale sign. He agreed. She then met with a real estate broker and arranged to buy Ben's property, if and when it came up for sale, through the broker without using her name. She took a room near the hospital and bought some decent wine.

What the hell.

After two weeks of grieving alone, Emily emerged from the silence of her sorrow and met with the hospital president. She proposed a conditional arrangement for the Prindiville money. He was ecstatic, but cautioned, "I will need to advise the board and hire a law firm to manage the transfer and investments, Emily. I'm not sure how keeping your name confidential will work out. I'll ask for legal advice there and let you know. We should probably meet privately from here on, don't you think? In the meantime, I will not mention your name."

Emily wanted the entire amount, minus the money needed to buy Ben's home and farm, if she got the opportunity, to be under the control of the hospital. She would keep three-hundred and fifty-thousand. The legal firm involved in the transfer disagreed and proposed that the hospital invest the money and receive all yearly profits for a period not less than twenty years, and then renegotiate or the entire remaining amount would revert to her control. The lawyers proposed that the gift should endure in Emily's name and could not be depleted below a four-hundred-million base. She would benefit from tax write-off laws for state and federal income taxes. Emily would probably never pay another dollar for income taxes. She would not have access to the money before the committed period of twenty years expired and the contract would have to be dissolved or renegotiated. She was content. The hospital board and president were jubilant. Emily signed and walked away with no guilt or soul-searching. It was over.

The worst time of her life kept right on stinging:

Losing Mark, and then Allen, and then Ben. Her dreams had ceased to exist. She desperately needed Ben, the one constant in her life. Emily had never felt so alone, not even while lying on that cold sidewalk the day Ben found her.

Chapter Fifteen

A CHANGE OF HABIT

The FBI agent in charge of Iris's case called several times to check with Emily about possible contacts with her mother. She had no contact. Iris had disappeared. Emily no longer had Ben to converse with and Allen had not called even once. She needed a solution to the continuing disturbance Iris was creating in her life and decided to visit the FBI office.

"I guess I don't know what you expect from me. On one hand, I want to protect my mother. On the other, I do not want to become an accessory. I don't want to be trapped here. I am thinking about leaving. I am torn and need advice."

"It is very simple, Miss Prindiville. We, you included, are dealing with the law here. Either you do the right thing or you don't. There really is no choice. You need to do the right thing so we can do the right thing. Truthfully, I doubt she will ever contact you again unless she desperately needs money. She is one smart cookie and must know we are looking for her. Oh, she knows."

"It's the law, you say? Black and white, then?"

"Absolutely. Stay on the right side of the law. It's your life. Stay on the right side so we don't muck it up for you."

Emily stood. "I expect to do the right thing. Thank you."

The agent stood and offered her hand. "Oh, I read about you in the Wall Street Journal today. That is quite a story. Amazing, actually."

Emily felt sick and sat. After a few deep breaths, she said, "Tell me, please. What did you read? I need to know."

The agent looked surprised. "The article about your money. It is above the fold on the front page of the Wall Street Journal. The seven-hundred and fifty-million dollars. You didn't know? I mean about the article?"

Emily turned pale and nearly passed out. The agent ran for water and assistance.

Shortly, with color returning to her face, Emily said, "Tell me what else the story said. There must be more than just the amount. How did they find out?"

"Apparently one of the hospital board members told a local reporter. The reporter made a deal with the WSJ. I'm guessing whoever it was made a few extra bucks there. They paid her–did I fail to mention it was a her? They probably checked it out and paid her for the information, and then revealed that you are the sole heir of a mining enterprise. They apparently have proof. That's all I know. Congratulations."

Emily drove straight to the hospital and quit her job, and then on to the president's office with plans to have a talk with him about privacy, and then think about withdrawing her offer.

He was taken by surprise. The Journal release had not made it to him. "Excuse me, Emily, but this seems awfully abrupt. We have nearly finished all legal requirements to transfer the money. We have agreed to all of your demands. Please take some time to reconsider."

"Really? How about the demand I made to keep my name confidential? Did you or did you not share the information with your Board?"

"Of course. I had to."

"You said you would keep the secret."

"I said I would try."

"The leak came out at a board party the day I told you about the offer. Could that be right?"

"I did mention the gift, but with the warning that it remain secret."

"Well, it obviously didn't and now I am a public target. What I intended to do when I came here today was withdraw my offer. I thought about placing the entire amount in a long term low yield government bond account of some sort. That way maybe your board could not rat me out again and people would leave me alone once they learned the money was out of my control. Anyway, I have decided not to be an ass. I intend to leave it with you. However, I need to find something else to do with my life now. Something more secure than hanging around here to become a slow moving target for moochers. I resigned today and will leave the money the way we planned."

He stood and thanked her, and then said, "The board has approved lifetime full coverage medical insurance for you and your immediate family, husband and children, Emily. Just so you know."

"In writing?"

"Yes. I'll have the documents forwarded to you. Please leave an address."

She started looking for a job the next day; employment far from Springfield.

Before leaving town, she stopped for lunch at the hospital cafeteria to say goodbye to some friends. Colin sat with them for a few moments and then whispered, "I need a few words with you Emily, in private, before you leave. I'll wait over there." He sat at a secluded table.

Emily joined him as soon as she could get away. "Is it something serious, Colin?"

"For a fact. Look, I know a little about your relationship with Allen. He knew we are friends and pulled me aside before he left. He asked me to tell you something. But first, are you aware of his suspension?"

"Yes. I am aware of that."

"The hospital suspended him as soon as they learned from the police department that he has been skimming drugs. You know, taking a few each time from patients. It got out of hand when he started writing prescriptions and picking them up himself. Allen is a drug addict, Emily. He admitted it to me. He is way gone. His life is really messed up. He spoke to me the day before the cops came for him. He is losing his license and is scheduled by the feds to be indicted. Remember, Emily, he asked me to tell you this. He wanted me, most of all, to tell you that you are well off without him. He told me to tell you that you were right when you thought you had something good going and wanted you to know that he thought you were good together. He was definitely in love with you. He is sorry about not being honest about the money. He just could not understand throwing all that money away. His words, Emily."

"That is mostly news I already knew, Colin. Not about the being in love part, though. Thank you. That helps my self-image a little bit. And you say he is gone?"

"Yep, he went home first, but that didn't last long. The feds came for him. He is presently incarcerated. Sorry to bring bad news, Emily, but he wanted you to know."

While scanning the net for possible employment, The New York City Barr & Embry agency for international governesses, nannies and companions attracted her attention. She texted a request for qualifications. They texted a formal application. She sent it back the next day. They answered by phone the day after that. "We will need to meet in person for an interview at your convenience, Miss Prindiville."

"Will I need to travel?"

"No. Our team will meet you at a location you specify."

"When?"

"Again, with no less than one day's notice, at a location you designate."

"I can have a hotel conference room scheduled here the day after tomorrow."

"That is acceptable. Early afternoon if possible so the team may be able to return that day. We will need approximately two hours with you. Please bring two forms of legal identification and your birth certificate. We also will need your school records and work history. I will forward our flight schedule. And, if you will, send reservations made in our name for two rooms at the hotel along with the conference room. We will take care of the expenses upon arrival. Have we done business?"

"Good enough for me."

A rather pompous middle-aged man and a matronly older woman, probably younger than she looked, both immaculately dressed and well spoken, arrived at the conference room and filled out a two hour long list of questions concerning everything about Emily. All very professional. They returned to New York that evening and she waited three days for an answer.

"Miss Prindiville, we believe we have located the perfect position for you in Washington DC. If that is an acceptable location, we are ready to organize a meeting with your prospective employer."

Emily was disappointed, hoping for something overseas. "May I ask about the position?"

"Of course. We believe you could be a perfect match for an eighteen-year-old Spanish girl. She is the daughter of the Spanish Ambassador to The United States and requires an English instructor and companion to introduce her to American culture. She speaks halting English. We understand that you are fluent in Spanish, having grown up with a Mexican maid, so we believe you two may be an excellent match. The Ambassador has been informed and would like to interview you personally. This coming Friday afternoon if you are available."

"That suits me. What about travel arrangements. Do you make them or do I?"

"We will forward vouchers and tickets for– air travel first class. You will have everything you need from us by registered mail by noon tomorrow. Please bring clothes to accommodate almost any diplomatic situation. I'm terribly sorry to be so inexact, but all we know is that the Ambassador is hosting some dignitaries Saturday. Semiformal if you are invited. Also, he may want to delay your departure until he and his wife are quite satisfied with the interviews. You should be prepared to stay several days."

"How educated is the girl."

"Ah, a good question. By our standards, possibly not very. She has been in private Catholic girl's schools her entire life and may be somewhat challenged socially insofar as cultural standards are concerned, even for her country. We are confident that you will find her to be quite bright, however. Her academic history is excellent."

"Do you know what the family expects of me, exactly?"

"Yes and no. The Ambassador asks that we leave those answers to him and his wife. Good luck, Miss Prindiville. We believe, should you accept, the time spent should be an exciting and rewarding assignment."

Emily found the Ambassador's uniformed chauffeur, Claude, an older black man, waiting at the arrival terminal holding a sign with her name. They were good friends before arriving in the suburbs of Falls Church

Virginia just outside Washington DC, close to the Ambassador's elegant home and parklike grounds.

The Ambassador and his wife, a very attractive statuesque blonde, observed Emily's arrival with interest and not a little uneasiness. The chauffeur carried Emily's bags and hanging clothes up the imposing steps onto the marble entrance where he surrendered the luggage to two houseboys being directed by the butler. Emily walked back to the limousine with him, arms linked, talking and lively all the way. She hugged him and returned to chat with the butler and head mistress, shaking hands and smiling, refusing to let them maintain their stiff stately manners and bearing.

The ambassador's wife watched the performance with unmistakable displeasure. He, on the other hand, seemed delighted and said so. "Oh, this young woman promises to be interesting. She obviously is not going to play the aristocracy game with us. I say, good for her. Now, Dolores, we desire that Elizabeth learns the ways of American girls. I suspect everyone here is about to find out. Come on, let's go down and meet her. Come on, smile, Dolores. Smile! This should be very entertaining."

Emily managed to be somewhat less effervescent in the company of the refined couple, and yet somewhat disturbed that the girl was not present. She ended the stiff encounter by asking if they had a pending schedule that she should be aware of.

"Oh, yes," he said. "Please forgive me. Would you be available for dinner this evening, Miss Prindiville?"

"I am, yes. Thank you. And please call me Emily. Will I need formal or informal dress?"

He looked to his wife who answered, "Informal, I think. Elizabeth will not be present. About Seven in the dining room."

Emily pointed both directions with a questioning look.

"Your maid will direct you. She is waiting there for you now." Dolores nodded toward a rather portly younger woman standing by the staircase.

"Seven, then. So nice to meet both of you. She curtsied slightly and departed, breathing a sigh of relief, thinking, What the hell have I done.

The maid, a local American girl, introduced herself as Janet and said, "I am assigned to you, Miss Prindiville. Permanently by the way. You are, or will be if you are hired, in fact my entire job. You are my duties. You are my mistress and I am at your disposal twenty-four-seven. I listened in to your conversation with the ambassador from the staircase and think you are going to be a breath of fresh air around here. This place is awfully stuffy. Everyone here is way too methodical for my taste. Now, the first thing you need to know is that the Ambassador is a great guy. No, really, he is. He may not seem it now, but he is laid-back and funny. The wife...? Well, maybe you can break though her snootiness. She is old school aristocracy all the way. And, by the way, Elizabeth will not be joining you until tomorrow. Don't ask, because I don't know where she is. I have not seen her. She arrived only yesterday from Spain with her maid. I think they have her checked into a hospital doing medical checkups. I have not been privileged to meet her. Her mother hates informality, but I expect you already know that much. You and Elizabeth will be living in adjoining rooms. Did I say rooms? That's a laugh. Apartments would be closer to the truth. Pretty lavish living."

"I am supposed to dress informally for dinner with them tonight, Janet. I probably ought to know what informal means around here?"

"A somewhat subdued party dress will work. No cleavage, though. Discreet. Okay, boring. And now we better hustle. Time is running out. I'll hang your clothes so you can pick."

The ambassador and wife were waiting for the evening meal when she arrived, right on time. Uniformed attendants stood at the ready behind designated chairs. The ambassador sat first, at table's end, the wife next to him and the Emily across from her.

This is informal? This is military precision. This is intimidating. This is ridiculous.

The meal was served and eaten with very little conversation.

I'm dying here.

The Ambassador placed his napkin on the table and the noticeably formal routine was over. He smiled and said, "Let us now move to a more comfortable setting." The ever-present attendants automatically stepped forward and pulled the chairs. He led the way to an adjoining sitting room. Emily declined the wine as did the wife. He opened the examination by smiling, and then presented his glass to her. "Welcome to our home, Miss Prindiville. Now, if you please, tell us about yourself."

"Very well. First, I am Emily. I would like to know how to address you."

"I am a descendent of a duke named Luis de Lima De Silva. Spain once had a recognized aristocracy that still exists more or less as tradition. So, De Silva it is."

She noted he had not given his first name. "Perhaps I

can condense what you need to know about me if I knew how much you already know about me. Please."

He nodded, seemingly undisturbed by her taking control. "Yes, Emily. Of course you must be aware that we have received a rather thorough briefing from the agency. We know that you are a registered nurse. We know that you are an accomplished musician, if not professional. We know that you finished at the top of your high school class and received the highest SAT score in the state, and we know that you also received honors throughout nurse training and college level studies." He looked to his wife.

Her eyes narrowed. She entered the conversation with, "We are curious about your social life, particularly with men. And you might also mention your religious preferences, if any."

Emily nearly laughed and could not suppress an amazed smile. "I will be happy to tell all about my religion–none–but I am neither for or against it. I was not raised in a religious environment and have not developed an interest. I have attended church a few times with friends and frankly found it to be a little too mysterious and, from my perspective, possibly behind the times. I will also happily tell you about my male friends, but first must ask if you are aware of my financial status?"

The ambassador shook his head. "We are not aware of the exact numbers, but have some idea about a medical worker's compensation in America. Is that what you mean?"

How interesting. The agency obviously was not aware of the Wall Street Journal news. I might as well get this over with. "You have no knowledge of my affiliation with R. Frederik Prindiville Enterprises?"

They glanced at each uneasily and shook their heads. He said, "We have no knowledge of that organization. Should we?"

"I think you should. Yes, definitely." She cleared her throat. "I am the sole heir to that enterprise. My father was R. Frederick Prindiville, the owner of several coal and mineral mines. You should google his name. R. Frederick Prindiville. He died late last year and left his entire estate to me. I recently sold it and have the money assigned to a trust under control of a hospital for the coming twenty years." She watched their facial expressions go from polite interest to uncertainty, to dismay. They both seemed bewildered and Emily decided to press on, telling them about the money. "As it stands, I was heir to seven-hundred and fifty million dollars."

You could hear a pin drop for the next thirty seconds.

The Ambassador was clearly perplexed. He self-consciously cleared his throat and said, "Why, then, Miss Prindiville–Emily–why are you here? You obviously don't need the money."

"I do, though. I have no intention of ever using the coal mining money for my personal gain. I have given it away, all of it, keeping just enough to buy a conventional home someday. In the meantime, I need work and this opportunity appeals to me. Oh, and part of the reason I am here is that I also needed to separate myself from my previous employer for personal reasons. Truth is, they allowed my name and the amount of money to leak to the news. The reason I left the hospital has nothing to do with my work, and...!" She held up her forefinger. "And there is also the recent and unhappy ending to the only love affair of my life. He wanted me to keep the money and I refused. He walked away. Add to that, the best friend I ever had died and I needed to get away. So, here I am. The agency found me qualified for this position. There you have it." She sat back.

They were both lost for words, shifting uncomfortably, needing time to think. Emily recognized their dilemma. "I expect that should give you enough to think about for the time being. Shall we take this up again tomorrow?"

No answer.

"The agency brief I received mentioned that I should be capable of teaching your daughter about the behavior and practices of young American women, along with teaching English and being her companion. Again, I am qualified and would like the opportunity. Now, I will stop talking." She sat back, folded her hands and waited.

The Ambassador regained his bearing first. "Thank you, Emily. Yes, some time to think is a good idea. In the meantime, I believe it would also be a good time for you to meet Elizabeth. She should be back in her room by now. If you would, please introduce yourself." He stood. "We wish you a good night. I will take an early for breakfast and would appreciate your presence. Say about Eight?"

Eight is early? "I'll be there. I look forward to it. Thank you both for a pleasant evening. Good night." She affected another half-way curtsey. Ben would have called it half-assed.

She tapped on Elizabeth's door and waited. Then tapped again, waited, and then stepped back preparing to leave.

"Who is it?"

"Elizabeth, my name is Emily. I am here to see about becoming your English instructor and companion. I would like to say hello, if you like."

The door opened slowly. A very tall slender girl dressed in the most unbecoming green plaid skirt, knee-high green woolen stockings and a long-sleeved white blouse buttoned all the way to the top stood silently, eyes narrowed, backing away. She was clearly apprehensive and said nothing. Emily paused only a moment before stepping through the door. She went directly to the girl and hugged. The girl stood stock still, arms at her side. Emily kissed her lightly on the neck, stepped back and delivered the most welcoming smile she could generate under the circumstances. The girl stepped father back, still not smiling. She didn't invite Emily in.

"Well then, I will see you sometime tomorrow morning, Elizabeth. I look forward to our relationship. Have a good night." After the door closed, Emily distinctly heard Elizabeth say in Spanish, "I do not hug."

Oh, yes you do.

The ambassador was alone at the table when Emily arrived the next morning. He stood and offered his hand, smiling warmly. "Please have a seat. I am looking forward to this. Please."

She sat, surprised somewhat by his casual friendliness. *Janet said he was laid-back.*

Food had already been served in large compartmented Lazy Susan turntable centered between them. He selected his breakfast and spun the device toward Emily. She followed his lead.

"In less formal settings like this, Emily, I much prefer you call me Albert. Dolores will not be joining us this morning. How did your introduction with Elizabeth go last night?"

"She seemed restrained. I think she was exhausted. We didn't progress beyond a brief meeting at her door. She was dressed in what I consider to be Catholic school girl clothes. Am I correct?"

"You are. Her school is out for three months and she flew in only yesterday from Madrid. She may have been overtired. I imagine things will go more smoothly for you today."

Three months? "Am I here for only three months, then? Are you planning to send her back to school?"

"Dolores is still weighing that possibility. However, I am not. I am depending on you, Emily, to help make it possible for me to keep her here in America. I want Elizabeth to remain in America for her college years. I hope that is not asking too much of you. I would also like you to conduct her during this...what do you call it? A gap year? Is that correct? Seems to be traditional off time between high school and college. Is that right? I want her to get out, to see and experience the world from a more ordinary viewpoint. She has been rather sheltered."

"That will take more than three months, but I can probably manage it. Does she want to spend her gap time in Europe?"

"No. She wants to see and understand America, particularly the habits and customs of young American women."

"I guess we need to see if the two of us are compatible first, won't we? I will do my very best. Now, about teaching her about the behavior and practices of

American girls. I read that job description on the agency brief and must tell you that our behaviors, as a whole, is all over the map. I do not believe you can categorize American girls by any fundamental or consistent behavior pattern. There are vast cultural differences here. I am limited, happily as I see it, to the more ordinary white middle class experiences. If that is your interest, then I am certainly qualified."

"Good! That is exactly what I want. Dolores is somewhat skeptical, but I have the lead and I would like it if you to introduce Elizabeth to American ways, particularly those of white middle-class younger women. Yes! I think she would be far better off if we start somewhere in the middle. The Good Lord certainly knows she has led a very sheltered and structured life up to now. Possibly too regimented in my eyes. I want you to...oh, how do you say this...loosen her up? Is that right?" He laughed and so did Emily.

"Just let me know when I begin, Albert. If, after today, you still want me. I have some ideas that should challenge Elizabeth's well-ordered world. This could be great fun for all of us."

Her conversation alone with Dolores later that morning did little to convince the girl's mother, but Emily finally received her unenthusiastic blessing and signed a contract.

All right! Game on!

She did not tap lightly on the door. When it began to open, Emily pushed through and right past Elizabeth. She sat on the bed, bouncing and smiling all the way. *Happy! Happy*! Elizabeth was still in her nightgown.

"I am told you play the violin, Elizabeth. Is that correct?"

She nodded.

"I would like to see it. Do you have it here?"

She nodded.

"Well, may I see it, please?"

The girl went to a closet, dropped the violin case on the bed, and stepped back. She still had not spoken a word.

Emily opened the case and marveled aloud over the instrument's quality. She tuned it, examined the bow, took a couple of preliminary strokes, and then began to play. The girls face slowly changed from the dour expression she had exhibited to the delighted smile of a teenager. She was thrilled. When Emily finished, the girl clapped and spoke.

"I didn't know you played. You play very good," she said.

"Play well. You say, you play well, Elizabeth, not good. Now, I have been confirmed by your parents as your new English instructor and companion, Elizabeth. Would you please play something for me? Let me hear you play. Here."

Elizabeth played for a few moments. She was obviously no beginner. Emily clapped and cheered. "This is so wonderful. When my instrument arrives, we are going to have a blast!"

"Blast? I do not understand."

"Blast! Fun. A good time. We will entertain everyone. A blast! Now, you get dressed and I will go to breakfast with you, and then we will think how to accomplish our mission."

"Mission? Again, I do not–"

"Mission. That means we are going to decide what to do with each other. That is our mission. We are supposed to get to know each other and I am supposed to teach you about American girls. Now, move it, girl. I need to fix my face."

"I don't–"

"Never mind. You will soon enough. Move it!" She skipped out of the room leaving a bewildered but smiling Elizabeth.

In the days following, Emily and Elizabeth established that, for the immediate future, Emily would speak only Spanish and Elizabeth would only speak English, each correcting the other's mistakes.

On the fourth day, Emily asked the De Silvas for permission to return to Springfield and gather her belongings. The ambassador trusted her by then and paid for a round trip. She flew out of Washington National to Chicago and then to Springfield where Emily tossed much of her clothing into a recycling bin. She saved her hospital wear, stored her car and packed everything else in suitcases and hanging bags. She hand-carried her two most important belongings: the violin and computer. Emily returned to DC the following day, again with United Airlines, sitting in the sparsely occupied first class section. COVID was still rampant and the airlines were suffering major passenger losses.

And then!

And then the copilot toured the cabin, chatting

casually with passengers–a corporate relations duty he seemed to enjoy. He stopped by Emily's seat and said, "I have seen you before, haven't I? You were on this same flight a few days ago if I remember correctly. Am I right? And yesterday you flew with us going the other direction. You got off at Springfield, I believe."

"I did, and I also remember you."

He smiled, seemed uncomfortable, waved and headed for the cockpit. He stopped after a few steps, turned and looked back. She smiled. He nodded, turned away and kept walking only to stop, pause for a moment, and then turn back and return.

She moved over to the center seat and patted the aisle seat.

He looked around nervously before taking the seat. "I really can't stay with you long. I would like to, but fraternization with the passengers is against regulations you know. I am the co-pilot, by the way. Tim Bradley."

Emily was aware that he had not offered his hand and gave him a positive nod. She offered hers. *Ladies choice.* She wondered if he knew. "I am Emily. Nice of you to stop by, Tim Bradley. I also remember seeing you yesterday, and the time before. So this is like old times. We go back."

"Are you headed to DC again?"

"Yes. And you?"

"Same. This is my regular route. Usually from Austin to Springfield to Chicago to DC. I layover one night in DC, and then do it again in reverse. Twice a week. I stay over two nights once and one night the other. Are you working and living in DC?"

"Yes, for most of the coming year. I work for the Spanish Ambassador."

His interest intensified. "Oh! That *is* interesting. Now, and I realize this is way too at ease with you, but if you are not already taken by some lucky fellow...." He glanced around the cabin. "And this is so against regulations, but I would like to visit with you for a few moments at the airport lounge after we land. That is if I am not intruding on someone else's territory and only if you are comfortable with it. Please tell me you are not taken and that you will actually consider joining me."

"I am not taken, Tim, and, yes, I would enjoy a few moments with you. Thank you. Now, you should probably get back to work." She patted his hand and they parted.

She stopped him by calling, "Tim!"

He stopped and turned back.

Emily took her mask off. "I want to see your face, Tim." He took it off. After a moment, she said, "Thank you. See you later."

Oh, he is the all-American boy—the guy most likely to succeed in the college yearbook.

A stewardess sat beside her minutes later and handed her a note with Tim's phone number. Emily recorded his number on her phone and wrote her number on the note and handed it back.

The stewardess, a woman in her forties, said, "I have flown with Tim almost a year. This is the first time that I am aware of that he has ever broken company rules. He's a catch, honey. Good luck, and I mean that."

Upon arrival, Emily called Claude and asked to be picked up in one hour, and then waited for Tim at the arrival gate. He escorted her to the luggage area, loaded her seemingly never-ending stack of luggage and then wheeled everything to the lounge. She refused a drink and Tim followed suit. By this time they knew they were both inoculated and took their masks off. They also recognized that they were unmistakably fascinated by each other, enjoying the time-honored signals of an escalating attraction: the effortless smiles, moving closer, almost but not quite touching, the eye contact.

"I have very little time this evening, Tim. Maybe forty-five minutes. I don't want to waste it doing anything but finding out about you."

"I'm good with that. But first tell me about your position with the ambassador. And then I hope you won't mind if I ask some personal questions, like who are you? In great detail."

She briefly reviewed her new job. He listened intently and then said, "That is definitely going to be interesting. Your primary duties appear to be to Americanize the daughter? That seems odd."

"I am officially hired to be her English teacher and companion. However, the Ambassador took me aside after the briefing, without his wife presence I might add, and made it clear that he mainly wants me to instruct his daughter about the ways of American girls. I think the companion part of my duties is where the Americanization of Elizabeth will take place. I really don't know how this is going to work. She seems...oh how do I say this? A wee bit stilted? Perhaps the result of her education years in all-girl Catholic schools? She is distressingly reserved. I need to get through her defensive sanctuary starting tomorrow—my first day on the job. A challenge, I think. I'm looking forward to it, though.

Now, where is your home? Where do you live, Tim Bradley with an E."

When Emily called a halt to the meeting in order to meet the chauffeur, they both knew enough to recognize that the foundation for a prospective relationship had been established. Tim transported her belongings and assisted until it was time to part.

"I want to see you again, Emily. I am in DC three nights a week and I have my own wheels here. Please say yes. I really want to know you. Please?"

"Yes. You need to call me a day ahead, though. But, yes, Tim. Call me." She patted his cheek and they parted.

On the way home, Claude focused the rear view mirror on her face. "That is one nice-looking young man, Miss Emily. Yes, Ma'am. He sure is."

"His name is Tim, Claude. He flew my airplane today. I think, with time, I could like him very much."

"Good for you, Miss Emily. Someone to party with, maybe?"

"Maybe. We shall see. And you, my friend, will undoubtedly be the first to know."

CHAPTER SIXTEEN

ELIZABETH

"When will you be eighteen, Liz?"

"My name is Elizabeth."

"Yes, and Elizabeth is a beautiful name. I truly admire your name, but that brings us to your first lesson in American girl culture, Elizabeth. Never name your children a name with more than two syllables. No, really. I am serious. If you do, everyone who knows her will ignore your precious name and shorten it. My name for instance. The closer a friend is to me, the shorter my name becomes. I am two syllables to most good friends. I am occasionally just called Em. One syllable, but only by my very best friends. The best friend I ever had called me Emy. So, whether you like it or not, if you form friendships with American young people, your name will become Liz. I can guarantee that. It is a sign they like you, Liz. Accept it, Liz. I like you, Liz."

"My mother will have a fit."

"Yes, as most mothers do. Your mother will always

238

call you Elizabeth, but she is about the only person who will. Believe me, in America you will be called Liz. Get used to it, Liz."

Tim called the following evening from Austin. After a short conversation, they exchanged email addresses. Emily began receiving mail if he was lonely–not that often–but she got to read some very interesting odds and ends from his newspaper opinion column. He eventually wanted to become a full-time writer. She enjoyed the give-and-take of writing. He was more often than not by himself late at night while on the road. He usually texted first to see if she was busy. She learned that he wanted her to call back if he asked by text if she was busy. When he was interested in a subject, she received essays, an occasional short story, or a prospective opinion piece for the newspaper. While on lay-over time in Austin, Tim rambled among old friends who went all the way back through high school and college, and of course his family: both parents and his only sibling, Pat. Pat was half way through his sophomore year at The University of Texas. Tim lived in an apartment not far from the University, equally close to his parent's home, the university and the airport. He was anything but lonely in Austin.

Every Sunday Tim emailed his weekly flight schedule. She missed him the first week. They had their first date with his crew at a lounge one night during the second week. Emily didn't need the limousine as Tim came for her in a beat up pickup truck inherited from his grandfather. The De Silvas were dismayed by the condition of the truck and said so, wondering if it was safe. Liz also laughed and made fun of the truck. Emily introduced Tim to everyone, including all the help. After saying goodbye to the ambassador and his wife, they drove off laughing.

"I bet they think I have hit bottom, Tim. Is this truck trustworthy?"

"Yes. Don't be fooled. Almost everything under the original body is practically new. I wouldn't let this old thing go for any reason. I grew up with it. Does it make you uncomfortable, Emily?"

"Are you kidding? No. My best friend had a truck like this. Well, maybe a bit cleaner and maybe polished and maybe several years newer. This is better, though, Tim. It has the bench seat. Ben's truck had bucket seats. I drove it a lot. Oh, I wish you could have met him."

"I want to meet him."

"Ben died this winter."

"Oh. I'm so sorry. What happened?"

"Age. Ben was nearing eighty-eight, Tim. He had lung cancer and died within two months of the time he was diagnosed. I miss him more than I can tell you; more than anyone I have ever known; more than is good for me. I still tear up or cry over Ben almost every day. He was the best friend I ever had. Did I mention that?"

"You have. I just didn't pick up on it. Not that your best friend was eighty-eight. Really? Eighty-eight? No way."

"Yes. It is a long story and I am anxious to tell you,

just not tonight. Tonight we party! Tonight I want to learn a few personal things about you."

He was busy driving and could only glance at her. She was not smiling and her eyes did not waver from his.

"Personal? Like what, Emily?"

"Like, I want to know how your lips feel on mine sometime soon. Not a kiss, Tim. Just touching at first. And then, if that is pleasant, I will probably want to know how it feels to kiss you. Nice and easy at first, and slow. And then I may want to find out what kind of a kisser you are. Yes, I think that is one of the first personal things I want to know. Let's see, we have known each other for three weeks and we have written and we have talked. Talking and texting are fine, Tim, and I do enjoy it, and I want to keep that in my life. But I want more now. I want to touch and I want to know personal things about you that you have not told me because they are personal. But first, I want to know what it's like to be close." She moved across the seat and snuggled against him.

Tim pulled into the nearest parking lot, turned the engine off and reached for her. They were a half hour late to meet his crew. When they arrived, Emily knew what his lips felt like and what kind of kisser he was. She was in high spirits, swaying and dancing across the room to meet his crew.

The first person Emily met was the older stewardess, the one who told her on the airplane that Tim was a catch. They hugged and the stewardess whispered, "Oh, you are good, Honey. This was quick. Tim never brings anyone to our little parties. Good for you. Now, let me introduce you to the crew."

Emily spent more time with the crew than with Tim

that evening. He watched her from afar, pleased by how quickly the team accepted her and how easily she fit in. He enjoyed watching her flow easily into the mix. Most of the crew came to him after meeting her.

"Hey, Timmy! Where did you find that? She is solid gold, Man. You should probably try to keep her around."

"You been keeping her secret from us, Tim? I can see why. I wouldn't let her out of my sight. Wow! She is hot."

"Is she going to be around, Tim? That is one sweet girl. You are a lucky man."

After they broke away, Tim told her, jokingly, that she might not ever see them again. "I'm not willing to share, Emily. I want time alone with you."

"Wasn't my idea, remember, but it was a good idea. I like them, Tim. Every single one of them. It was a good first date." I need to get back to the plantation now. Appearances, you know. What's the buzzword now? Optics?"

During his next two-night layover, Emily broke away from work and spent several hours alone with him. They didn't talk much. They did become more thoroughly acquainted, each discovering what was under the other's shirt and blouse. They understood enough by then to know the relationship held limitless promise and both, secretly, began to imagine the possibility of a lifetime arrangement. They knew by then, beyond doubt, that they were ready to move to the next level, and soon.

"How are we going to manage this, Emily? Teenage groping is wonderful and you are perfect, but what we are doing is going to drive me crazy."

"I know, Tim. Me too. I want more. Okay, let's make a plan. My place, obviously, is out. Any ideas?"

"Yes. I have scouted around. There is a nice upscale motel in Falls Church, half way between where we each live. That would save time for both of us. We could use my place, of course, but it is noisy and not all that private, and we would probably be targets for some infantile behavior. What I want to know is, how will staying out overnight to affect your employers?"

"That has been on my mind. I guess it's time for a mom and pop sit-down with them."

"How are you and Liz making it?"

"Moving on very well, I think. She is actually funny at times. Not so conventional as I thought. I like her and we are getting closer. When I have my talk with her parents, I'm going to beg them to let me take her clothes shopping. She has some stuffy stuff to wear. Awful, really. No way she can feel pretty. She has been taught to go way out of her way to look plain. She could be very pretty if she will."

"Another thing to think about, Emily, is that my brother starts spring break in two weeks. Mom refuses to let him go anywhere this year. Too much COVID. He has taken his first COVID shot while working with a hospital unit doing vaccination programs. He gets his second shot this week. I have my shots. You have yours. Liz has hers, thanks to her parent's celebrity status. What I'm thinking is, when I have a two-night stay-over, you might introduce Liz to Pat and the ways of American boys. I'm thinking that Pat would be happy to come with me and meet Liz. She's eighteen now and Pat is nineteen. He is several inches taller than I am, better looking and never stops smiling. He also knows his way around girls from what Mom tells me. What do you think? He would sure open her world up if she lets him. And she will, I guarantee that. He is habit forming and insistent."

"I think I need to think about it, Tim. Pat just might work out, but that means they would have to be with us. Dammit! And I am not about to turn an insistent guy who knows his way around girls loose on Liz. Maybe we could run around with them for a night. I'll ask Liz first. If she buys it, then I will go to the Ambassador. The two of them can carry the ball to Dolores, not me. And, by the way, exactly how tall is Pat?"

"Six four. Four inches taller than I am."

"Good. Liz is probably about five nine. She could wear heels around him. They might be a good fit. Hair and eye color?"

"Light brown and blue. Same as mine."

"We will make two odd couples. Dark and light. Not important."

Emily asked for a meeting with the Ambassador after speaking to Liz about a night out with Pat. Surprisingly, Liz required very little encouragement and asked everything Emily knew about Pat. Emily met the Ambassador the next day just before the evening meal. Even though she had asked for him alone, he brought Dolores.

How hard is this?

"Good evening to both of you! What I want to talk to you about is my friend, Tim. He is bringing his nineteen-year-old college student brother Pat to town in a couple of weeks. I would like to introduce Pat to Liz and have her come along with us for a night out. Just to eat out and maybe go to a discreet club to talk and maybe dance. I have never met his brother, but Tim says he is decent and I trust Tim. I think this is a perfect way to introduce Li...sorry, Elizabeth to the American dating culture. Any thoughts?"

The De Silvas looked at each other. She nodded to him and the Ambassador took the lead. "How long would she be out?"

"Oh, perhaps three or four hours, maybe a little longer. Quite a distance to travel from here to anywhere in the big city."

"And you would be with her at all times?"

"Absolutely. No chance for anything to get out of hand, even if they were interested, and they don't even know each other. I think it would be a good place for her to begin, don't you? We wouldn't go to any of the wilder clubs. You are somewhat acquainted with Tim. I hope you realize that he is one of the good guys."

Once again, Dolores nodded to Albert and he said, "We need to think about it. I happen to believe it would be good for her. Thank you, Emily. We will let you know."

"Great! Now, I hope you are not offended by what I am about to say next, but it also concerns Elizabeth and I think it's important."

The Ambassador nodded once again toward his wife. She nodded in return. Emily knew by then that the last one to nod was giving priority to the other. He said, "If it is important, Emily, please go ahead. We will not be offended. Please."

"Very well. I want to say something about her clothes.

May I speak freely about her clothes? That is, about my opinion of her clothes?"

"Certainly. We expect you to express your opinions honestly. Please go ahead."

Emily sighed. "All right. You expect me to chaperon your daughter into a different social world than she has experienced–the American middle-class young adult world. Am I correct?"

They nodded again. Her nod came last, as it did more often than not. He answered, "We have discussed this before, I believe. Our goals have not changed."

"Good. All right then. I want to take Elizabeth clothes shopping. I believe her clothes will make her uncomfortable in the social settings I am planning. What do you think?"

Dolores appeared to resent Emily's comments and sat back, frowning. Albert noticed, smiled to counter his wife's displeasure, and said, "What do you have in mind?"

"As I said–a shopping spree. I want to help her select clothes that she will be comfortable in around young Americans. I don't want her to stand out or be embarrassed. I have scanned the clothes in her closet and find them awfully plain for most semi-casual social outings anywhere in America." She watched and waited.

The Ambassador seemed uncomfortable, rubbing his chin, keeping his thoughts to himself. Dolores frowned and looked out the window. They were not ready.

"I see that you are both uncomfortable with the idea. Perhaps, Dolores, you could come with us? I don't plan to dress Elizabeth inappropriately–just stylishly in the current fashions of her age group. Nothing too expensive. Please say yes."

Albert suddenly stood, looked at his wife and said. "You two manage this. I am out of my element here." He smiled, waved both hands, wiping the problem away, and left them alone.

Dolores also stood. "No, Emily, this is exactly why we want you. I trust you and so does Albert. Elizabeth is obviously taken by you. You be Elizabeth's guide–or is it Liz now?" She closed one eye and looked at Emily accusingly from the other. "No, you do exactly as you feel appropriate, but please be at least somewhat conservative for my sake. You may take the limo. Have fun. Oh, and I will want a fashion show when you finish."

Emily was shocked. Dolores wasn't so straitlaced after all. Elizabeth jumped for joy, like a little girl. "My mother said that! I cannot believe. You are magical, Emily.

The shopping trip took two days. The fashion show took most of an afternoon. Dolores winced a time or two but never objected, even nodding appreciatively on several occasions.

"Now, Liz. Now we fix your hair and add a touch of cosmetics. You are going to be dazzling."

Another day passed before Emily asked the Ambassador if she and Liz could be permitted to attend the gathering of dignitaries he was to entertain that evening.

"I don't understand your purpose, Emily. I doubt there will be anyone of interest for you there."

"We won't be there long, Albert. What I am planning

is going to be something like a mini debutante coming-out party for Liz. Just say yes. You won't be disappointed. I promise. And Liz is so looking forward to it. Please?"

Later, Emily took the elevator down to the kitchen area and drifted into the crowded room of dignitaries. She planned to be near Albert at the exact time she and Liz had selected. As Liz began descending the staircase, Emily whispered to Albert, "Elizabeth is going to stop for a moment near the bottom half of the stairs, Mister Ambassador. You should take the opportunity to introduce her to your guests."

Dolores and Albert were shocked as Liz descended the massive curved staircase, stepping down carefully, floating, eyes straight ahead, not looking down at the stairs. She was dressed in a cocktail dress, perfect for the occasion. Emily had styled her hair, slightly curling in front, just a touch of silver coloring, touching her shoulders on both sides of her face.

As Liz paused, Emily tapped a spoon on an empty crystal wineglass. All conversation stopped and the gathering gazed about in anticipation of an announcement. Everyone present soon noticed Liz. She looked grown-up, striking, pausing on the stairs to smile. The Ambassador stepped through the crowd to be near and announced to the now silent gathering, "Ladies and gentlemen, my daughter Elizabeth, De Silva." His eyes were glistening.

Liz drifted through the gathering, speaking to all comers, and then departed unobtrusively before mealtime. She went directly to Emily's room where they celebrated.

"What did your mother say?"

"Oh, Mother was so pleased, Emily. She had tears. She hugged and hugged and told me I was beautiful. She has never done anything like that. You are magic!"

"Liz, you need to have your own phone. You also need to have a computer so you can be on-line and for college. There is so much going on with the internet. It's a must. Do I need to say something to your parents or will you?"

"No. Let me do it. First, why do I need these things? I have a house phone."

"Not good enough. Believe me, a phone and the internet are important parts of being an American girl. Your friends need to be confident that you are private, that they can say and write things that you might not want your parents to know. The sooner the better, Liz."

"I will talk to them. And by the way, what friends? You are my only American friend."

"Well, we are soon going to see about that. I have a plan. But I need to talk to you about something you may not like, Liz. Please don't be angry with me."

"It must be important. Tell me."

"Shaving, Liz. You are going to stand out unless you shave under your arms. I don't know exactly what your customs are, but women here shave under their arms and their legs. Particularly young women. The old saying goes, 'When in Rome, do as the Romans do.' This is one of those times, Liz."

"I'm not upset, Emy. I have noticed and I have been

nervous about it."

"Do you have the equipment you need?"

"No."

"Next time we are out, that's the first thing we do. Won't take long to learn. Good for you. I wondered how you would take it. How about your parents? What will they think?"

"I'm going to do it, Emy. Don't worry about them."

Tim called. "Pat's Spring Break begins next week, Emily. Any news about permitting Liz to run around with us–him?"

"I will let you know tonight. Is Pat into this or is he just doing you a favor?"

"He's good with it. Matter of fact, he has asked about Liz more than once. He will be here for two nights, Emily. Do we set him up with her both nights?"

"No, you Dodo! Two will definitely be one too many. Let him fend for himself the first night so you and I can have some time together. We can eat out and go to a club or two the next night with them. They are both underage, so you need to think about a place we can go to talk and dance without being tossed out."

Emily received an email message from Tim late that evening. A poem.

I KNEW
I knew you were there,
I have always known.
 Not the color of eyes or hair.
I watched and waited for you.

I have saved a place for you.
The link has always been there.
A cosmic bridge joins our souls.
Meet me in the middle.

Emily cried. She called Tim and told him that she knew the moment he took his mask off in the airplane. Later, she called and told him that the Ambassador was okay with taking Liz on Saturday night. Some place respectable and solid. "He trusts me, but Dolores didn't say anything. Tell Pat we are on for Saturday night. He should wear dining-out casual clothes. Now I need to motivate Liz about dancing."

They took Pat to a restaurant when he arrived about noon so Emily could become acquainted. He was everything she hoped for: very nice looking in an all-American way. And happy! He smiled and found something humorous about everything. Pat would overwhelm Liz in a good way. She almost envied Liz.

Emily did not agonize about the prospect of staying overnight with Tim, other than to say, "I hate to think how this is going to look to the De Silvas. How me staying out overnight will probably look to them, particularly right before they turn their daughter loose with us. What do you think?"

"Are you kidding? Yes. This makes me so happy, Emy. I need you."

"I came prepared to stay over, Tim."

"Great. I need to explain tonight to Pat. He won't be a problem. Great!"

Tim made the motel arrangements, dumped Pat, kissed

the world goodbye and drove too fast.

After he closed the motel room door, they both stood still, breathing deeply, looking at the only important item in the room.

The king-sized bed.

Emily said, "I suppose that will work. Okay, I'm going to bathe. Did you bring something to drink?"

"Yes, and glasses. Don't take all night."

Emily came out ten minutes later dressed in a sheer nightgown–a one-time-only nightgown.

Tim stood and reached for her. They held and kissed until she shooed him away. "Clean up, Airman. Let's do this. Make haste."

He came out wearing a towel and slipped into bed beside her. What clothes they had on were lying on the floor within minutes. Emily loved the gentle, easy, slow progress for a while, and then she turned the easy part into needy, and the slow part into a frenzy, writhing beneath him, tugging at him, moaning, begging.

"Give me your towel, Tim." She spread it on the bed and lay on it. Their first time was something neither would ever forget. They were both gasping for air after consummation, laughing, tears running, holding and elated.

"Oh, Tim. How perfect. I never imagined it would be so wonderful."

She sat up and inspected the towel. "I wondered if I would spot. She lay back and reached for him.

Tim remained silent for several seconds, his face a mixture of puzzlement and concern. "Wait a minute. Are you telling me this was your first time, Emy?"

She snuggled closer. "Yes, Tim. You are my first, and hopefully the only. Are you surprised?"

"Maybe. A little. I just never.... I wondered about the towel, Emy."

"I wasn't sure I was a virgin, Tim. One of my girlfriend's mother left her alone for two weeks. We used her vibrator. A rather substantial device. Intimidating at the time. I doubt any of us survived that thing still virgin. I'm happy it turned out this way. I was never all that into saving myself for marriage. R. Frederick made sure I had little opportunity to practice with boys."

They talked and held, had another sip of wine and did it all again. Emily commented after the second time, "Amazing. After all the years of wondering what it would be like, my body already knew. There has never been a mystery, Tim. Everything was instinctive. I didn't have to adapt, or learn, or wonder. I didn't have to be anxious about anything. I didn't have to be unsure of what to do next. My body already knew. Isn't that amazing? No training required. It's fundamental. "

"Damn, Emily! I should have taken my time. I should have been gentle. I'm sorry."

"Don't be. You were everything I ever dreamed of, Tim. Don't apologize. It was perfect for me. I discovered exactly what I hoped for. I'm happy."

Tim set his alarm for midnight. They talked until he slept with her head on his shoulder. Emily couldn't sleep. She became aware that she couldn't hear or feel him sleeping. She touched his chest. Normal. She leaned close to listen to his breathing. Barely audible. *A man who doesn't snore? How great will that be?*

The De Silvas never said anything about her night out.

Liz could not contain her curiosity. "Where were you last night, Emily? Did you party all night?"

"Oh, Liz. Someday I hope you go where I was last night. I went to the best place on earth."

"Is that a club?"

Emily laughed. "Best night out ever in my life. That's all I'm going to say about last night. Now, let's concentrate on today. Are you prepared to party! We are going to have such a good time tonight."

She called Tim. "We need to introduce Pat to the De Silvas before we head out the gate with their daughter tonight, don't you think?"

"Yes, I agree. Pat is up for anything, so you don't need to worry about how he will handle it. And, by the way, the company just announced that I am going to be furloughed sometime soon; maybe for several months. COVID has really taken a bite out of our schedule and I am a junior pilot. I can use company housing and fly anywhere for free, so you may expect to see me around DC a lot."

Pat handled meeting the De Silvas very well. Just discreet enough, and friendly enough, and comfortable enough. Emily could tell Dolores was not only surprised, but charmed.

Oh, Liz is never going to get a chance to be timid–not with Pat.

The club was seriously following COVID rules, social distancing, masking and twenty-five percent occupancy. The band was very good and only turned up the volume when people danced. The dance floor remained sparsely occupied.

As the evening progressed, Pat did overwhelm Liz in every good way. Before the meal was over, Liz was studying every move he made, thoroughly entranced by his directness and humor. Emily caught Liz watching Pat like he was a rock star; almost in a daze; dreamy; lost in her own world; utterly taken.

Pat pulled Liz reluctantly onto the dance floor where she stood for the longest time watching him dance. She began smiling, picking up the beat, watching his feet, slowly beginning to move with the music. Everything about her movements changed in stages, and then the most remarkable thing happened: Liz, swaying gracefully, her eyes now mischievous, locked to Pat's eyes. She began stamping her feet, whirling, clapping and snapping her fingers, blending fluid flamenco moves with her arms.

It worked! Whatever the steps were, if any, didn't matter at all. She loosened up and began enjoying herself, in her own world. Suddenly liberated. People began pointing, watching and whispering. Oh, Liz loved it! Dancing to moderated rock music came to her naturally. The crowd clapped when the music stopped.

Later, crashed on Emily's bed reviewing the night, Liz sat up, hands over her eyes, and cried. Emily couldn't console her. Finally, Liz wiped her eyes and said, "I am so happy! And I am also so sad, Emy. Think of all I have missed. Pat, and fun, and dancing. All so innocent and so much fun. I have missed all of it. This has been the best night of my life, Emy. The best ever. I am so happy."

"Emy? See! I told you. So now I am Emy. Well, you certainly changed during the evening, Liz. You are going to have no trouble with our American ways. I'm proud of you. You were remarkable. Now, I have some information that is going to make you appreciate why I want you to have a phone and internet. Pat asked me for your phone number. You don't have one, other than your room phone, and you are not going to be spending your life in a room anymore. Those days are over. You need a cell phone."

"Pat asked for my number? Did he really? Oh, that makes everything even better. Are all American boys like Pat?"

"Oh, God, no. How we wish. But, no, Pat is in a league all his own. He is a special guy, Liz, and you are lucky that he was the first one to come along. Well, lucky in a way. He sets the bar awfully high for other guys if that's what you expect. You will find, as time goes on, that there are not many Pats in this world. He is special and he was perfect for this night, and for you. Pat will probably be back in DC, Liz, and Pat will probably want to see you, and Pat will probably want to be friendlier, and Pat will be difficult to contain, and…well, you can take it from there. You know him better than I do."

"Oh, Emy, I think I would run away with him. I don't think I care at all about the ways of American girls anymore. I think I am going to like the boys much better."

"Go to bed, silly. It probably won't do you any good, but you should at least try to get some sleep. Now go!"

Emily asked for the limousine for half a day. When Dolores asked, she massaged her answer a wee bit and said, "Just for an outing around DC with Elizabeth to see some things she might be interested in."

She asked Claude to take them across the Potomac to Georgetown University. After cruising most of the campus, Liz said, "This is beautiful, Emy. Very beautiful, but why are we here?"

"For several reasons. First, this is a Catholic university and your parents won't have good reason to reject it. Second, it is close to your home. And third, this is where I think you belong. But most importantly, your father has talked to me about Georgetown and I think he would like it if you began college here. You can get a great education at a highly rated university, and you can hang out with students you will have a lot in common with. Many of the dignitaries send their kids here. You don't have to live at home, but it is close enough if you want to, or if your parents want you to live at home. I think, no matter if you decide to go here or not, that when you do go to school you should live on campus and not at home with your parents. So, pay attention, Liz. We are going next to the admin building to see about entrance requirements, and then we will talk."

"Do I have any choice?"

"Of course you do, but no! I want you to do this and your father wants you to do this and it's time, Liz! You are college age and you need to get on with it. Anyway, let's go in and see about it. Come on! You need to do this."

By the end of the day Liz was on board. "I love this place, Emy. I could probably go here."

"Of course you could, but your parents need to be

involved, and there are other great schools. You can go to any American school you want to because of your father's status. I think this would be my choice for you, though. But it's your ball game. I will go anywhere with you to look at other schools. From here on, it's up to you. How hard can it be? Just do it."

The Ambassador was thrilled. Dolores was not all that unhappy. Liz considered other schools, but didn't ask to visit. She applied at Georgetown and was accepted for the summer orientation program along with two freshman year required courses. She would begin a full schedule in the fall semester. Liz wanted to study international relations. The De Silvas were happy and organized their lives to keep the estate until after Elizabeth graduated and before returning to Spain.

Emily could see an end to her job and started planning her next step. She would initiate her plan by showing Liz some of the most famous movies beginning with *SLEEPLESS IN SEATTLE.* Liz, predictably, was captivated and wanted to see the Empire State building.

The De Silvas did not object when Emily suggested inviting Tim and Pat to come along, provide they had separate rooms.

Of course.

She called Tim and launched the plan. Yes, Pat could get a week off, and yes, Tim was free, having just been furloughed.

Game on. Thank you COVID.

"I can still ride for free, Emily. I am coming to DC. Be free in DC Emily."

"How cute. When will you be here?"

"Tomorrow."

Her heart skipped. They had known each other for two months. She wanted to be with him. She needed to be with him. She would be with him.

Tim Time.

Tim and Pat were invited by the De Silva's for dinner and arrived at the Ambassador's estate after Tim's late afternoon DC arrival. The ambassador, his wife Emily and Liz were waiting on the marble entryway. No one was surprised that Tim and Emily embraced and kissed. Everyone, including Liz, looked surprised when Pat took Liz in his arms and kissed her on the cheek. The dinner went smoothly. The after-dinner drinks went smoothly. The two young men departed later without incident. The Ambassador went to bed. Emily went to bed. Dolores asked Liz to sit with her.

"We need to talk, young lady."

"Have I done something wrong, Mother?"

"No, my Dear, and you are not going to do anything wrong. We need to have a sincere mother-daughter talk. Let's begin with me wondering if you realize how close you are to having sex?"

"Mother! For heaven's sake! What are you thinking?"

"I am thinking, in your shoes, I would probably think about sex with him. I am not encouraging you to do that, but I am well aware of the way you two look at each other. Oh, I still remember all of the signals. You are leaving for New York tomorrow for three days and two nights. I know Emily will not encourage you to be all alone with Pat, but I also know Emily is in love with Pat's brother and they will probably find a way to be together. Sex is a wonderful thing with the right person and I won't deny it for you in the right circumstances. You are old enough, but I am not encouraging it, Elizabeth, and you know what the church believes. Now, that said, I want to know that you are aware that the circumstances in New York will be tempting. A mother worries. There, I said it. I want you to have a good time in New York, Dear, but a mother worries."

Liz woke Emily and told her about the conversation with her mother. "I don't know what to do, Emy. This is all so maddening. What can I say to her?"

"Are you thinking about sex with Pat? Be honest."

"Not really. Well, I have, I guess, but just…. Oh, I suppose I have."

"Too many mistakes are made during this stage of life, Liz. Too many lives are ruined. Do not think for one moment that sex means marriage. It does not. This is what I want you to think about: You and Pat are in different lanes of life. Pat is a great guy and a good place for you to start, but you are destined by heritage to stay in your own lane, Liz. Love Pat if you want to, but he is probably not your destiny. Do you know what I am saying? You have a life that is far different than anything here. Do you hear me?"

"I think so, Emy. I will probably stay awake all night thinking about it. I will never forget what you just said. Thank you."

"Don't thank, me, Liz. Thank your mother. Now get out of here and let me try to sleep."

Emily and Tim asked to see Dolores alone the next morning early. Emily opened the conversation. "Liz spoke to me last night about the conversation you had with her yesterday–about your worries. Tim and I are both aware of the potential for something damaging happening that Liz and Pat would both regret–that all of us would regret. We want to assure you that we are also concerned." She looked at Tim and nodded.

Tim leaned closer to Dolores. "I have spoken with Pat, Mrs. De Silva. He also understands your concern and will not take advantage of your daughter, even if he could. I promise. There will be no sex in New York. Not by Pat and not by me. There will be no boys and girls sleeping together. Emily and I intend to act suitably. You have my word."

Emily spoke before Dolores answered. "Liz is not going to have the opportunity to make a mistake, Dolores. You also have my word. We are going to have fun and I hope Liz will never forget the visit. She may fall in love and learn about American boys, but nothing to be ashamed of is going to happen to her in New York

City. Not on my watch."

Getting to the top of the Empire State building took time and effort. COVID regulations limited the number allowed. Only Liz's ambassadorial connection finally worked.

Emily whispered to Pat, "You kiss her for real while we are up here, Pat. She will never forgive you if you don't."

He did. Tim also performed well. They all had a lasting memory. They went to the Statue of Liberty next, and then to the hotel for a dinner that no one would remember, and then to two rooms with two beds. Boys in one room, girls in the other. And then they flew back to DC where Elizabeth and her mother became lifetime confidants. Liz told her mother what Emily said about being her being in a different life lane than Pat, about what she said about her family's aristocratic functions and obligations. She also told her mother that she was deliriously in love with Pat. He was her first love, but she recognized that he probably wouldn't be her only love.

Time together with Tim in New York was different for Emily. She felt relaxed and comfortable. She no longer harbored doubts about her feelings, or his. She knew what was going to happen next. The next time Tim came for her, they sat in his truck and talked for hours. Emily had a list. First, she wanted to know more about his parents.

"My father is Doctor Bradley. Harold Bradley. Hal. He teaches and heads the Creative Writing department at the University of Texas. My mother is also Doctor Bradley. Naomi. Dad calls her Omi. She once taught in the same creative writing department but retired when I was born. She has been an independent editor since. She makes better money than my dad by editing for some major publishers and occasionally for well-known writers. My parents are, and always have been, in love with each other. I want what they have.

"You know almost everything about my brother, Emy, other than he is seriously thinking about professional soccer overseas. He is a goalie and will probably make All American this year. He is really quick for a big man. If he is not a success at soccer, he will have an education in business administration."

"I envy you, Tim. I never had a home life, or siblings, or parents like that. Now, what about you? I know personal things, but what about your life goals?"

"My plans? I do not want to spend my working years flying for the airlines, Emy. As you well know, I would always be on a schedule, not unlike a bus driver with days and nights away from home. I want to be able, financially, to quit flying by age thirty. And then I want to write. I am making some fairly good money now with articles and short stories. I have already been published in the New York Times opinion section. I have also been published in The New Yorker and several lesser magazines. I wrote assignments for the Armed Forces News while I was in the Air Force. I want to become well enough known and respected to make a good living writing."

"Tell me about the Air Force. That just doesn't seem like something you would do. How did that happen?"

"I really never thought that much about flying. After I graduated, and after realizing a good paying job writing was not going to happen right away, I walked into a recruiter's office and signed up for pilot training. Shocked my parents. I was twenty-one and free, so, as you say, 'What the hell.'"

"Where did you serve?"

"All over the world flying the C-5, the largest airplane in America's inventory. Good training and some very interesting places. I didn't have to train long to be qualified to fly civilian airliners. When I got out after four years, I was only twenty-five. I have been with United for a year and a half."

"You mention a home in Austin. I presume that is your plan?"

"Yes, first choice. Somewhere else if being with my family requires a change. Where I live is secondary to family."

"So, family? Wife and kids, then?

"Wife first, of course, but kids are on my list of must-haves. Yes. I want kids before I'm too old to enjoy them. Mid-thirties, I think."

"Guess you won't be writing for *NATIONAL GEOGRAPHIC*."

"No, not and be married."

"I am not attempting to give you the third-degree, Tim, but I would like to know if you have ever googled me."

"No."

"Really? Why not?"

"I wanted to learn about you by myself. I don't want

outside interference to have anything to do with my own judgement."

"How am I doing?"

"You are way out in first place. I can easily see myself living with you, Emy. I know it's too soon, but I could start right now."

"Not so fast, Pilgrim. No early proposals, please. I want you to google me, Tim. Now. Right now.

"Sounds serious."

"Just do it, please."

He typed her name, waited a moment, read for several seconds, and then flopped back on the bed. "Holy sh...! And you have been keeping this secret from me? Why?"

"Because it has already cost me the first guy I ever fell in love with. I think he had googled me before we met. I didn't know that at the time. He liked my looks to begin with, and then learned my name and then googled. He read what you just read, Tim, only before it became widely known that I was the sole heir and would inherit everything. I think he, Allen, was in the relationship for the prospect of money, not just for me. He had dreams of being rich."

"What happened? Why did you break up, or were you ever that tight?"

"I thought we were the real thing, but he faded as soon as I gave the money away, Tim. I kept just enough to buy a decent home. All the rest I gave to a hospital to invest. The contract will be renegotiated in twenty years. So, effectively, it's still mine. Allen couldn't understand how anyone could be that cavalier with money. I didn't know until the end that he knew about the money before we became acquainted. A friend of mine told me. Anyway, I have not grieved all that much over him. He has been suspended from medicine. Lost his license over drug use. Does my association with so much money change anything, Tim?"

"Yes. What you did makes me love you more. I suppose you have to count that as a change. What prompted you to give it away?"

"My adoptive father's money came mainly from coal mining, Tim. I do not want to be associated with it. Coal is pollution and I absolutely do believe in global warming."

"Good enough for me. Anything else?"

"Yes, I want to meet your parents. Are you ready for that?"

"Just say when. I'm pleased and excited, Em. You will love them. I know they will love you, particularly my Mom."

"That's the first time you have called me Em."

SUMMER NUDE

I sleep unfettered now,

Zephyr's caressing fingers

sliding across naked skin,

slipping over my meekness,

modifying old modesties -

a brazen emancipation.

Timid patterns capitulate

as reticence recedes.

Dated innocence disrobed

betrays a lust for life.

I sleep unfettered now,

unbridled by modesties mantle.

Kite-winds rise, and I to meet them.

Lee Anne Russell 2017

CHAPTER SEVENTEEN

TIM TIME

Liz began school at Georgetown in June. Three classes a day. She met another Spanish diplomat's daughter the first day and liked her. Emily counseled her not to become part of a Spanish clique. "You will separate yourself from the other kids. Make friends with everyone. I'm not telling you to ignore your new friend, just…well, you know what I mean."

After the first week of school, Emily realized that Liz's English was good enough. She also recognized that and other than being there for Liz as a friend, she could find little reason for remaining in DC with the De Silvas. She informed them at supper that evening that her services were no longer needed, that she felt of little use. "I have been happy here; I love Elizabeth like a sister. I always will, but she doesn't need me now. She needs to be off on her own. She is in control of her life and I have every confidence in her. So, yes, I should probably leave."

Albert didn't appear to be surprised. "We wondered if you would stay after Elizabeth started school. She has mentioned living in the dorm and we agreed. We believe living away from home will be a healthy, fundamental part of college."

Dolores asked what Emily planned to do. "Are you going to stay here in Washington?"

"No. I plan to return to nursing. I'm not sure where yet, but not to the hospital in Springfield."

Albert, always practical, said, "You still have three months on your contract, Emily. If you are sure about leaving, we will happily pay the remaining three months. You have been a wonderful friend to Elizabeth. We, particularly Elizabeth, will never forget you. She has made such remarkable changes under you guidance, and all for the better. She has grown strong under your coaching. Elizabeth is a happy, confident person now. You have been more like a sister to her. Dolores and I are delighted with what you have done, most particularly the example you have set. We both believe you are the best thing that ever happened to her. Are you so sure about leaving?"

"Yes. I think that would be best for me and for Elizabeth. She is on her own now. So, yes, I am planning to leave. I will always remember you with pleasure. Both of you have provided a great place for me to stop and solve some of my own life problems. Thank you. I will speak to Liz this evening and plan to leave tomorrow."

Dolores's eyes were wet when she said, "Where will you go, Emily."

Emily laughed. "Like you don't know. I am going to Austin to meet Tim's parents and friends. I am going to take a job at an Austin hospital. I am going to take my time and learn every possible thing I can about Tim Bradley. When I am satisfied, I plan to marry him, as I am certain you undoubtedly already know. I love him. Tim enriches my life in every way. I also like his brother very much, as you know your daughter does as well. Now, it's time for me to learn about Tim's parents."

Emily and Elizabeth both cried when she announced her intentions that evening.

"You can't go, Emy! You can't just leave me. You are my sister. You are my model. How will I ever–"

"Stop it! Please stop! You had to know I would leave when you didn't need me. You don't need me anymore, Liz, not as a teacher or a companion, and if you ever do, just pick up the damned phone. How hard is it?"

After much hugging and crying, they both went to Emily's room and packed after she called Tim and told him to pack. He called back minutes later with their flight schedule.

The entire staff stood in an ordered line the next morning at the mansion entryway and hugged goodbye. Her maid, Janet, started a chant, "Speech! Speech! Speech!"

Emily found herself alone, facing everyone. The Ambassador urged her to say something.

"Leave us with your thoughts, Emily."

"Thank you, Mister De... Albert. And thank you Dolores for everything, but most of all for being my friends and for letting me be free to say and do what I thought best, even though I know you both cringed and bit your tongues. Thank you." She turned to the staff. "And for all of you. You have been good friends and I will miss you." She turned to Elizabeth and asked her to step forward. After hugging her, she turned again to the gathering and said, "The night I met Elizabeth, as I closed her door after hugging her, I heard her say, 'I am not a hugger.' That may have been true then, but I can tell you from six months of experience that she is definitely a hugger now." She turned to Elizabeth. "My dear friend. My sister. I love you and I always will. My last bit of knowledge to pass on to you is this: There is only one ideal sex in this world, and it is women. Only a woman can come close to human perfection. Men, bless their hearts, and my apologies to those present, are poor tortured, testosterone-soaked souls. They must have toys, whether their toys be a country, armies and navies, yachts, guns, airplanes or a need for public recognition. The list is endless. Each male, you will find, is flawed and in need of stability that can only be provided by a woman. First by their mother, and then, hopefully, someone not unlike their mother. Men may occasionally be more intelligent than we women, but they are seldom ever smarter than we are, Liz. You have all the qualities to be the perfect woman, and I believe that is your destiny.

"I am leaving you now to go to Texas to see if I can round up a man of my own. I already know who he is, and though he is not perfect, I know I must have him to be complete. I know that. And there you have it–the perfect woman's flaw. Men. We cannot live without them, and I certainly do not want to live without the man I have chosen. Please keep that to yourselves as I have not told him yet. He makes me happy." Everyone present laughed.

"You make me happy Liz. You have a great destiny. Goodbye. Now give me a hug and let me go."

Claude teared up that morning after wheeling her

baggage into the airport. "I'm sure going to miss you, Miss Emily. I sure am."

Emily didn't get off at the Springfield stop. She planned to come back and retrieve the remainder of her belongings and her car, if her plans in Austin worked out.

One step at a time.

Harold Bradley, in his sixties and very nice looking, came alone to pick Emily up at the airport, thoughtfully leaving room in his car for her pile of luggage. After an open-arms greeting, he said, "I have been warned by the woman at home, anxiously awaiting your arrival, that I am not to talk to you until she is present, Emily. She doesn't want to miss anything. I am so happy to meet you. Tim has spent some interesting evenings showing pictures and telling us all about you. You are no stranger to us. Anyway, welcome to Austin. I hope you stay." He loaded her luggage and asked if there was anything else. No, he said with a flourish, "Okay! Get in and let's go! Tim has gone to the parking lot to look for his car. He'll be along shortly. And, by the way, please call me Hal."

Naomi, not much larger than Emily, met them in the drive. She seemed overcome for a few moments, hunting for words, finally giving up and embracing. "Oh, I have so looked forward to this. You cannot possibly be everything Tim says you are, but your photos have certainly not been deceiving. You are as beautiful as he assured us you were. Come in! Let's get out of this Texas heat." She turned to her husband. "Hal! You let Tim take care of that luggage. Now, I mean it!" She turned to Emily. "You will stay with us of course until Tim has that mess he lives in cleaned up, won't you? Please say yes."

"Does Tim know about that arrangement?"

"Well, of course he doesn't! He's a guy. And, for your information, Pat won't be here for several days. Some sort of a soccer camp. So the upstairs will be all yours." She paused. "I am assuming that you and Tim are on friendly enough terms to sleep together? Am I right? Oh, for God's sake! Would you listen to me? I'm really not that dense. Well, if you have been sleeping together, Hal and I expect you to go right on with your life here. Now, what would you like to drink? Sit down right there so I can see you from the kitchen." She directed Emily to a small easy chair. "Tea? Water? Something stronger?"

"I think I will just wait for Tim, Naomi. I'm not thirsty." She felt like a train had run over her, not realizing yet–she would soon enough–that she was, in many ways, a carbon copy of Naomi, full of energy and in control.

She was still sitting in the chair when Tim arrived and kissed her.

"Everything under control here?"

Emily laughed out loud. "You must be kidding. This is where Naomi lives."

Tim nodded. "Welcome to the house of busy. You two will be perfect together."

"Are we going to stay here tonight, Tim?"

"What did Mom say?"

"She says we are."

"Well then,

there you have it, Emy. She is going to love you to death, but not before I do. Don't worry, she might be just a little bit more wound up than usual. You are a huge deal to her. I never brought a girl or woman home before, at least not someone I was serious about. Let's just go with what she wants for a day or two. What she *needs* is probably a better term for it."

"So, this is her? Is she like this all the time? Does she ever slow down?"

"No, this isn't her. She's just excited right now. Mom knows so much about you, and for your information, you are just like her. You will always know how she feels about everything. She is almost as happy as you are–just a senior version." He looked around. "So, she wants us to stay here tonight?"

"Yes. And she expects that we probably will sleep together. And Pat won't be here. And I will take a drink now. And please make it a half a glass of something not too strong."

Tim departed and Hal came in. "You must be tired, Emily. Can I get something?"

"Tim is in the kitchen taking care of that."

"I know what you must be feeling right now, Emily. Relax. Just go with the flow. She is thrilled to have you here. Really, Omi is quite normal, as you will soon see. I am also thrilled you are here, just perhaps somewhat more laid-back." He turned and yelled, "What the hell is taking you so damned long in there, Tim!" He turned back to Emily and smiled. "How hard can it be, right?"

My, God! A carbon copy of Ben.

Emily asked, "What happened to Naomi? Does she need help?"

Hal shook his head. "If I know her, and I do, she is

probably in the bedroom crying."

Emily leaned forward, alarmed. "Is something wrong?"

"No. Everything in Omi's world at this moment is perfect. Absolutely nothing is wrong. You are here and she is overjoyed, that' all. She is happy. She cries when happy. But, it might speed things up if you tap on the door and see about her. Omi is not going to let you out of her sight for days. Just go with it, Emy, if you can."

Good heavens! She is Omi and I am Emy? Perhaps an omen?

Naomi was still patting her face and drying her eyes. She held and hugged Emily for the longest time before sighing deeply and stepping away. "Okay, I'm good to go now. Ready to face the world again. Oh, I am so glad you are here, Emily. I have been worried that Tim might be too involved with you and committed too soon. I have worried that he could be hurt. I have never seen him so crazy over a girl before. I'm sure this is going to be a long evening for you, but I– we–have so many things to discover. Come on. Let's join the guys. She suddenly stopped.

"No, wait. I have to tell you what Tim told us about you. Just one of the many things he has told us, but you will love this. This is Tim the writers' description of your expressions. 'Her face is an orchestral performance, Mom. Every little movement of her face means something. Her eyes tell what she is thinking. The wrinkles on her nose tell something else. The wrinkles on her brow something else. Her mouth and lips are an entire orchestra section. I know her well enough now to close my eyes while listening to her talk while imagining what her face is doing. And I see me in her eyes, Mom.

She has gypsy eyes. Oh, that's not all. Her expressions go all the way to the floor. She twists and sways while walking up to me, or any of her good friends, sometimes followed by a twirl before she hugs. And her body moves, always part of a performance that she is unaware of.

Naomi, as promised, returned to normal. She was not flighty, but she was definitely in control of her world. She was also a near replica of Emily. At one point in the evening, Hal led both women to the bedroom mirror and forced then to notice what he and Tim had known all along. They were not precise duplicates, but favored each other much like closely related relatives. Tim had deliberately kept pictures of his mother from Emily, waiting for this moment.

Upon entering Tim's apartment the next day, Emily expressed surprise. "I thought you lived in a mess. I wasn't looking for this."

"Oh, Mom thinks I still live in the rubble of my adolescent upstairs bedroom. I have four years of military training, so you will never have to pick up after me."

"I am impressed. Now, I want to see that great office you have talked about. Show me." Her mouth fell open. "Oh, I'm not ready for this, Tim. What is all of this? It looks like the cockpit of an airliner."

"Nothing like that. Almost all this equipment is dedicated to writing, printing, publishing, researching. I could live in this room forever."

She stepped through a half open door. "And what is this empty room for? And why is it empty?"

"That's for you. You get to pick your own furniture. What equipment you put in there is up to you. That's your office, Emy."

"How long has it been like this, Tim?"

"Since I moved in. A year now."

"You didn't know me a year ago."

"Oh, I knew you were coming, Emy. I have planned all my life for you."

"What if I don't stay?"

"Don't tease me about that. I knew from the day I sat with you flying to DC, and so did you, that we would end up together. Tell me I'm wrong."

"You were right then and you still are. Yes, I knew. I wanted to know you from first sight. I am deliriously happy with you, Tim, but I don't want to live with your parents. Now, answer me this, Tim: Are you as tight with your parents as it seems? It's almost like you still live at home and never left."

"Yes, I am. But I am not thinking about them when I talk about *my* family, Emily. I'm talking about *my* family. *My* wife and kids."

"Oooooo! Now I want to run naked."

They went to sleep almost the same way every night. Slowing down; reviewing their day; voices becoming softer until only one would be talking, murmuring, getting slower and lower. The other, on the cusp of sleep, replied in muttered hums, still engaged, but barely. The speaker needed nothing more than to know the other was listening.

The Springfield office of the FBI called Emily the following morning.

"Just to bring you up to date, Miss Prindiville. We have Iris Brooks now. One of Driscoll's helpers gave the information hoping for a better sentence. We found her in Cancun Mexico. Her trial date is not set yet, but she has turned State's Evidence. I expect she will have to serve some time–maybe a five year sentence. She was way too involved to go free. And I also expect she will probably be released before serving the full sentence."

"Is there any chance I might be called?"

"I can't say. The prosecutor will decide. I doubt it, though. Driscoll was involved in a new scheme with fentanyl and a Mexican cartel that Iris didn't know about and was not part of. Iris knew about some of his other arrangements, though. Giving evidence there will help her cause."

"Will I be able to see her?"

"I can't say about that, either. When a prosecutor is assigned, you will have to go through that office. Anyway, we want you to keep the same phone number so we can contact you, or if you change, notify us."

Emily became best friends with Naomi. They shopped together. They exercised together. They lunched together. Omi became more than Tim's mother. She was Emily's new Bestie.

"We can be friends, Omi, but we cannot be a confidante concerning Tim. I expect he already believes he has no secrets."

"That's just plain silly. Tim has never had a secret

from me in his life. Why start now?"

"I'm just saying. I may not want Tim telling you everything about me."

"Oh, that. I know you two are not going to tell me everything and that's okay. Just don't keep any secrets from me."

They both laughed and it was settled.

So, no secrets from Omi. What the hell.

Emily went to Springfield within the week and returned with her belongings and the car. While there, she stopped at the hospital and had lunch in the cafeteria with old friends. She learned Allen was being held without bond and had been indicted.

Upon return to Austin, she applied for and was accepted as an RN at St. David's Center hospital. She also scheduled her first classes to become a Physician Assistant–PA.

During the murmuring moments before sleep, Emily said, "I have started getting tons of mail asking for money. Didn't take them long to track me down. The mail office told me today, in no uncertain terms, that I must get a private box. They don't want to handle the influx."

"Ummmm."

"Did you hear me, Tim? The hospital mailroom says I have to get my own address."

"Umm huh. What are you going to do about it?"

"I need to change my name, I guess."

He became semi alert. His breathing slowed. "What? Just like that? Isn't that a big deal legally, Emy?

Changing your name?"

"Yup."

"What name are you planning to use? Have you already picked one?"

Long pause.

She whispered, "I have. Bradley, I think."

His breathing slowed further. "As in, Bradley with an e?"

"Eeeyup."

"When is this all of this going to happen?"

"We have to wait seventy-two hours after applying for the license."

"We? I see. When are *we* going to apply?" He still wasn't taking her seriously.

"Tomorrow works for me."

A very long pause.

"Wait!" He switched on the reading light by her bed. "Are you serious? Open your eyes, Emy! This is not a game to me." He stared at her.

"Never been more serious, Tim. Are you free tomorrow morning for a couple of hours?"

"Emy! What about a wedding? What about time to plan a wedding?"

"I don't care about a big wedding or any other kind of wedding, Tim. I have never once dreamed about a big wedding. I just want to go to the courthouse tomorrow, apply for a license and three day later get married by a Justice of The Peace or some small church pastor. I want your parents to stand up with us. If you have friends you want to invite, just do it. Do you want a big wedding? Do you, Tim?"

"No, but I never thought about it one way or another." He turned her face toward his. "Now you just wait a minute here, Emy! Zip, pop, just like that? We get married?"

"Yes. Absolutely. That is exactly what I want. I just want to be married and I want to do it as soon as I can and I want to marry you, Tim. What's so hard about that?"

He turned the light off, flopped back, pulled the covers up and said, "So, we get the license, wait seventy-two hours and get married. That's all there is to it?"

"That works for Texas and that works just fine for me, Tim. I am as serious I can be about this. Let's do it."

"What do you think Mom will have to say about it?"

"Oh, Omi is behind it one-hundred percent. She already has a new outfit and is thrilled to be the bridesmaid."

Another long pause.

"Well I'll be damned. I should have known. You two."

"Wasn't her idea, flyboy. Now, are you in or out?"

"You don't have to ask. You know I will always be in, Emy."

She snuggled her face into his neck. "All right then. Let's get some sleep. We are going to start your family tomorrow."

ABOUT THE AUTHOR

Larry Cunningham is a retired Marine Corps Lt. Colonel, fighter squadron commander. He wrote USMC plans for the evacuation of Vietnam, Cambodia and Laos. He flew many combat missions and served as Air Officer during the siege of Khe Sanh.

He is an ex-cattle rancher, high school science teacher, college fiction writing instructor and poet. He often speaks at writer's meetings and conferences.

* * * * *

Look for Cunningham's next book coming soon!

https://www.jameslarrycunningham.com
Cunningham has written four novels.

www.ingramcontent.com/pod-product-compliance
Lightning Source LLC
Chambersburg PA
CBHW030112180626
46812CB00002B/392